AMERIKA

Franz Kafka

AMERIKA

TRANSLATED BY WILLA AND EDWIN MUIR

PREFACE BY KLAUS MANN

AFTERWORD BY MAX BROD

ILLUSTRATIONS BY EMLEN ETTING

Schocken Books

NEW YORK

CONTENTS

ILLUSTRATIONS

PREFACE

THE atmosphere of Prague was, in the first quarter of this century, more thoroughly impregnated with literary savour than that of any other European city, except Paris. That weird settlement at the entrance of Eastern Europe—Prague, gloomy and picturesque, full of ancient glory and present struggle—produced an abundance of good or even excellent literature, and also a few writers of genius, such as Rainer Maria Rilke, Franz Werfel—and Franz Kafka.

Kafka was no "professional writer"—which means that he did not regard the occupation of writing as a form of career or business. In the day-time he worked in a dreary office—as long as a virulent disease did not prevent him from doing so—his evenings, however, and long hours of the night were dedicated to the at once exhausting and elevating endeavour of producing a few pages of immaculate German prose. His zealous conscientiousness in all matters concerning style reminds us of Gustave Flaubert's radical aestheticism, while his passionate concern with the problem of our spiritual existence makes him akin to Sören Kierkegaard—two masters, by the way, whom Kafka admired most ardently.

In his lifetime only a dozen initiated friends and connoisseurs grasped the puzzling phenomenon of his greatness. Only those selected few realized the philosophic and artistic significance of his short prose compositions and his three fragmentary novels, *The Castle, The Trial,* and *Amerika*—forming in their entity a sublime "trilogy of human solitude," to use a formula of the novelist and critic Max Brod. To the rank and file of *literati,* Kafka was just another curious character whom one met occasionally at a café—a sickly youth of an aristocratic Jewish type: melancholy, shy, gifted with an almost frightening seriousness and a bizarre sense of humour. He was no bohemian . . . rather pedantic in the tidiness of his appearance; unpresuming, amiable and reserved; sometimes enchanting by the natural gracefulness of his manners— sometimes disquieting through the profound sadness of his eye and smile. He always looked younger than he really was. Even a picture taken in the last year of his fatal disease—in 1924—shows a juvenile figure—slightly stooping but elastic and elegant. He was forty-one when he died. At that time most of his works were still unpublished.

It was partly his mysterious pride partly his genuine modesty that made him averse to any kind of publicity. His friends had to struggle with him for a manuscript they wanted to send to a literary magazine or a publishing-house. He left no will—except the strict injunction that all of his posthumous papers should be burned. His nearest, most trusted and understanding friend, Max Brod, had to meet the agonizing dilemma. Should he neglect Kafka's imperious and cruel wish? Was he to destroy a literary treasure the singularity of which he fully recognized?

The decision he finally made—to save and edit the manuscripts—was, of course, the only right and honorable one. It is to him, to Max Brod, that we actually owe the preservation of Kafka's work; he is chiefly responsible for the gradual, belated growing of Kafka's fame.

May we speak of "fame" in the peculiar case of an author who neither sought nor gained popularity and never was "a success" in the ordinary sense of the word? Kafka's books were not best-sellers—not even in pre-Nazi Germany, so impressionable and eagerly opened to all kinds of artistic experiments. Yet the actual effect of his works has been more intense and lasting than that of many a literary sensation of the day: his subterranean influence has proven penetrating and mysteriously strong. One critic has called him "the secret king of modern German prose." But awareness of this inconspicuous greatness gradually crossed the boundaries of the German-speaking world. Most of his writings were translated into many languages; essays on Kafka were written, not only in German but also in English and French, Spanish, Czech, Swedish and Hungarian. His personal style—that unmistakable compound of baroque and classic elements, of dreamlike romanticism and realistic exactness—has inspired and influenced young writers on both sides of the Atlantic.

"What we call Fame is nothing but the sum of all mistakes circulating about one individual." These words, haughty and resigned, are Rainer Maria Rilke's—another genius whose princely shyness despised and banished the clamorous approach of mass curiosity. Even Kafka, for all his aristocratic reserves, was not spared awkward misinterpretations. He has been identified with the Surrealists, and with a certain decadent Viennese school: there were even attempts at analysing from a Marxist angle certain enigmatic passages in his books. All such interpretations are, of course, erroneous, and utterly fail to define the true substance of his being and writing.

He never meant to surprise and startle his readers by macabre tricks. He wanted to be plastic, plain and simple. His literary masters were Flaubert and Tolstoi rather than Baudelaire and

Dostoievski. He has been compared with Edgar Allan Poe, but he admired Dickens. His supreme ambition was to describe the dismay and ecstasy of his inward adventures as thoroughly and realistically as Flaubert described all the details of Madame Bovary's appearance, or Tolstoi the face and smell of a Russian peasant. Kafka is no surrealist but the most realistic explorer of spheres that are not less real for their being inaccessible to average travellers. His topography of nightmare landscapes is as precise as any scientific report.

The humorous, grotesque element in his descriptions—disturbing to some of his admirers, and overestimated by others—is nothing but the natural consequence of his sober honesty. His own experiences taught him that even the Mystery has comic aspects—aspects well known, by the way, to medieval saints and sculptors. The Devil, or at least his minor emissaries, can assume a very clownish appearance—funny as well as fiendish. There are Gothic statues in which we recognize that horrified laughter characteristic of Kafka's sinister wit. What inconceivable tribulation must have frozen his tears, numbed the outcry of his despair, and left him that lurid jocularity as his only solace!

Kafka was haunted by all sorts of fears and apprehensions. Ideas of Original Sin, of Guilt and Punishment were the very basis of his feeling and thinking. The God to whom he sent his almost hopeless prayers and whose Holy name he hardly ever mentioned, is Jehova, the Lord of Revenge, and there is no Savior to reconcile doomed mortal creatures with their merciless Father. Human beings have constantly to atone for crimes the gravity and even the names of which they cannot know. Our mysterious guilt is examined in an eternal trial; there is a hierarchy of hidden judges—and even the lowest is of such overwhelming majesty that we could not bear to see him face to face.

These fixed ideas and creative torments are deeply rooted, of course, in many circumstances and experiences of Kafka's personal life. The autobiographic content of his narratives is stronger than it may seem at first. Any psychoanalyst could define Kafka's religious pathos—his humble and yet mistrustful fear of God—as the productive "sublimation" of an obvious "father complex." The patriarchal figure of his father played, indeed, a predominant role in Kafka's biography. He admired and dreaded the father because of his solid strength, his well-balanced vitality. The father was the one who had lived as a man *should* live—who had mastered life: whereas the son, for all the problematic rapture of his inspiration, considered himself a failure in all matters that really count.

A failure he was, indeed, as far as crude realities of life are concerned: he could not stand the work in a gloomy office; he had no spectacular success as an author, never made enough money to support himself; his poor health prevented him from marrying: the one great romance of his life was doomed to dreary frustration.

He suffered—not only from his disease, but from life itself—life as a Jew, in Prague, in the tumultuous period of World War and Revolution. He was scarcely interested in politics. Social problems appear in his books only indirectly—disguised, transposed into a remote and mysterious sphere. His vision of *The Trial* and *The Castle,* in which the invisible Power hides, was influenced, not only by the esoteric wisdom of the Cabala, but also by his own experiences as a minor functionary of the ancient Austrian Bureaucracy. His vast and meticulous epic of a capricious tyranny has no seditious verve nor is it really satirical. Kafka's attitude toward the worldly authorities expresses the same half-ironic apprehension and critical respect characteristic of his devotion to the inscrutable Father, human or divine.

The city of Prague meant to him, in a weird and definite way, the microcosm in which he recognized the tragedy and struggle of mankind. Prague was actually *all he knew*—his entire world, his paradise and his prison. He yearned for other landscapes, for a lighter and brighter beauty. But the few journeys he could afford, in the company of friends or alone, were short and hardly satisfactory.

The most extensive journey he ever made took place wholly in his mind. The goal of his bold excursion was the United States. His friends were highly surprised when he confided to them his secret—that he was going to write a novel entitled *Amerika:* in fact, he had already begun.

"What do you know about America?" they asked. And he answered, cheerfully: "I know the autobiography of Benjamin Franklin, and I always admired Walt Whitman, and I like the Americans because they are healthy and optimistic." He imagined that all Americans wore a perpetual smile. Later, in the years of his fatal disease, he met in a sanatorium several Americans who quite often grumbled and complained. He was deeply disappointed. But when he conceived his novel *Amerika,* in 1913, he knew no Americans at all and understood very little English. His only sources of information were the few books he had read—and his own poetic imagination.

He seemed unusually cheerful and confident while working on *Amerika.* His friends were pleased to notice that his looks and mood had improved almost miraculously. His relative optimism, however, did not entirely protect him from qualms and scruples. He was at that time reading, or re-reading, several novels by Dickens, and made the following remarks in his diary:

"Dickens, *Copperfield*. 'The Stoker, a plain imitation of Dickens: even more so than the planned novel." (The first chapter of the America novel was published as a special little volume, called 'The Stoker', before the novel appeared.) . . . My intention was, as I now see, to write a Dickens novel, enriched by the sharper lights which I took from our modern times, and by the pallid ones I would have found in my own interior.—Dickens' wealth and naive, sweeping power: but, consequently, moments of horrible weakness . . . The impression of the senseless whole is barbaric—a barbarism which I was able to avoid thanks to my decadence . . ."

Strangely enough, in Kafka's mind the figure and the works of Dickens were vitally connected with the American atmosphere and landscape. It was not Dickens' biting satire on America, in *Martin Chuzzlewit*, that lay behind this odd identification. The picture that Kafka cherished was of a fatherly genius called Charles Dickens being welcomed to New York with wild enthusiasm by thousands of his American readers. Kafka often described to his friends the hilarious spectacle of all that exuberant public jammed on the dock, eagerly awaiting a new chapter of *David Copperfield*, waving and shouting as the boat with its literary treasure slowly pulls in.

As to his own novel, *Amerika*, he was far from accurate when he called it an "imitation of Dickens." For the resemblance to Dickens is only accidental and superficial—while the differences between the sentimental or humorous circumstantiality of Dickens' style and Kafka's visionary precision are basic and essential.

The adolescent heroes of the English master-novelist have to endure suffering and adventures because the world is wicked—and because the great narrator had to offer an exciting plot. But Karl Rossmann, the leading character of Kafka's story, is harassed by more profound and complicated dangers: the problem of guilt *as such,* the mystic curse of Original Sin follows him over the ocean. We see this naive but observant lad as he arrives in New York, welcomed by "the free breezes" of America and a Statue of Liberty furnished most surprisingly (and perhaps symbolically?), with an upraised sword. He seems almost happy, in spite of the hardships ahead—happy, at least, as compared with his tragic relatives, the doomed heroes of Kafka's two other novels, *The Castle* and *The Trial.* Both of these remain strangely anonymous—or rather, they hide their mysterious identity with the author behind the obvious initial "K"; while young Karl Rossmann is permitted a name of his own, in which the fatal "K" appears, but does not predominate. He is a younger, more fortunate brother of that nameless being, K., for whom there will be no America: the one who must remain in Europe, in Prague, to endure the merciless decisions of the inscrutable judges.

It may be, however, that Karl is guilty as well—notwithstanding the maid-servant's confession that she was the active party in the sordid affair that precipitated the youth's departure from Europe. He is not responsible—according to human judgment. But our judgment is, of course, subject to error and is easily refuted by the sentence of the higher authorities.

What is our guilt? Who defines its roots, its consequences, and the chastisement it may deserve? Nobody knows if the stoker, that pathetic hero of the introductory chapter, is innocent or guilty—and the wayward laws dominating Karl Rossmann's life are not less mysterious. At first he seems favoured by a playful fate as he meets, almost miraculously, his benign and wealthy uncle, a certain Senator Jacob. But the uncle repudiates him as surprisingly as he offered him his protection—and we find the young adventurer, abandoned by his mighty benefactor, penniless and friendless on the highways, in a vast and unknown country.

What an amazing panorama!—this American landscape seen through the clairvoyant eyes of a naive and sensitive youth. Every detail of Kafka's description of American life is quite inaccurate, and yet the picture as a whole has poetical truth. The hyper-modern desk which the generous uncle puts at his nephew's disposal looks like a grotesque piece of furniture in a Charlie Chaplin film: it is an alarming object with innumerable technical tricks—secret drawers that pop open when one touches a hidden button, little trapdoors, complicated locks. The country house of a millionaire near New York is built like an ancient European castle—a typical Kafka castle in fact—confusing, frightening, with countless corridors and galleries, tremendous staircases and an unfinished chapel. And those astounding streets of American cities, with the Gothic lines of steel-constructed skyscrapers profiled against a wan, colourless sky, like cathedrals from another planet where people are praying to another God! Those endless highways, flanked by little inns and dusty gardens where dirty men hastily swallow indescribable liquids and waiters run around with distorted faces as if in permanent pain.

Yet, in the midst of this bewitched scenery, the great Trial continues—that tremendous drama of Justice which is also a farce—full of a sardonic irony; puzzling, terrifying and funny. Friendly and evil ghosts seem to fight with each other for the possession of Karl's soul, just as God and the Devil dispute for Doctor Faust in the medieval miracle-play. And a miracle-play it is, comic and profound, in which Karl acts as hero, victim, sinner, martyr and clown. The benign *Oberköchin,* the Supreme Cook in the Hotel Occidental, represents the principle of Good. But even this efficient guardian angel proves incapable of helping her protegé when he finds himself in an alarming mess brought about by two fiendish demons, Delamarche and Robinson, who keep tagging behind the child-like wanderer. The grand and appalling chapter, describing Karl's humiliation as a servant of these two ghastly crooks and their prodigious mistress, represents the burlesque and moving climax of the adventurous story.

But as though the author found it intolerable to continue this macabre report, he suddenly breaks off his narrative, and when Karl re-appears—months, perhaps years later—he is looking for a new job, and finds one in *The Great Nature Theatre of Oklahoma*—a kind of gigantic WPA project, organized and financed by invisible but extremely powerful benefactors. Kafka was especially fond of this concluding chapter, and his friends tell us that he used to read it aloud in an "unforgettable manner." With an enigmatic smile he declared that his young hero, Karl Rossmann, might well find again, "in this almost boundless theatre," his profession, his security and freedom, and perhaps even his homeland and parents—"as by a celestial spell."

Kafka himself was not in a position to describe these happy developments. The novel had to remain a fragment as did all of his greater compositions, according to their imperative inherent law. The very themes of these works—the topics of Guilt and Atonement, human loneliness and the unfathomable riddle of the Supreme Law—prohibit them from finding an end: they are essentially and necessarily *endless. Amerika,* however, is the only one of Kafka's fragmentary novels on the last pages of which a confident mood prevails. The youthful hero disappears—running, capering like a reckless foal in the midst of a vast, heroic landscape. His tragic brother and creator, Franz Kafka, watches the agile figure gradually shrinking between the huge hills, trees and buildings. Finally the poet turns away his beautiful, shadowed forehead, bidding a plaintive farewell of mingled tenderness and renunciation.

Kafka's excursion to the New World has come to an end. Here they are again—the gloomy streets of Prague, the familiar background of his suffering. The city, numb and solemn, welcomes her prodigal son. The baroque statues, the cathedrals, the mysterious dwellings of the alchemists, the libraries, the strange and sweetish smells of the ghetto—all this well-known beauty, well-known horror, receive him with a faint, unfathomable smile: Here you are—our son, our prisoner, our poet; this is Europe—your chain, your curse and your love: Europe, your bitter love: you must bear it, accept it. *Here,* you must continue your writing, your meditations and prayers; seeking and fearing God. *Here* you must bear the torments of your religious persecution mania, and must transform your constant agonies into the brittle beauty of your lucid prose. Here, you must serve and perish, to earn at last the gloomy crown—the dark glory of your own destruction. Bow your head! Recognize your fate! There is no escape.

He accepts his lot. He is brave—the delicate but tenacious son of an ancient, heroic race, most experienced in suffering, humiliation, and long endurance. But sometimes, surely, his loving, sorrowful thoughts must have wandered over the ocean, to visit that errant youth whom he had created and abandoned there. To him he sends his wishes and his hopes. He wants Karl to be courageous—as courageous, indeed, as in his own place his elder brother—"K"—is obliged to be. The poet and prophet must glorify and analyze his doom; must continue his dialogue with a hidden God—indefatigable, witty, passionate, desperate, and yet faithful. But Karl has to *live*—no easy task either. And he must live in America. He has, therefore, a special chance. His creator hopes that he may prove worthy of it. He does not want him to perish. For the poet, in all his glory and misery, deeply and simply loves his innocent creature, his favourite dream, his heir.

KLAUS MANN

Brentwood, Los Angeles, August 1940

AMERIKA

As Karl Rossmann, a poor boy of sixteen who had been packed off to America by his parents because a servant girl had seduced him and got herself a child by him, stood on the liner slowly entering the harbour of New York, a sudden burst of sunshine seemed to illumine the Statue of Liberty, so that he saw it in a new light, although he had sighted it long before. The arm with the sword rose up as if newly stretched aloft, and round the figure blew the free winds of heaven.

"So high!" he said to himself, and was gradually edged to the very rail by the swelling throng of porters pushing past him, since he was not thinking at all of getting off the ship.

A young man with whom he had struck up a slight acquaintance on the voyage called out in passing: "Not very anxious to go ashore, are you?"—"Oh, I'm quite ready," said Karl with a laugh, and being both strong and in high spirits he heaved his box on to his shoulder. But as his eye followed his acquaintance, who was already moving on among the others lightly swinging a walking stick, he realised with dismay that he had forgotten his umbrella down below. He hastily begged his acquaintance, who did not seem particularly gratified, to oblige him by waiting beside the box for a minute, took another survey of the situation to get his bearings for the return journey, and hurried away. Below decks he found to his disappointment that a gangway which made a handy short cut had been barred for the first time in his experience, probably in connection with the disembarkation of so many passengers, and he had painfully to find his way down endlessly recurring stairs, through corridors with countless turnings, through an empty room with a deserted writing-table, until in the end, since he had taken this route no more than once or twice and always among a crowd of other people, he lost himself completely. In his bewilderment, meeting no one and hearing nothing but the ceaseless shuffling of thousands of feet above him, and in the distance, like faint breathing, the last throbbings of the engines, which had already been shut off, he began unthinkingly to hammer on a little door by which he had chanced to stop in his wanderings.

"It isn't locked," a voice shouted from inside, and Karl opened the door with genuine relief. "What are you hammering at the door for, like a madman?" asked a huge man, scarcely even glancing at Karl. Through an opening of some kind a feeble glimmer of daylight, all that was left after the top decks had used it up, fell into the wretched cubbyhole in which a bunk, a cupboard, a chair and the man were packed together, as if they had been stored there. "I've lost my way," said Karl, "I never noticed it during the voyage, but this is a terribly big ship."—"Yes, you're right there," said the man with a certain pride, fiddling all the time with the lock of a little sea-chest, which he kept pressing with both hands in the hope of hearing the wards snap home. "But come inside," he went on, "you don't want to stand out there!"—"I'm not disturbing you?" asked Karl. "Why, how should you disturb me?"—"Are you a German?" Karl asked to reassure himself further, for he had heard a great deal about the perils which threatened newcomers to America, particularly from the Irish. "That's what I am, yes," said the man. Karl still hesitated. Then the man suddenly seized the door handle and pulling the door shut with a hasty movement swept Karl into the cabin.

4

"I can't stand being stared at from the passage," he said, beginning to fiddle with his chest again, "people keep passing and staring in, it's more than a man can bear."—"But the passage is quite empty," said Karl, who was standing squeezed uncomfortably against the end of the bunk. "Yes, now," said the man. "But it's now we were speaking about," thought Karl, "it's hard work talking to this man."—"Lie down on the bunk, you'll have more room there," said the man. Karl scrambled in as well as he could, and laughed aloud at his first unsuccessful attempt to swing himself over. But scarcely was he in the bunk when he cried: "Good Lord, I've quite forgotten my box!"—"Why, where is it?"—"Up on deck, a man I know is looking after it. What's his name again?" And he fished a visiting-card from a pocket which his mother had made in the lining of his coat for the voyage. "Butterbaum, Franz Butterbaum."—"Can't you do without your box?"—"Of course not."—"Well, then, why did you leave it in a stranger's hands?"—"I forgot my umbrella down below and rushed off to get it; I didn't want to drag my box with me. Then on top of that I got lost."—"You're all alone? Without anyone to look after you?"—"Yes, all alone."—"Perhaps I should join up with this man," the thought came into Karl's head, "where am I likely to find a better friend?"—"And now you've lost the box as well. Not to mention the umbrella." And the man sat down on the chair as if Karl's business had at last acquired some interest for him. "But I think my box can't be lost yet."—"You can think what you like," said the man, vigorously scratching his dark, short, thick hair. "But morals change every time you come to a new port. In Hamburg your Butterbaum might maybe have looked after your box; while here it's most likely that they've both disappeared."—"But then I must go up and see about it at once," said Karl, looking round for the way out. "You just stay where you are," said the man, giving him a push with one hand on the chest, quite roughly, so that he fell back on the bunk again. "But why?" asked Karl in exasperation. "Because there's no point in it," said the man, "I'm leaving too very soon, and we can go together. Either the box is stolen and then there's no help for it, or the man has left it standing where it was, and then we'll find it all the more easily when the ship is empty. And the same with your umbrella."—"Do you know your way about the ship?" asked Karl suspiciously, and it seemed to him that the idea, otherwise plausible, that his things would be easier to find when the ship was empty must have a catch in it somewhere. "Why, I'm a stoker," said the man. "You're a stoker!" cried Karl delightedly, as if this surpassed all his expectations, and he rose up on his elbow to look at the man more closely. "Just outside the room where I slept with the Slovaks there was a little window through which we could see into the engine-room."—"Yes, that's where I've been working," said the stoker. "I have always had a passion for machinery," said Karl, following his own train of thought, "and I would have become an engineer in time, that's certain, if I hadn't had to go to America."—"Why did you have to go?"—"Oh, that!" said Karl, dismissing the whole business with a wave of the hand. He looked with a smile at the stoker, as if begging his indulgence for not telling. "There was some reason for it, I suppose," said the stoker, and it was hard to tell whether in saying that he wanted to encourage or discourage Karl to tell. "I could be a stoker now too," said Karl, "it's all one now to my father and mother what becomes of me."—"My job's going to be free," said the stoker, and to point his full consciousness of it, he stuck his hands into his trouser pockets and flung his legs in their baggy, leather-like trousers on the bunk to stretch them. Karl had to shift nearer to the

6

wall. "Are you leaving the ship?"—"Yes, we're paid off to-day."—"But why? Don't you like it?"—"Oh, that's the way things are run; it doesn't always depend on whether a man likes it or not. But you're quite right, I don't like it. I don't suppose you're thinking seriously of being a stoker, but that's just the time when you're most likely to turn into one. So I advise you strongly against it. If you wanted to study engineering in Europe, why shouldn't you study it here? The American universities are ever so much better than the European ones."—"That's possible," said Karl, "but I have hardly any money to study on. I've read of someone who worked all day in a shop and studied at night until he became a doctor, and a mayor, too, I think, but that needs a lot of perseverance, doesn't it? I'm afraid I haven't got that. Besides, I wasn't a particularly good scholar; it was no great wrench for me to leave school. And maybe the schools here are more difficult. I can hardly speak any English at all. Anyhow, people here have a prejudice against foreigners, I think."—"So you've come up against that kind of thing too, have you? Well, that's all to the good. You're the man for me. See here, this is a German ship we're on, it belongs to the Hamburg-American Line; so why aren't the crew all Germans, I ask you? Why is the Chief Engineer a Roumanian? A man called Schubal. It's hard to believe it. A measly hound like that slave-driving us Germans on a German ship! You mustn't think"—here his voice failed him and he gesticulated with his hands—"that I'm complaining for the sake of complaining. I know you have no influence and that you're a poor lad yourself. But it's too much!" And he brought his fist several times down on the table, never taking his eyes from it while he flourished it. "I've signed on in ever so many ships"—and he reeled off twenty names one after the other as if they were one word, which quite confused Karl—

7

"and I've done good work in all of them, been praised, pleased every captain I ever had, actually stuck to the same cargo-boat for several years, I did"—he rose to his feet as if that had been the greatest achievement of his life—"and here on this tub, where everything's done by rule and you don't need any wits at all, here I'm no good, here I'm just in Schubal's way, here I'm a slacker who should be kicked out and doesn't begin to earn his pay. Can you understand that? I can't."—"Don't you put up with it!" said Karl excitedly. He had almost lost the feeling that he was on the uncertain boards of a ship, beside the coast of an unknown continent, so much at home did he feel here in the stoker's bunk. "Have you seen the Captain about it? Have you asked him to give you your rights?"—"Oh, get away with you, out you get, I don't want you here. You don't listen to what I say, and then you give me advice. How could I go to the Captain?" Wearily the stoker sat down again and hid his face in his hands.

"I can't give him any better advice," Karl told himself. And it occurred to him that he would have done better to go and get his box instead of handing out advice that was merely regarded as stupid. When his father had given him the box for good he had said in jest: "How long will you keep it?" and now that faithful box had perhaps been lost in earnest. His sole remaining consolation was that his father could hardly learn of his present situation, even if he were to enquire. All that the shipping company could say was that he had safely reached New York. But Karl felt sorry to think that he had hardly used the things in the box yet, although, to take an instance, he should long since have changed his shirt. So his economies had started at the wrong point, it seemed; now, at the very beginning of his career, when it was essential to show himself in clean clothes, he would have to appear in a dirty shirt. Otherwise the loss of the box would not have been so serious, for the suit which he was wearing was actually better than the one in the box, which in reality was merely an emergency suit that his mother had hastily mended just before he left. Then he remembered that in the box there was a piece of Veronese salami which his mother had packed as an extra tid-bit, only he had not been able to eat more than a scrap of it, for during the voyage he had been quite without any appetite, and the soup which was served in the steerage had been more than sufficient for him. But now he would have liked to have the salami at hand, so as to present it to the stoker. For such people were easily won over by the gift of some trifle or other; Karl had learned that from his father, who deposited cigars in the pockets of the subordinate officials with whom he did business, and so won them over. Yet all that Karl now possessed in the way of gifts was his money, and he did not want to touch that for the time being, in case he should have lost his box. Again his thoughts turned back to the box, and he simply could not understand why he should have watched it during the voyage so vigilantly that he had almost lost his sleep over it, only to let that same box be filched from him so easily now. He remembered the five nights during which he had kept a suspicious eye on a little Slovak, whose bunk was two places away from him on the left, and who had designs, he was sure, on the box. This Slovak was merely waiting for Karl to be overcome by sleep and doze off for a minute, so that he might manoeuvre the box away with a long, pointed stick which he was always playing or practising with during the day. By day the Slovak looked innocent enough, but hardly did night come on than he kept rising up from his bunk to cast melancholy glances at Karl's box. Karl had seen this quite clearly, for every now and then someone would light a little candle, al-

9

though it was forbidden by the ship's regulations, and with the anxiety of the emigrant would peer into some incomprehensible prospectus of an emigration agency. If one of these candles was burning near him, Karl could doze off for a little, but if it was farther away or if the place was quite dark, he had to keep his eyes open. The strain of this task had quite exhausted him, and now perhaps it had all been in vain. Oh, that Butterbaum, if ever he met him again!

At that moment, in the distance, the unbroken silence was disturbed by a series of small, short taps, like the tapping of children's feet; they came nearer, growing louder, until they sounded like the tread of quietly marching men. Men in single file, as was natural in the narrow passage, and a clashing as of arms could be heard. Karl, who had been on the point of relaxing himself in a sleep free of all worries about boxes and Slovaks, started up and nudged the stoker to draw his attention, for the head of the procession seemed just to have reached the door. "That's the ship's band," said the stoker, "they've been playing up above and have come back to pack up. All's clear now, and we can go. Come!" He took Karl by the hand, snatched at the last moment a framed picture of the Madonna from the wall above the bed, stuck it into his breast pocket, seized his chest, and with Karl hastily left the cubby-hole.

"I'm going to the office now to give them a piece of my mind. All the passengers are gone; I don't need to care what I do." The stoker kept repeating this theme with variations, and as he walked on kicked out his foot sideways at a rat which crossed his way, but merely drove it more quickly into its hole, which it reached just in time. He was slow in all his movements, for though his legs were long they were massive as well.

They went through part of the kitchen, where some girls in dirty white aprons—which they splashed deliberately—were washing dishes in great tubs. The stoker hailed a girl called Lina, put his arm round her waist, and since she coquettishly resisted the embrace dragged her a part of the way with him. "It's pay-day; aren't you coming along?" he asked. "Why take the trouble; you can bring me the money here," she replied, squirming under his arm and running away. "Where did you pick up that good-looking boy?" she cried after him, but without waiting for an answer. They could hear the laughter of the other girls, who had all stopped their work.

But they went on and came to a door above which there was a little pediment, supported by tiny, gilded caryatides. For a ship's fitting it looked extravagantly sumptuous. Karl realised that he had never been in this part of the ship, which during the voyage had probably been reserved for passengers of the first and second class; but the doors that cut it off had now been thrown open to prepare for the cleaning down of the ship. Indeed, they had already met some men with brooms on their shoulders, who had greeted the stoker. Karl was amazed at the extent of the ship's organisation; as a steerage passenger he had seen very little of it. Along the corridors ran wires of electric installations, and a little bell kept sounding every now and then.

The stoker knocked respectfully at the door, and when someone cried "Come in!" urged Karl with a wave of the hand to enter boldly. Karl stepped in, but remained standing beside the door. The three windows of this room framed a view of the sea, and gazing at the cheerful motion of the waves his heart beat faster, as if he had not been looking at the sea without interruption for five long days. Great ships crossed each other's courses in either direction, yielding to the assault of the waves only as far as their ponderous weight permitted them. If one almost shut one's eyes, these ships seemed to be staggering under their own weight. From their masts flew long, narrow pennants which, though kept taut by the speed of their going, at the same time fluttered a little. Probably from some battleship there could be heard salvoes, fired in salute, and a warship of some kind passed at no great distance; the muzzles of its guns, gleaming with the reflection of sunlight on steel, seemed to be nursed along by the sure, smooth motion, although not on an even keel. Only a distant view of the smaller ships and boats could be had, at least from the door, as they darted about in swarms through the gaps between the great ships. And behind them all rose New York, and its skyscrapers stared at Karl with their hundred thousand eyes. Yes, in this room one realised where one was.

At a round table three gentlemen were sitting, one a ship's officer in the blue ship's uniform, the two others harbour officials in black American uniforms. On the table lay piles of various papers, which the officer first glanced over, pen in hand, and then handed to the two others, who read them, made excerpts, and filed them away in portfolios, except when they were not actually engaged in taking down some kind of protocol which one of them dictated to his colleagues, making clicking noises with his teeth all the time.

By the first window a little man was sitting at a desk with his back to the door; he was busy with some huge ledgers ranked on a stout book-shelf on a level with his head. Beside him stood an open safe which, at first glance at least, seemed empty.

The second window was vacant and gave the better view. But near the third two gentlemen were standing conversing in low tones. One of them was leaning against the window; he was wearing the ship's uniform and playing with the hilt of his sword. The man to whom he was speaking faced the window, and now and then a movement of his disclosed part of a row of decorations on the breast of his interlocutor. He was in civilian clothes and carried a thin bamboo cane which, as both his hands were resting on his hips, also stood out like a sword.

Karl did not have much time to see all this, for almost at once an attendant came up to them and asked the stoker, with a glance which seemed to indicate that he had no business here, what he wanted. The stoker replied as softly as he had been asked that he wished to speak to the Head Purser. The attendant made a gesture of refusal with his hand, but all the same tiptoed towards the man with the ledgers, avoiding the round table by a wide detour. The ledger official—this could clearly be seen—stiffened all over at the words of the attendant, but at last turned round towards this man who wished to speak to him and waved him away violently, repudiating the attendant too, to make quite certain. The attendant then sidled back to the stoker and said in the voice of one imparting a confidence: "Clear out of here at once!"

At this reply the stoker turned his eyes on Karl, as if Karl were his heart, to whom he was silently bewailing his grief. Without stopping to think, Karl launched himself straight across the room, actually brushing against one of the officers' chairs, while the attendant chased after him, swooping with wide-spread arms as if to catch an insect; but Karl was the first to reach the Head Purser's desk, which he gripped firmly in case the attendant should try to drag him away.

The whole room naturally sprang to life at once. The ship's officer at the table leapt to his feet; the harbour officials looked on calmly but attentively; the two gentlemen by the window moved closer to each other; the attendant, who thought it was no longer his place to interfere, since his masters were now involved, stepped back. The stoker waited tensely by the door for the moment when his intervention should be required.

And the Head Purser at last made a complete rightabout turn in his chair.

From his secret pocket, which he did not mind showing to these people, Karl hauled out his passport, which he opened and laid on the desk in lieu of further introduction. The Head Purser seemed to consider the passport irrelevant, for he flicked it aside with two fingers, whereupon Karl, as if that formality were satisfactorily settled, put it back in his pocket again.

"May I be allowed to say," he then began, "that in my opinion an injustice has been done to my friend the stoker? There's a certain man Schubal aboard who bullies him. He has a long record of satisfactory service on many ships, whose names he can give you, he is diligent, takes an interest in his work, and it's really hard to see why on this particular ship, where the work isn't so heavy as on cargo boats, for instance, he should get so little credit. It must be sheer slander that keeps him back and robs him of the recognition that should certainly be his. I have confined myself, as you can see, to generalities; he can lay his specific complaints before you himself." In saying this Karl had addressed all the gentlemen present, because in fact they were all listening to him, and because it seemed much more likely that among so many at least one just man might be found, than that the one just man should be the Head Purser. Karl also guilefully concealed the fact that he had known the stoker for such a short time. But he would have made a much better speech had he not been distracted by the red face of the man with the bamboo cane, which was now in his line of vision for the first time.

"It's all true, every word of it," said the stoker before anyone even asked him, indeed before anyone so much as looked at him. This over-eagerness on his part might have proved a great mistake if the man with the decorations who, it now dawned on Karl, was of course the Captain, had not clearly made up his mind to hear the case. For he stretched out his hand and called to the stoker: "Come here!" in a voice as firm as a rock. Everything now depended on the stoker's behaviour, for about the justice of his case Karl had no doubt whatever.

Luckily it appeared at this point that the stoker was a man of some worldly experience. With exemplary composure he drew out of his sea-chest, at the first attempt, a little bundle of papers and a notebook, walked over with them to the Captain as if that were a matter of course, entirely ignoring the Head Purser, and spread out his evidence on the window-ledge. There was nothing for the Head Purser to do but also to come forward. "The man is a notorious grumbler," he said in explanation, "he spends more time in the pay-room than in the engine-room. He has driven Schubal, who's a quiet fellow, to absolute desperation. Listen to me!" here he turned to the stoker. "You're a great deal too persistent in pushing yourself forward. How often have you been flung out of the pay-room already, and serve you right too, for your impudence in demanding things to which you have no right whatever? How often have you gone running from the pay-room to the Purser's office? How often has it been patiently explained to you that Schubal is your immediate superior, and that it's him you have to deal with, and him alone? And now you actually come here, when the Captain himself is present, to pester him with your impudence, and as if that weren't enough you bring a mouthpiece with you to reel off the absurd grievances you've drilled into him, a boy I've never even seen on the ship before!"

Karl forcibly restrained himself from springing forward. But the Captain had already intervened with the remark: "Better hear what the man has to say for himself. Schubal's getting a good deal too big for his boots, these days, but that doesn't

15

mean I think you're right." The last words were addressed to the stoker; it was only natural that the Captain should not take his part at once, yet everything seemed to be going the right way. The stoker began to state his case and controlled himself so far at the very beginning as to call Schubal "Mr. Schubal." Standing beside the Head Purser's vacant desk, Karl felt so pleased that in his delight he kept pressing the letter-scales down with his finger.—Mr. Schubal was unfair! Mr. Schubal gave the preference to foreigners! Mr. Schubal ordered the stoker out of the engine-room and made him clean water-closets, which was not a stoker's job at all!—At one point even the capability of Mr. Schubal was called in question, as being more apparent than real. At this point Karl fixed his eyes on the Captain and stared at him with earnest deference, as if they had been colleagues, to keep him from being influenced against the stoker by the man's awkward way of expressing himself. All the same, nothing definite emerged from the stoker's out-pourings, and although the Captain still listened thoughtfully, his eyes expressing a resolution to hear the stoker this time to the end, the other gentlemen were growing impatient and the stoker's voice no longer dominated the room, which was a bad sign. The gentleman in civilian clothes was the first to show his impatience by bringing his bamboo stick into play and tapping, though only softly, on the floor. The others still looked up now and then; but the two harbour officials, who were clearly pressed for time, snatched up their papers again and began, though somewhat absently, to glance over them; the ship's officer turned to his desk, and the Head Purser, who now thought he had won the day, heaved a loud ironical sigh. From the general dispersion of interest the only one who seemed to be exempt was the attendant, who sympathised to some extent with this poor man confronting the great, and gravely nodded to Karl as though trying to explain something.

Meanwhile outside the windows the life of the harbour went on; a flat barge laden with a mountain of barrels, which must have been wonderfully well packed, since they did not roll off, went past, almost completely obscuring the daylight; little motor-boats, which Karl would have liked to examine thoroughly if he had had time, shot straight past in obedience to the slightest touch of the man standing erect at the wheel. Here and there curious objects bobbed independently out of the restless water, were immediately submerged again and sank before his astonished eyes; boats belonging to the ocean liners were rowed past by sweating sailors; they were filled with passengers sitting silent and expectant as if they had been stowed there, except that some of them could not refrain from turning their heads to gaze at the changing scene. A movement without end, a restlessness transmitted from the restless element to helpless human beings and their works!

But everything demanded haste, clarity, exact statement; and what was the stoker doing? Certainly he was talking himself into a sweat; his hands were trembling so much that he could no longer hold the papers he had laid on the window-ledge; from all points of the compass complaints about Schubal streamed into his head, each of which, it seemed to him, should have been sufficient to dispose of Schubal for good; but all he could produce for the Captain was a wretched farrago in which everything was lumped together. For a long time the man with the bamboo cane had been staring at the ceiling and whistling to himself; the harbour officials now detained the ship's officer at their table and showed no sign of ever letting him go again; the Head Purser was clearly restrained from letting fly only by the Captain's composure; the attendant stood at attention, waiting every moment for the Captain to give an order concerning the stoker.

At that Karl could no longer remain inactive. So he advanced slowly towards the group, running over in his mind the more rapidly all the ways in which he could most adroitly handle the affair. It was certainly high time; a little longer, and they might quite well both of them be kicked out of the office. The Captain might be a good man and might also, or so it seemed to Karl, have some particular reason at the moment to show that he was a just master; but after all he wasn't a mere instrument to be recklessly played on, and that was exactly how the stoker was treating him in the boundless indignation of his heart.

Accordingly Karl said to the stoker: "You must put things more simply, more clearly; the Captain can't do justice to what you are telling him. How can he know all the mechanics and ship's boys by name, far less by their first names, so that when you mention so-and-so he can tell at once who is meant? Take your grievances in order, tell the most important ones first and the lesser ones afterwards; perhaps you'll find that it won't be necessary even to mention most of them. You always explained them clearly enough to me!" If boxes could be stolen in America, one could surely tell a lie now and then as well, he thought in self-excuse.

But was his advice of any use? Might it not already be too late? The stoker certainly stopped speaking at once when he heard the familiar voice, but his eyes were so blinded with tears of wounded dignity, of dreadful memory, of extreme present grief, that he could hardly even recognise Karl. How could he at this stage—Karl silently realised this, facing the now silent stoker—how could he at this stage suddenly change his style of argument, when it seemed plain to him that he had already

18

said all there was to say without evoking the slightest sympathy, and at the same time that he had said nothing at all, and could not expect these gentlemen to listen to the whole rigmarole over again? And at such a moment Karl, his sole supporter, had to break in with so-called good advice which merely made it clear that everything was lost, everything.

"If I had only spoken sooner, instead of looking out of the window," Karl told himself, dropping his eyes before the stoker and letting his hands fall to his sides as a sign that all hope was ended.

But the stoker mistook the action, feeling, no doubt, that Karl was nursing some secret reproach against him, and, in the honest desire to disabuse him, crowned all his other offences by starting to wrangle at this moment with Karl. At this very moment, when the men at the round table were completely exasperated by the senseless babble that disturbed their important labours, when the Head Purser was gradually beginning to find the Captain's patience incomprehensible and was just on the point of exploding, when the attendant, once more entirely translated to his masters' sphere, was measuring the stoker with savage eyes, and when, finally, the gentleman with the bamboo cane, whom even the Captain eyed now and then in a friendly manner, already quite bored by the stoker, indeed disgusted at him, had pulled out a little notebook and was obviously pre-occupied with quite different thoughts, glancing first at the notebook and then at Karl.

"I know," said Karl, who had difficulty in turning aside the torrent which the stoker now directed at him, but yet could summon up a friendly smile for him in spite of all dissension, "that you're right, you're right, I have never doubted it." In his fear of being struck by the stoker's gesticulating hands he would have liked to catch hold of them, and still better to force the man into a corner so as to whisper a few soothing, re-assuring words to him which no one else could hear. But the stoker was past all bounds. Karl now began actually to take a sort of comfort in the thought that in case of need the stoker could overwhelm the seven men in the room with the very strength of his desperation. But on the desk, as he could see at a glance, there was a bell-arrangement with far too many buttons; the mere pressure of one hand on them would raise the whole ship and call up all the hostile men that filled its passageways.

But here, in spite of his air of bored detachment, the gentleman with the bamboo cane came over to Karl and asked, not very loudly yet clearly enough to be heard above the stoker's ravings: "By the way, what's your name?" At that moment, as if someone behind the door had been waiting to hear this remark, there was a knock. The attendant looked across at the Captain; the Captain nodded. Thereupon the attendant went to the door and opened it. Outside was standing a middle-sized man in an old military coat, not looking at all like the kind of person who would attend to machinery—and yet he was Schubal. If Karl had not guessed this from the expression of satisfaction which lit up all eyes, even the Captain's, he must have recognised it with horror from the demeanour of the stoker, who clenched his fists at the end of his out-stretched arms with a vehemence that made the clenching of them seem the most important thing about him, to which he was prepared to sacrifice everything else in life. All his strength was concentrated in his fists, including the very strength that held him upright.

And so here was the enemy, fresh and gay in his shore-going clothes, a ledger under his arm, probably containing a statement of the hours worked and the wages due to the stoker, and he was openly scanning the faces of everyone present, a frank admission that his first concern was to discover on which side they stood. All seven of them were already his friends, for even though the Captain had raised some objections to him earlier, or had pretended to do so because he felt sorry for the stoker, it was now apparent that he had not the slightest fault to find with Schubal. A man like the stoker could not be too severely repressed, and if Schubal were to be reproached for anything, it was for not having subdued the stoker's recalcitrance sufficiently, since the fellow had dared to face the Captain after all.

Yet it might still be assumed that the confrontation of Schubal and the stoker would achieve, even before a human tribunal, the result which would have been awarded by divine justice, since Schubal, even if he were good at making a show of virtue, might easily give himself away in the long run. A brief flare-up of his evil nature would suffice to reveal it to these gentlemen, and Karl would arrange for that. He already had a rough and ready knowledge of the shrewdness, the weaknesses, the temper of the various individuals in the room, and in this respect the time he had spent there had not been wasted. It was a pity that the stoker was not more competent; he seemed quite incapable of decisive action. If one were to thrust Schubal at him, he would probably split the man's hated skull with his fists. But it was beyond his power to take the couple of steps needed to bring Schubal within reach. Why had Karl not foreseen what so easily could have been foreseen: that Schubal would inevitably put in an appearance, if not of his own accord, then by order of the Captain? Why had he not outlined an exact plan of campaign with the stoker when they were on their way here, instead of simply walking in, hopelessly unprepared, as soon as they found a door, which was what they had done? Was the stoker even capable of saying a word by this time, of answering yes and no, as he must do if he were now to be cross-examined, although, to be sure, a cross-examination was almost too much to hope for? There he stood, his legs a-sprawl, his knees uncertain, his head thrown back, and the air flowed in and out of his open mouth as if the man had no lungs to control its motion.

But Karl himself felt more strong and clear-headed than perhaps he had ever been at home. If only his father and mother could see him now, fighting for justice in a strange land before men of authority, and, though not yet triumphant, dauntlessly resolved to win the final victory! Would they revise their opinion of him? Set him between them and praise him? Look into his eyes at last, at last, these eyes so filled with devotion to them? Ambiguous questions, and this the most unsuitable moment to ask them!

"I have come here because I believe this stoker is accusing me of dishonesty or something. A maid in the kitchen told me she saw him making in this direction. Captain, and all you other gentlemen, I am prepared to show papers to disprove any such accusation, and, if you like, to adduce the evidence of unprejudiced and incorruptible witnesses, who are waiting outside the door now." Thus spake Schubal. It was, to be sure, a clear and manly statement, and from the altered expression of the listeners one might have thought they were hearing a human voice for the first time after a long interval. They certainly did not notice the holes that could be picked in that fine speech. Why, for instance, had the first relevant word that occurred to him been "dishonesty"? Should he have been accused of that, perhaps, instead of nationalistic prejudice? A maid in the kitchen had seen the stoker on his way to the office, and Schubal had immediately divined what that meant? Wasn't it his consciousness of guilt that had sharpened his apprehension? And he had immediately collected witnesses, had he, and then called them unprejudiced and incorruptible to boot? Imposture, nothing but imposture! And these gentlemen were not only taken in by it, but regarded it with approval? Why had he allowed so much time to elapse between the kitchen-maid's report and his arrival here? Simply in order to let the stoker weary the gentlemen, until they began to lose their powers of clear judgment, which Schubal feared most of all. Standing for a long time behind the door, as he must have done, had he deliberately refrained from knocking until he heard the casual question of the gentleman with the bamboo cane, which gave him grounds to hope that the stoker was already despatched?

Everything was clear enough now and Schubal's very behaviour involuntarily corroborated it, but it would have to be proved to these gentlemen by other and still more palpable means. They must be shaken up. Now then, Karl, quick, make the best of every minute you have, before the witnesses come in and confuse everything!

At that very moment, however, the Captain waved Schubal away, and at once—seeing that his case seemed to be provisionally postponed—he stepped aside and was joined by the attendant, with whom he began a whispered conversation involving many side glances at the stoker and Karl, as well as the most impressive gestures. It was as if Schubal were rehearsing his next fine speech.

"Didn't you want to ask this youngster something, Mr. Jacob?" the Captain said in the general silence to the gentleman with the bamboo cane.

"Why, yes," replied the other, with a slight bow in acknowledgement of the Captain's courtesy. And he asked Karl again: "What is your name?"

Karl, who thought that his main business would be best served by satisfying his stubborn questioner as quickly as possible, replied briefly, without, as was his custom, introducing himself by means of his passport, which he would have had to tug out of his pocket: "Karl Rossmann."

"But really!" said the gentleman who had been addressed as Jacob, recoiling with an almost incredulous smile. The Captain too, the Head Purser, the ship's officer, even the attendant, all showed an excessive astonishment on hearing Karl's name. Only the Harbour Officials and Schubal remained indifferent.

"But really!" repeated Mr. Jacob, walking a little stiffly up to Karl, "then I'm your Uncle Jacob and you're my own dear nephew. I suspected it all the time!" he said to the Captain before embracing and kissing Karl, who dumbly submitted to everything.

"And what may your name be?" asked Karl when he felt himself released again, very courteously, but quite coolly, trying hard to estimate the consequences which this new development might have for the stoker. At the moment, there was nothing to indicate that Schubal could extract any advantage out of it.

"But don't you understand your good fortune, young man?" said the Captain, who thought that Mr. Jacob was wounded in his dignity by Karl's question, for he had retired to the window, obviously to conceal from the others the agitation on his face, which he also kept dabbing with a handkerchief. "It is Senator Edward Jacob who has just declared himself to be your uncle. You have now a brilliant career in front of you, against all your previous expectations, I dare say. Try to realise this, as far as you can in the first shock of the moment, and pull yourself together!"

"I certainly have an Uncle Jacob in America," said Karl,

turning to the Captain, "but if I understand rightly, Jacob is only the surname of this gentleman."

"That is so," said the Captain, encouragingly.

"Well, my Uncle Jacob, who is my mother's brother, had Jacob for a Christian name, but his surname must of course be the same as my mother's, whose maiden name was Bendelmayer."

"Gentlemen!" cried the Senator, coming forward in response to Karl's explanation, quite cheerful now after his recuperative retreat to the window. Everyone except the Harbour Officials laughed a little, some as if really touched, others for no visible reason.

"Yet what I said wasn't so ridiculous as all that," thought Karl.

"Gentlemen," repeated the Senator, "you are involved against my will and your own in a little family scene, and so I can't but give you an explanation, since, I fancy, no one but the Captain here"—this reference was followed by a reciprocal bow—"is fully informed of the circumstances."

"Now I must really attend to every word," Karl told himself, and glancing over his shoulder he was delighted to see that life was beginning to return to the figure of the stoker.

"For the many years of my sojourn in America—though sojourn is hardly the right word to use of an American citizen, and I am an American citizen from my very heart—for all these many years, then, I have lived completely cut off from my relatives in Europe, for reasons which, in the first place, do not concern us here, and in the second, would really give me too much pain to relate. I actually dread the moment when I may be forced to explain them to my dear nephew, for some frank criticisms of his parents and their friends will be unavoidable, I'm afraid."

"It is my uncle, no doubt about it," Karl told himself, listening eagerly, "he must have had his name changed."

"Now, my dear nephew has simply been turned out—we may as well call a spade a spade—has simply been turned out by his parents, just as you turn a cat out of the house when it annoys you. I have no intention of extenuating what my nephew did to merit that punishment, yet his transgression was of a kind that merely needs to be named to find indulgence."

"That's not too bad," thought Karl, "but I hope he won't tell the whole story. Anyhow, he can't know much about it. Who would tell him?"

"For he was," Uncle Jacob went on, rocking himself a little on the bamboo cane which was braced in front of him, a gesture that actually succeeded in deprecating any unnecessary solemnity which otherwise must have characterised his statement, "for he was seduced by a maidservant, Johanna Brummer, a person of round about thirty-five. It is far from my wishes to offend my nephew by using the word 'seduced,' but it is difficult to find another and equally suitable word."

Karl, who had moved up quite close to his uncle, turned round to read from the gentlemen's faces the impression the story had made. None of them laughed, all were listening patiently and seriously. After all, one did not laugh at the nephew of a Senator on the first possible opportunity. It was rather the stoker who now smiled at Karl, though very faintly, but that was satisfactory in the first place, as a sign of reviving life, and excusable in the second place, since in the stoker's bunk Karl had tried to make an impenetrable mystery of this very story which was now being made so public.

"Now this Brummer," Uncle Jacob went on, "had a child by my nephew, a healthy boy, who was given the baptismal name of Jacob, evidently in memory of my unworthy self, since my nephew's doubtless quite casual references to me had managed to make a deep impression on the woman. Fortunately, let me add. For the boy's parents, to avoid paying alimony or being personally involved in any scandal—I must insist that I know neither how the law stands in their district nor their general circumstances—to avoid the scandal, then, and the payment of alimony, they packed off their son, my dear nephew, to America, shamefully unprovided-for, as you can see, and the poor lad, but for the signs and wonders which still happen in America if nowhere else, would have come to a wretched end in New York, being thrown entirely on his own resources, if this servant girl hadn't written a letter to me, which after long delays reached me the day before yesterday, giving me the whole story, along with a description of my nephew and, very wisely, the name of the ship as well. If I were setting out to entertain you, gentlemen, I could read a few passages to you from this letter"—he pulled out and flourished before them two huge, closely-written sheets of letter-paper. "You would certainly be interested, for the letter is written with somewhat simple but well-meant cunning and with much loving care for the father of the child. But I have no intention either of entertaining you for longer than my explanation needs, or of wounding at the very start the perhaps still sensitive feelings of my nephew, who if he likes can read the letter for his own instruction in the seclusion of the room already waiting for him."

But Karl had no feelings for Johanna Brummer. Hemmed in by a vanishing past, she sat in her kitchen beside the kitchen dresser, resting her elbows on top of it. She looked at him whenever he came to the kitchen to fetch a glass of water for his father or do some errand for his mother. Sometimes, awk-

wardly sitting sideways at the dresser, she would write a letter, drawing her inspiration from Karl's face. Sometimes she would sit with her hand over her eyes, heeding nothing that was said to her. Sometimes she would kneel in her tiny room next the kitchen and pray to a wooden crucifix; then Karl would feel shy if he passed by and caught a glimpse of her through the crack of the slightly open door. Sometimes she would bustle about her kitchen and recoil, laughing like a witch, if Karl came near her. Sometimes she would shut the kitchen door after Karl entered, and keep hold of the door-handle until he had to beg to be let out. Sometimes she would bring him things which he did not want and press them silently into his hand. And once she called him "Karl" and, while he was still dumbfounded at this unusual familiarity, led him into her room, sighing and grimacing, and locked the door. Then she flung her arms round his neck, almost choking him, and while urging him to take off her clothes, she really took off his and laid him on her bed, as if she would never give him up to anyone and would tend and cherish him to the end of time. "Oh Karl, my Karl!" she cried; it was as if her eyes were devouring him, while his eyes saw nothing at all and he felt uncomfortable in all the warm bedclothes which she seemed to have piled up for him alone. Then she lay down by him and wanted some secret from him, but he could tell her none, and she showed anger, either in jest or in earnest, shook him, listened to his heart, offered her breast that he might listen to hers in turn, but could not bring him to do it, pressed her naked belly against his body, felt with her hand between his legs, so disgustingly that his head and neck started up from the pillows, then thrust her body several times against him—it was as if she were a part of himself, and for that reason, perhaps, he was seized with a terrible feeling of yearning. With the tears running down his cheeks he reached his own bed at last, after many entreaties from her to come again. That was all that had happened, and yet his uncle had managed to make a great song out of it. And it seemed the cook had also been thinking about him and had informed his uncle of his arrival. That had been very good of her and he would make some return for it later, if he could.

"And now," cried the Senator, "I want you to tell me candidly whether I am your uncle or not?"

"You are my uncle," said Karl, kissing his hand and receiving a kiss on the brow. "I'm very glad to have found you, but you're mistaken if you think my father and mother never speak kindly of you. In any case, you've got some points quite wrong in your story; I mean that it didn't all happen like that in reality. But you can't really be expected to understand things at such a distance, and I fancy it won't do any great harm if these gentlemen are somewhat incorrectly informed about the details of an affair which can't have much interest for them."

"Well spoken," said the Senator, leading Karl up to the Captain, who was visibly sympathetic, and asking: "Haven't I a splendid nephew?"

"I am delighted," said the Captain, making a bow which showed his military training, "to have met your nephew, Mr. Senator. My ship is highly honoured in providing the scene for such a reunion. But the voyage in the steerage must have been very unpleasant, for we have, of course, all kinds of people travelling steerage. We do everything possible to make conditions tolerable, far more, for instance, than the American lines do, but to turn such a passage into a pleasure is more than we've been able to manage yet."

"It did me no harm," said Karl.

"It did him no harm!" repeated the Senator, laughing loudly.

"Except that I'm afraid I've lost my box——" and with that he remembered all that had happened and all that remained to be done, and he looked round him and saw the others still in the same places, silent with respect and surprise, their eyes fixed upon him. Only the Harbour Officials, in so far as their severe, self-satisfied faces were legible, betrayed some regret at having come at such an unpropitious time, and the watch which they had laid on the table before them was probably more important to them than everything that had happened in the room or might still happen there.

The first to express his sympathy, after the Captain, was curiously enough the stoker. "I congratulate you heartily," he said, and shook Karl's hand, making the gesture a token of something like gratitude. Yet when he turned to the Senator with the same words the Senator drew back, as if the stoker were exceeding his rights; and the stoker immediately retreated.

But the others now saw what should be done and at once pressed in a confused throng round Karl and the Senator. So it happened that Karl actually received Schubal's congratulations, accepted them and thanked him for them. The last to advance in the ensuing lull were the Harbour Officials, who said two words in English, which made a ludicrous impression.

The Senator now felt moved to extract the last ounce of enjoyment from the situation by refreshing his own and the others' minds with the less important details, and this was not merely tolerated but of course welcomed with interest by everyone. So he told them that he had entered in his notebook, for consultation in a possible emergency, his nephew's most distinctive characteristics as enumerated by the cook in her letter. Bored by the stoker's ravings, he had pulled out the notebook simply to distract himself, and had begun for his own amusement to compare the cook's descriptions, which were not so exact as a detective might wish, with Karl's appearance. "And that's how to find a nephew!" he concluded proudly, as if he wanted to be congratulated all over again.

"What will happen to the stoker now?" asked Karl, ignoring his uncle's last remarks. In his new circumstances he thought he was entitled to say whatever came into his mind.

"The stoker will get what he deserves," said the Senator, "and what the Captain considers to be right. I think we have had enough and more than enough of the stoker, a view in which every gentleman here will certainly concur."

"But that's not the point in a question of justice," said Karl. He was standing between his uncle and the Captain, and, perhaps influenced by his position, thought that he was holding the balance between them.

And yet the stoker seemed to have abandoned hope. His hands were half stuck into the belt of his trousers, which together with a strip of checked shirt had come prominently into view during his excited tirade. That did not worry him in the least; he had displayed the misery of his heart, now they might as well see the rags that covered his body, and then they could thrust him out. He had decided that the attendant and Schubal, as the two least important men in the room, should do him that last kindness. Schubal would have peace then and no longer be driven to desperation, as the Head Purser had put it. The Captain could take on crowds of Roumanians; Roumanian would be spoken all over the ship; and then perhaps things would really be all right. There would be no stoker pestering the head office any more with his ravings, yet his last effort would be held in almost friendly memory, since, as the Senator expressly declared, it had been the direct cause of his recognising his nephew. The nephew himself had several times tried to help him already and so had more than repaid him beforehand for his services in the recognition scene; it did not even occur to the stoker to ask anything else from him now. Besides, even if he were the nephew of a senator, he was far from being a captain yet, and it was from the mouth of the Captain that the stern verdict would fall. And thinking all this, the stoker did his best not to look at Karl, though unforunately in that roomful of enemies there was no other resting-place for his eyes.

"Don't mistake the situation," said the Senator to Karl, "this may be a question of justice, but at the same time it's a question of discipline. On this ship both of these, and most especially the latter, are entirely within the discretion of the Captain."

"That's right," muttered the stoker. Those who heard him and understood smiled uneasily.

"But we have already obstructed the Captain for too long in his official duties, which must be piling up considerably now that he has reached New York, and it's high time we left the ship, instead of adding to our sins by interfering quite unnecessarily in this petty quarrel between two mechanics and so making it a matter of importance. I understand your attitude perfectly, my dear nephew, but that very fact justifies me in hurrying you away from here immediately."

"I shall have a boat lowered for you at once," said the Captain, without deprecating in the least the Senator's words, to Karl's great surprise, since his uncle could be said to have humbled himself. The Head Purser rushed hastily to his desk and telephoned the Captain's order to the bos'un. "There's hardly any time left," Karl told himself, "but I can't do anything without offending everybody. I really can't desert my uncle now, just when he's found me. The Captain is certainly polite, but that's all. In matters of discipline his politeness fades out. And my uncle certainly meant what he said. I don't want to speak to Schubal; I'm sorry that I even shook hands with him. And the other people here are of no consequence."

Thinking these things he slowly went over to the stoker, pulled the man's right hand out of his belt and held it gently in his.

"Why don't you say something?" he asked. "Why do you put up with everything?"

The stoker merely knitted his brows, as if he were seeking some formula for what he had to say. While doing this he looked down at his own hand and Karl's.

"You've been unjustly treated, more than anyone else on this ship; I know that well enough." And Karl drew his fingers backwards and forwards between the stoker's, while the stoker gazed round him with shining eyes, as if blessed by a great happiness that no one could grudge him.

"Now you must get ready to defend yourself, answer yes and no, or else these people won't have any idea of the truth. You must promise me to do what I tell you, for I'm afraid, and I've good reason for it, that I won't be able to help you any more." And then Karl burst out crying and kissed the stoker's hand, taking that seamed, almost nerveless hand and pressing it to his cheek like a treasure which he would soon have to give up. But now his uncle the Senator was at his side and very gently yet firmly led him away.

"The stoker seems to have bewitched you," he said, exchanging an understanding look with the Captain over Karl's head. "You felt lonely, then you found the stoker, and you're grateful to him now; that's all to your credit, I'm sure. But if only for my sake, don't push things too far, learn to understand your position."

Outside the door a hubbub had arisen, shouts could be heard; it sounded even as if someone were being brutally banged against the door. A sailor entered in a somewhat disheveled state with a girl's apron tied round his waist. "There's a mob outside," he cried, thrusting out his elbows as if he were still pushing his way through a crowd. He came to himself with a start and made to salute the Captain, but at that moment he noticed the apron, tore it off, threw it on the floor and shouted: "This is a bit too much; they've tied a girl's apron on me." Then he clicked his heels together and saluted. Someone began to laugh, but the Captain said severely: "This is a fine state of things. Who is outside?"

"It's my witnesses," said Schubal, stepping forward. "I humbly beg your pardon, sir, for their bad behaviour. The men sometimes go a bit wild when they've finished a voyage."

"Bring them in here at once!" the Captain ordered, then immediately turning to the Senator said, politely but hastily: "Have the goodness now, Mr. Senator, to take your nephew and follow this man, who will conduct you to your boat. I need hardly say what a pleasure and an honour it has been to me to make your personal acquaintance. I only wish, Mr. Senator, that I may have an early opportunity to resume our interrupted talk about the state of the American fleet, and that it may be again interrupted in as pleasant a manner."

"One nephew is quite enough for me, I assure you," said Karl's uncle, laughing. "And now accept my best thanks for your kindness, and goodbye. Besides, it isn't altogether impossible that we"—he put his arm warmly round Karl—"might see quite a lot of you on our next voyage to Europe."

"That would give me great pleasure," said the Captain. The two gentlemen shook hands with each other, Karl barely touched the Captain's hand in silent haste, for the latter's attention was already engrossed by the fifteen men who were now being shepherded into the room by Schubal, somewhat chastened but still noisy enough. The sailor begged the Senator to let him lead the way and opened a path through the crowd for him and Karl, so that they passed with ease through ranks of bowing men. It seemed that these good-natured fellows regarded the quarrel between Schubal and the stoker as a joke, and not even the Captain's presence could make them take it seriously. Karl noticed among them the kitchen-maid Lina, who with a sly wink at him was now tying round her waist the apron which the sailor had flung away, for it was hers. Still following the sailor, they left the office and turned into a small passage which brought them in a couple of steps to a little door, from which a short ladder led down to the boat that was waiting for them. Their conductor leapt down into the boat with a single bound, and the sailors in the boat rose and saluted. The Senator was just warning Karl to be careful how he came down, when Karl, as he stood on the top rung, burst into violent sobs. The Senator put his right hand under Karl's chin, drew him close to him and caressed him with his left hand. In this posture they slowly descended step by step and, still clinging together, entered the boat, where the Senator found a comfortable place for Karl, immediately facing him. At a sign from the Senator the sailors pushed off from the ship and at once began rowing at full speed. They were scarcely a few yards from the ship when Karl made the unexpected discovery that they were on the side of the ship towards which the windows of the office looked out. All three windows were filled with Schubal's witnesses, who saluted and waved in the most friendly way; Uncle Jacob actually waved back and one of the sailors showed his skill by flinging a kiss towards the ship without interrupting the regular rhythm of his rowing. It was now as if there were really no stoker at all. Karl took a more careful look at his uncle, whose knees were almost touching his own, and doubts came into his mind whether this man would ever be able to take the stoker's place. And his uncle evaded his eye and stared at the waves on which their boat was tossing.

IN his uncle's house Karl soon became used to his new circumstances. But indeed his uncle indulged his slightest wishes and Karl had never to learn by hard experience, which so much embitters one's first acquaintance with foreign countries.

Karl's room was on the sixth floor of a house whose five other floors, along with three more in the basement, were taken up by his uncle's business. It was so light, what with its two windows and a door opening on a balcony, that Karl was filled with fresh astonishment every morning on coming into it out of his tiny bedroom. Where might he not have had to stay, if he had landed in this country as a destitute little emigrant? Indeed, as his uncle, with his knowledge of the emigration laws, thought highly probable, Karl might not have been admitted into the United States at all and might have been sent home again without regard to the fact that he no longer had a home. In this country sympathy was something you could not hope for; in that respect America resembled what Karl had read about it; except that those who were fortunate seemed really to enjoy their good fortune here, sunning themselves among their care-free friends.

A narrow outside balcony ran along the whole length of Karl's room. But what would have been at home the highest vantage point in the town allowed him here little more than a view of one street, which ran perfectly straight between two rows of squarely chopped buildings and therefore seemed to be fleeing into the distance, where the outlines of a cathedral loomed enormous in a dense haze. From morning to evening and far into the dreaming night that street was the channel for a constant stream of traffic which, seen from above, looked like an inextricable confusion, for ever newly improvised, of fore-shortened human figures and the roofs of all kinds of vehicles, sending into the upper air another confusion, more riotous and complicated, of noises, dust and smells, all of it enveloped and penetrated by a flood of light which the multitudinous objects in the street scattered, carried off and again busily brought back, with an effect as palpable to the dazzled eye as if a glass roof stretched over the street were being violently smashed into fragments at every moment.

Cautious in all things, Uncle Jacob advised Karl for the time being to take up nothing seriously. He should certainly examine and consider everything, but without committing himself. The first days of a European in America might be likened to a re-birth, and though Karl was not to worry about it unduly, since one got used to things here more quickly than an infant coming into the world from the other side, yet he must keep in mind that first judgments were always unreliable and that one should not let them prejudice the future judg-ments which would eventually shape one's life in America. He himself had known new-comers, for example, who, instead of following these wise precepts had stood all day on their bal-conies gaping down at the street like lost sheep. That was bound to lead to bewilderment! The solitary indulgence of idly gazing at the busy life of New York was permissible in any-one travelling for pleasure, perhaps even advisable within lim-its; but for one who intended to remain in the States it was sheer ruination, a term by no means too emphatic, although it might be exaggerated. And, indeed, Uncle Jacob frowned with annoyance if ever he found Karl out on the balcony when

he paid one of his visits, which always occurred once daily and at the most diverse hours. Karl soon noticed this and in consequence denied himself as much as possible the pleasure of lingering on the balcony.

However, it was by no means the sole pleasure that he had. In his room stood an American writing-desk of superior construction, such as his father had coveted for years and tried to pick up cheaply at all kinds of auction sales without ever succeeding, his resources being much too small. This desk, of course, was beyond all comparison with the so-called American writing-desks which turned up at auction sales in Europe. For example, it had a hundred compartments of different sizes, in which the President of the Union himself could have found a fitting place for each of his state documents; there was also a regulator at one side and by turning a handle you could produce the most complicated combinations and permutations of the compartments to please yourself and suit your requirements. Thin panels sank slowly and formed the bottom of a new series or the top of existing drawers promoted from below; even after one turn of the handle the disposition of the whole was quite changed and the transformation took place slowly or at delirious speed according to the rate at which you wound the thing round. It was a very modern invention, yet it reminded Karl vividly of the traditional Christmas panorama which was shown to gaping children in the market-place at home, where he too, well wrapped in his winter clothes, had often stood enthralled, closely comparing the movement of the handle, which was turned by an old man, with the changes in the scene, the jerky advance of the Three Holy Kings, the shining out of the Star and the humble life of the Holy Manger. And it had always seemed to him that his mother, as she stood behind him, did not follow every detail with sufficient attention. He would draw her close to him, until he could feel her pressing against his back, and shouting at the top of his voice would keep pointing out to her the less noticeable occurrences, perhaps a little hare among the grass in the foreground, sitting up on its hind legs and then crouching as if to dart off again, until his mother would cover his mouth with her hand and very likely relapse into her former inattention. The desk was certainly not made merely to remind him of such things, yet in the history of its invention there probably existed some vague connection similar to that in Karl's memory. Unlike Karl, Uncle Jacob by no means approved of this particular desk; he had merely wanted to buy a well-appointed writing-desk for Karl, but nowadays these were all furnished with this new apparatus, which had also the advantage that it could be fitted to more old-fashioned desks without great expense. At any rate, Karl's uncle never omitted to advise him against using the regulator at all, if possible, and re-inforced his advice by pointing out that the mechanism was very sensitive, could easily be put out of order and was very expensive to repair again. It was not hard to guess that these remarks were merely pretexts, though on the other hand it would have been quite easy to lock the regulator and yet Uncle Jacob refrained from doing so.

In the first few days, during which Karl and his uncle naturally had a good number of talks together, Karl mentioned that at home he had been fond of playing the piano, though he had not played it much, having had no teaching except his mother's rudimentary instructions. Karl was quite well aware that to volunteer this information was virtually to ask for a piano, but he had already used his eyes sufficiently to know that his uncle could afford to be lavish. Yet this suggestion was not acted upon at once; but some eight days later his uncle said, almost as if making a reluctant admission, that the piano had just arrived and Karl, if he liked, could supervise its transport. That was an easy enough task, yet not much easier than the transport itself, for the building had a furniture lift in which, without any difficulty, a whole furniture van could have been accommodated, and in this lift the piano soared up to Karl's room. Karl could have gone up himself in the same lift as the piano and the workmen, but just beside it there was an ordinary lift free, so he went up in that instead, keeping himself at the same elevation as the other by means of a lever and staring fixedly through the glass panels at the beautiful instrument which was now his property. When he had it safely in his room and struck the first notes on it, he was filled with such foolish joy that instead of going on playing he jumped up and with his hands on his hips gazed rapturously at the piano from a little distance. The acoustics of the room were excellent and they had the effect of quite dispelling his first slight discomfort at living in a steel house. True, in the room itself, despite the external appearance of the building, one could see not the slightest sign of steel, nor could one have discovered in the furnishings even the smallest detail which did not harmonise with the comfort of the whole. At first Karl set great hopes on his piano playing and sometimes unashamedly dreamed, at least before falling asleep, of the possibility that it might exert a direct influence upon his life in America. When he opened his windows and the street noises came in, it certainly sounded strange to hear on the piano an old army song of his native country which soldiers, sprawling of an evening at barrack windows and gazing into the darkness of some square outside, sang to each other from window to window,—but the street, if he looked down it afterwards, remained unchanged, only one small section of a great wheel which afforded no hand-hold unless one knew all the forces controlling its full orbit. Uncle Jacob tolerated the piano playing and said not a word against it, especially as Karl indulged very seldom in it; indeed, he actually brought Karl the scores of some American marches, among them the national anthem, but pure love of music could hardly explain the fact that he asked Karl one day, quite seriously, whether he would not like to learn the violin or the French horn as well.

The learning of English was naturally Karl's first and most important task. A young teacher from a neighbouring commercial college appeared in his room every morning at seven and found him already over his exercise books at the desk, or walking up and down the room committing words to memory. Karl saw clearly that if he were to acquire English there was no time to be lost and that this was also his best chance of giving his uncle especial pleasure by making rapid progress. And indeed, though he had to confine himself at first to the simplest greetings, he was soon able to carry on in English an increasingly large part of his conversation with his uncle, whereupon more intimate topics simultaneously came up for discussion. The first American poem,—a description of a fire—which Karl managed to recite to his uncle one evening, made that gentleman quite solemn with satisfaction. They were both standing at a window in Karl's room, Uncle Jacob was looking out at the sky, from which all brightness had already faded, bringing his hands together slowly and regularly in time with the verses, while Karl stood erect beside him and with eyes fixed on vacancy delivered himself of the difficult lines.

The better Karl's English became, the greater inclination his uncle showed to introduce him to his friends, arranging only that on such occasions the English teacher should always be at his elbow. The first person to whom Karl was introduced one morning was a slender, incredibly supple young man, whom Uncle Jacob brought into the room with a string of fulsome compliments. He was obviously one of these many million-aires' sons who are regarded as failures by their parents' standards and who lead strenuous lives which an ordinary man could scarcely endure for a single average day without breaking down. And as if he knew or divined this and faced it as best he could, there was always about his lips and eyes an unchanging smile of happiness, which seemed to embrace himself, anyone he was speaking to and the whole world.

With the unconditional approval of Uncle Jacob, it was arranged that this young man, whose name was Mr. Mack, should take Karl out riding every morning at half-past five, either in the riding school or in the open air. Karl hesitated at first before consenting, since he had never sat on a horse and wished first to learn a little about riding, but as his uncle and Mack insisted so much, arguing that riding was simply a pleasure and a healthy exercise and not at all an art, he finally agreed. Of course, that meant that he had now to leave his bed at half-past four every morning, which was often a great hardship to him, since he suffered from an actual longing for sleep, probably in consequence of the unremitting attention which he had to exercise all day long; but as soon as he came into his bathroom he ceased to be sorry for himself. Over the full length and breadth of the bath stretched the spray—which of his schoolmates at home, no matter how rich, had anything equal to it and for his own use alone?—and there Karl could lie out-stretched—this bath was wide enough to let him spread out his arms—and let the stream of luke-warm, hot, and again luke-warm and finally ice-cold water pour over any part of him at pleasure, or over his whole body at once. He lay there as if in a still faintly surviving enjoyment of sleep and loved to catch with his closed eyelids the last separately falling drops, which as they broke flowed down over his face.

At the riding school, where his uncle's towering motor-car deposited him, the English teacher would be already waiting, while Mack invariably arrived later. But Mack could be late with an easy mind, for the actual life of the riding-school did not begin until he came. The horses started out of their semi-slumber when he entered, the whips cracked more loudly through the room, and on the gallery running round it single figures suddenly appeared, spectators, grooms, riding-pupils, or whatever they were. Karl employed the time before Mack's arrival in practising riding a little, though only the most rudimentary first exercises. There was a tall man who could reach the backs of the biggest horses almost without raising his arm, and he invariably gave Karl his scanty quarter-of-an-hour's instruction. The results which Karl achieved were not impressive and he learned by heart many exclamations of pain in English, gasping them out to his English teacher, who always leant against the door, usually in a very sleepy condition. But almost all his dissatisfaction with riding ceased once Mack appeared. The tall man was sent away and soon nothing could be heard in the hall, which was still half in darkness, but the hoofs of galloping horses and hardly anything seen but Mack's uplifted arm, as he signalled his orders to Karl. After half an hour of this pleasure, fleeting as a dream, a halt was called. Mack was then always in a great hurry, said goodbye to Karl, patted him a few times on the cheek if he was particularly pleased with his riding, and vanished, too pressed for time even to accompany Karl through the door. Then Karl and the English teacher climbed into the car and drove to their lesson, generally round byways, for if they had plunged into the traffic of the great street which led directly from the riding-school to his uncle's house it would have meant too great a loss of time. In any case, the English teacher soon ceased to act as escort, since Karl, who blamed himself for needlessly forcing the tired man to go with him to the riding-school, especially since the English required in his intercourse with Mack was very simple, begged his uncle to absolve the man from that duty. And after some reflection his uncle acceded to his wish.

It took a relatively long time before Uncle Jacob would consent to allow Karl even the slightest insight into his business, although Karl often begged him to do so. It was a sort of commission and despatch agency such as, to the best of Karl's knowledge, was probably not to be found in Europe. For the business did not consist in the transference of wares from the producer to the consumer or to the dealer, but in the handling of all the necessary goods and raw materials going to and between the great manufacturing trusts. It was consequently a business which embraced simultaneously the purchasing, storing, transport and sale of immense quantities of goods and had to maintain the most exact, unintermittent telephonic and telegraphic communication with its various clients. The telegraphists' hall was not smaller but larger than the telegraphic office of Karl's native town, through which he had once been shown by one of his schoolmates, who was known there. In the telephone hall, wherever one looked, the doors of the telephone boxes could be seen opening and shutting, and the noise was maddening. His uncle opened the first of these doors and in the glaring electric light Karl saw an operator, quite oblivious to any sound from the door, his head bound in a steel band which pressed the receivers against his ears. His right arm was lying on a little table as if it were strangely heavy and only the fingers holding the pencil kept twitching with inhuman regularity and speed. In the words which he spoke into the

47

mouthpiece he was very sparing and often one noticed that though he had some objection to raise or wished to obtain more exact information, the next phrase that he heard compelled him to lower his eyes and go on writing before he could carry out his intention. Besides he did not need to say anything, as Uncle Jacob explained to Karl in a subdued voice, for the same conversation which this man was taking down was being taken down at the same time by two other operators and would then be compared with the other versions, so that errors might as far as possible be eliminated. At the moment when Uncle Jacob and Karl emerged from the box a messenger slipped into it and came out with the notes which the operator had just written. Through the hall there was a perpetual tumult of people rushing hither and thither. Nobody said good day, greetings were omitted, each man fell into step behind anyone who was going the same way, keeping his eyes on the floor, over which he was set on advancing as quickly as he could, or giving a hurried glance at a word or figure here and there on the papers he held in his hand, which fluttered with the wind of his progress.

"You have really gone far," Karl once said on one of these journeys through the building, which took several days to traverse in its entirety, even if one did nothing more than have a look at each department.

"And let me tell you I started it all myself thirty years ago. I had a little business at that time near the docks and if five crates came up for unloading in one day I thought it a great day and went home swelling with pride. Today my warehouses cover the third largest area in the port and my old store is the restaurant and storeroom for my sixty-fifth group of porters."

"It's really wonderful," said Karl.

"Developments in this country are always rapid," said his uncle, breaking off the conversation.

One day his uncle appeared just before dinner, which Karl had expected to take alone as usual, and asked him to put on his black suit at once and join him for dinner, together with two of his business friends. While Karl was changing in the next room, his uncle sat down at the desk and looked through the English exercise which Karl had just finished, then brought down his hand on the desk and exclaimed aloud: "Really first-rate!"

Doubtless Karl's changing went all the more smoothly on hearing these words of praise, but in any case he was now pretty certain of his English.

In his uncle's dining-room, which he could still remember from the evening of his arrival, two tall, stout gentlemen rose to their feet, one of them called Green, the other Pollunder, as appeared during the subsequent conversation. For Uncle Jacob hardly ever dropped a word about any of his acquaintances and always left it to Karl to discover by his own observation whatever was important or interesting about them. During the dinner itself only intimate business matters were discussed, which meant for Karl an excellent lesson in commercial English, and Karl was left silently to occupy himself with his food, as if he were a child who had merely to sit up straight and empty his plate; but Mr. Green leaned across to him and asked him in English, unmistakably exerting himself to pronounce every word with the utmost distinctness, what in general were his first impressions of America? With a few side glances at his uncle, Karl replied fairly fully in the dead silence that followed and in his gratitude and his desire to please used several characteristic New York expressions. At one of his phrases all three gentlemen burst out laughing together and Karl was afraid that he had made a gross mistake; but no, Mr. Pollunder explained to him that he had actually said something very smart.

Mr. Pollunder, indeed, seemed to have taken a particular fancy to Karl, and while Uncle Jacob and Mr. Green returned once more to their business consultations Mr. Pollunder asked Karl to bring his chair nearer, asked him countless questions about his name, his family and his voyage and at last, to give him a reprieve, began hastily, laughing and coughing, to tell about himself and his daughter, with whom he lived in a little country house in the neighbourhood of New York, where, however, he was only able to pass the evenings, for he was a banker and his profession kept him in New York the whole day. Karl was warmly invited to come out to the country house; an American so new and untried as Karl must be in need of occasional recuperation from New York. Karl at once asked his uncle's leave to accept the invitation and his uncle gave it with apparent pleasure, yet without naming any stated time or even letting it come into consideration, as Karl and Mr. Pollunder had expected.

But the very next day Karl was summoned to one of his uncle's offices (his uncle had ten different offices in that building alone), where he found his uncle and Mr. Pollunder reclining somewhat monosyllabically in two easy chairs.

"Mr. Pollunder," said Uncle Jacob, who could scarcely be distinguished in the evening dusk of the room, "Mr. Pollunder has come to take you with him to his country house, as was mentioned yesterday."

"I didn't know it was to be today," replied Karl, "or else I'd have got ready."

"If you're not ready, then perhaps we'd better postpone the visit to some other time," remarked his uncle.

"What do you need to get ready?" cried Mr. Pollunder. "A young man is always ready for anything."

"It isn't on his account," said Uncle Jacob, turning to his

guest, "but he would have to go up to his room again, and that would delay you."

"There's plenty of time for that," said Mr. Pollunder, "I allowed for a delay and left my office earlier."

"You see," said Uncle Jacob, "what a lot of trouble this visit of yours has caused already."

"I'm very sorry," said Karl, "but I'll be back again in a minute," and he made to rush away.

"Don't hurry yourself," said Mr. Pollunder, "you aren't causing me the slightest trouble; on the contrary, it's a pleasure to have you visiting me."

"You'll miss your riding lesson tomorrow. Have you called it off?"

"No," said Karl; this visit to which he had been looking forward so much was beginning to be burdensome, "I didn't know——"

"And you mean to go in spite of that?" asked his uncle.

Mr. Pollunder, that kind man, came to Karl's help.

"We'll stop at the riding-school on the way and put everything right."

"There's something in that," said Uncle Jacob. "But Mack will be expecting you."

"He won't be expecting me," said Karl, "but he'll turn up anyhow."

"Well then?" said Uncle Jacob, as if Karl's answer had not been the slightest excuse.

Once more Mr. Pollunder solved the problem: "But Clara" —she was Mr. Pollunder's daughter—"expects him too, and this very evening, and surely she has the preference over Mack?"

"Certainly," said Uncle Jacob. "Well then, run away to your room," and as if involuntarily, he drummed on the arm

51

of his chair several times. Karl was already at the door when his uncle detained him once more with the question: "Of course you'll be back here again tomorrow morning for your English lesson?"

"But my dear sir!" cried Mr. Pollunder, turning round in his chair with astonishment, as far as his stoutness would permit him. "Can't he stay with us at least over tomorrow? Couldn't I bring him back early in the morning the day after?"

"That's quite out of the question," retorted Uncle Jacob. "I can't have his studies broken up like this. Later on, when he has taken up a regular profession of some kind, I'll be very glad to let him accept such a kind and flattering invitation even for a long time."

"What a contradiction!" thought Karl.

Mr. Pollunder looked quite melancholy. "But for one evening and one night it's really hardly worth while."

"That's what I think too," said Uncle Jacob.

"One must take what one can get," said Mr. Pollunder, and now he was laughing again. "All right, I'll wait for you," he shouted to Karl, who, since his uncle said nothing more, was hurrying away.

When he returned in a little while, ready for the journey, he found only Mr. Pollunder in the office; his uncle had gone. Mr. Pollunder shook Karl quite gaily by both hands, as if he wished to assure himself as strongly as possible that Karl was coming after all. Karl, still flushed with haste, for his part wrung Mr. Pollunder's hands in return; he was elated at the thought of the visit.

"My uncle wasn't annoyed at my going?"

"Not at all! He didn't mean all that very seriously. He has your education so much at heart."

"Did he tell you himself that he didn't mean it seriously?"

"Oh yes," said Mr. Pollunder, drawling the words, and thus proving that he could not tell a lie.

"It's strange how unwilling he was to give me leave to visit you, although you are a friend of his."

Mr. Pollunder too, although he did not admit it, could find no explanation for the problem, and both of them, as they drove though the warm evening in Mr. Pollunder's car, kept turning it over in their minds for a long time, although they spoke of other things.

They sat close together and Mr. Pollunder held Karl's hand in his while he talked. Karl was eager to hear as much as he could about Miss Clara, as if his impatience with the long journey could be assuaged by listening to stories that made the time appear shorter. He had never driven through the streets of New York in the evening, but though the pavements and roadways were thronged with traffic changing its direction every minute, as if caught up in a whirlwind and roaring like some strange element quite unconnected with humanity, Karl, as he strained his attention to catch Mr. Pollunder's words, had no eye for anything but Mr. Pollunder's dark waistcoat, which was peacefully spanned by a gold chain. Out of the central streets where the theatre-goers, urged by extreme and unconcealed fear of being late, hurried along with flying steps or drove in vehicles at the utmost possible speed, they came by intermediate stages to the suburbs, where their car was repeatedly diverted by mounted police into side alleys, as the main roadway was occupied by a demonstration of metal-workers on strike and only the most necessary traffic could be permitted to use the cross-roads. When the car, emerging out of dark, dully echoing narrow lanes, crossed one of these great thoroughfares which were as wide as squares, there opened out on both sides an endless perspective of pavements filled with a moving mass of people, slowly shuffling forward, whose singing was more homogeneous than any single human voice. But in the road-way, which was kept free, mounted policemen could be seen here and there sitting on motionless horses, or banner-bearers, or inscribed streamers stretching across the street, or a labour leader surrounded by colleagues and stewards, or an electric tram which had not escaped quickly enough and now stood dark and empty while the driver and the conductor lounged on the platform. Small groups of curious spectators stood at a distance watching the actual demonstrators, rooted to their places although they had no clear idea of what was really happening. But Karl merely leaned back happily on the arm which Mr. Pollunder had put round him; the knowledge that he would soon be a welcome guest in a well-lighted country house surrounded by high walls and guarded by watch-dogs filled him with extravagant well-being, and although he was now beginning to feel sleepy and could no longer catch perfectly all that Mr. Pollunder was saying, or at least only intermittently, he pulled himself together from time to time and rubbed his eyes to discover whether Mr. Pollunder had noticed his drowsiness, for that was something he wished to avoid at any price.

"WELL, here we are," said Mr. Pollunder in one of Karl's most absent moments. The car was standing before a house which, like the country houses of most rich people in the neighbourhood of New York, was larger and taller than a country house designed for only one family has any need to be. Since there were no lights except in the lower part of the house, it was quite impossible to estimate how high the building was. In front of it rustled chestnut trees and between them —the gate was already open—a short path led to the front-door steps. Karl felt so tired on getting out that he began to suspect the journey must have been fairly long after all. In the darkness of the chestnut avenue he heard a girl's voice saying beside him: "So this is Mr. Jacob at last."

"My name is Rossmann," said Karl, taking the hand held out to him by a girl whose silhouette he could now perceive.

"He is only Jacob's nephew," said Mr. Pollunder in explanation, "his own name is Karl Rossmann."

"That doesn't make us any the less glad to see him," said the girl, who did not bother much about names.

All the same Karl insisted on asking, while he walked towards the house between Mr. Pollunder and the girl: "Are you Miss Clara?"

"Yes," she said, and now a little light from the house picked out her face, which was inclined towards him, "but I didn't want to introduce myself here in the darkness."

"Why, has she been waiting for us at the gate?" thought Karl, gradually wakening up as he walked along.

"By the way, we have another guest this evening," said Clara.

"Impossible!" cried Pollunder irritably.

"Mr. Green," said Clara.

"When did he come?" asked Karl, as if seized by a premonition.

"Just a minute ago. Didn't you hear his car in front of yours?"

Karl looked up at Mr. Pollunder to discover what he thought of the situation, but his hands were thrust into his trouser pockets and he merely stamped his feet a little on the path.

"It's no good living just outside New York; it doesn't save you from being disturbed. We'll simply have to get a house farther away; even if I have to spend half the night driving before I get home."

They remained standing by the steps.

"But it's a long time since Mr. Green was here last," said Clara, who obviously agreed with her father yet wanted to soothe him and take him out of himself.

"Why should he come just this evening?" said Pollunder, and the words rolled furiously over his sagging lower lip, which like all loose, heavy flesh was easily agitated.

"Why indeed!" said Clara.

"Perhaps he'll soon go away again," remarked Karl, himself astonished at the sympathy uniting him to these people who had been complete strangers to him a day ago.

"Oh no," said Clara, "he has some great business or other with Papa which will probably take a long time to settle, for he has already threatened me in fun that I'll have to sit up till morning if I'm going to play the polite hostess."

"That's the last straw. So he's going to stay all night!" cried Pollunder, as if nothing could be worse. "I really feel half inclined," he said, and the idea restored some of his good humour, "I really feel half inclined, Mr. Rossmann, to put you in the car again and drive you straight back to your uncle. This evening's spoilt beforehand, and who knows when your uncle will trust you here again. But if I bring you back tonight he won't be able to refuse us your company next time."

And he took hold of Karl's hand, to carry out his plan on the instant. But Karl made no move and Clara begged her father to let him stay, since she and Karl at least need not let Mr. Green disturb them at all, and finally Pollunder himself grew aware that his resolution was not of the firmest. Besides— and that was perhaps the decisive thing—they suddenly heard Mr. Green shouting from the top of the steps down into the garden: "Where on earth are you?"

"Coming," said Pollunder and he began to climb the steps. Behind him came Karl and Clara, who now studied each other in the light.

"What red lips she has," Karl said to himself and he thought of Mr. Pollunder's lips and how beautifully they had been metamorphosed in his daughter.

"After dinner," she said, "we'll go straight to my room, if you would like that, so that we at least can be rid of Mr. Green, even if Papa has to put up with him. And then perhaps you'll be so kind as to play the piano for me, for Papa has told me how well you can play; I'm sorry to say I'm quite incapable of practising and never touch my piano, much as I really love music."

Karl was quite prepared to fall in with Clara's suggestion, though he would have liked to have Mr. Pollunder join them as well. But the sight of Green's gigantic figure—he had already got used to Pollunder's bulk—which gradually loomed above them as they climbed the steps, dispelled all Karl's hopes of luring Mr. Pollunder away from the man that evening.

Mr. Green hailed them in a great hurry, as if much time had already been lost, took Mr. Pollunder's arm, and pushed Karl and Clara before him into the dining-room which, chiefly because of the flowers on the table rising from sprays of green foliage, looked very festive and so made the presence of the importunate Mr. Green doubly regrettable. Karl was just consoling himself, as he waited beside the table until the others were seated, with the thought that the great glass doors leading to the garden would remain open, for a strong fragrance was wafted in as if one sat in an arbour, when Mr. Green snorted and rushed to close these very glass doors, bending down to the bolts at the bottom, stretching up to the ones at the top, and all with such youthful agility that the servant, when he hurried across, found nothing left to do. Mr. Green's first words when he returned to the table expressed his astonishment that Karl had obtained his uncle's permission to make this visit. He raised one spoonful of soup after another to his mouth and explained to Clara on his right and to Mr. Pollunder on his left why he was so astonished, and how solicitously Uncle Jacob watched over Karl, so that his affection for Karl was too great to be called the mere affection of an uncle.

"Not content with his uncalled-for interference here, he insists on interfering between me and my uncle, too," thought Karl, and he could not swallow a drop of the golden-coloured soup. But then, not wishing to show how upset he felt, he began silently to pour the soup down his throat. The meal went on with torturing slowness. Mr. Green alone, assisted by Clara, showed any liveliness and found occasion for a short burst of laughter now and then. Mr. Pollunder let himself be drawn into the conversation once or twice, when Mr. Green started to talk about business. But he soon withdrew even from such discussions and Mr. Green had to surprise him into speech by bringing them up again unexpectedly. Moreover, Mr. Green kept insisting on the fact (and at this point Karl, who was listening as intently as if something were threatening him, had to be told by Clara that the roast was at his elbow and that he was at a dinner party) that he had had no intention beforehand of paying this unexpected visit. For though the business he came to discuss was of special urgency, yet the most important part of it at least could have been settled in town that day, leaving the minor details to be tackled next day or later. And so, long before closing hours, he had actually called at Mr. Pollunder's office, but had not found him there, and so he had had to telephone home that he would not be back that night and to drive out here.

"Then I must ask your pardon," said Karl loudly, before anyone else had time to answer, "for I am to blame that Mr. Pollunder left his office early today, and I am very sorry."

Mr. Pollunder tried to cover his face with his table napkin, while Clara, though she smiled at Karl, smiled less out of sympathy than out of a desire to influence him in some way.

"No apology is required," said Mr. Green, carving a pigeon with incisive strokes of the knife, "quite the contrary, I am delighted to pass the evening in such pleasant company instead of dining alone at home, where I have only an old housekeeper to wait on me, and she's so old that it's as much as she can do to get from the door to the table, and I can lean right back in my chair for minutes at a time to watch her making the journey. It wasn't until recently that I managed to persuade her to let my man carry the dishes as far as the door of the dining-room; but the journey from the door to the table is her perquisite, so far as I can make out."

"Heavens," cried Clara, "what fidelity!"

"Yes, there's still fidelity in the world," said Mr. Green, putting a slice of pigeon into his mouth, where his tongue, as Karl chanced to notice, took it in charge with a flourish. Karl felt nearly sick and got up. Almost simultaneously Mr. Pollunder and Clara caught him by the hands.

"It's not time to get up yet," said Clara. And when he had sat down again she whispered to him: "We'll escape together in a little while. Have patience."

Meanwhile Mr. Green had calmly gone on eating, as if it were Mr. Pollunder's and Clara's natural duty to comfort Karl after he had made him sick.

The dinner was lingered out particularly by the exhaustiveness with which Mr. Green dissected each course, which did not keep him however from attacking each new course with fresh energy; it really looked as if he were resolved radically to recuperate from the offices of his old housekeeper. Now and again he bestowed praise on Miss Clara's expertness in housekeeping, which visibly flattered her, while Karl on the contrary felt tempted to ward it off, as if it were an assault. Mr. Green, however, was not content with attacking Clara, but deplored frequently, without looking up from his plate, Karl's extraordinary lack of appetite. Mr. Pollunder defended Karl's lack of appetite, although as the host he should have encouraged him to eat. And because of the constraint under which he had suffered during the whole dinner, Karl grew so touchy that against his better knowledge he actually construed Mr. Pollunder's words as an unkindness. And it was another symptom of his condition that all at once he would eat far too much with indecorous speed, only to sit drooping for a long time afterwards, letting his knife and fork rest on the plate, quite silent and motionless, so that the man who served the dishes often did not know what to do with him.

"I'll have to tell your uncle the Senator tomorrow how you offended Miss Clara by not eating your dinner," said Mr. Green, and he betrayed the facetious intention of his words only by the way in which he plied his knife and fork.

"Just look at the girl, how downcast she is," he went on, chucking Clara under the chin. She let him do it and closed her eyes.

"Poor little thing!" he cried, leaning back, purple in the face, and laughing with the vigour of a full-fed man. Karl vainly sought to account for Mr. Pollunder's behaviour. He was sitting looking at his plate, as if the really important event were happening there. He did not pull Karl's chair closer to him and, when he did speak, he spoke to the whole table, while to Karl he had nothing particular to say. On the other hand he suffered Green, that disreputable old New York roué, deliberately to fondle Clara, to insult himself, Karl, Pollunder's guest, or at least to treat him like a child, and to go on from strength to strength, working himself up to who knew what dreadful deeds.

After rising from the table—when Green noticed the general intention he was the first to get up and as it were drew all the others with him—Karl turned aside to one of the great windows set in narrow white sashes which opened on to the terrace, and which in fact, as he saw on going nearer, were really doors. What had become of the dislike which Mr. Pollunder and his daughter had felt in the beginning for Green, and which had seemed at that time somewhat incomprehensible to Karl? Now they were standing side by side with the man and nodding at him. The smoke from Mr. Green's cigar, a present from Pollunder,—a cigar of a thickness which Karl's father in Austria had sometimes mentioned as an actual fact but had probably never seen with his own eyes,—spread through the room and bore Green's influence even into nooks and corners where he would never set foot in person. Far off as he was, Karl could feel his nose prickling with the smoke, and Mr. Green's demeanour, which he merely glanced at from the window with a hasty turn of the head, seemed infamous to him. He began to think it not at all inconceivable that his uncle had demurred for so long against giving permission for this visit simply because he knew Mr. Pollunder's weak character and accordingly envisaged as a possibility, even if he did not exactly foresee, that Karl might be exposed to insult. As for the American girl, Karl did not like her either, although she was very nearly as beautiful as he had pictured her. Ever since Mr. Green's gallantries began he had been actually surprised by the beauty of which her face was capable, and especially by the brilliance of her lively eyes. A dress which fitted so closely to its wearer's body he had never seen before; small wrinkles in the soft, closely-woven, yellowish material, betrayed the force of the tension. And yet Karl cared nothing for her and would gladly have given up all thought of going to her room, if instead he could only open the door beside him,—and he had laid his hands on the latch just in case—and climb into the car or, if the chauffeur were already asleep, walk by himself back to New York. The clear night with its benevolent full moon was free to everyone and to be afraid of anything out there, in the open, seemed senseless to Karl. He pictured to himself— and for the first time he began to feel happy in that room—how in the morning—he could hardly get back on foot sooner than that—he would surprise his uncle. True, he had never yet

been in his uncle's bedroom, nor did he even know where it was, but he would soon find that out. Then he would knock at the door and at the formal "come in" rush into the room and surprise his dear uncle, whom until now he had known only fully dressed and buttoned to the chin, sitting up in bed in his nightshirt, his astonished eyes fixed on the door. In itself that might not perhaps be very much, but one had only to consider what consequences it might lead to. Perhaps he might breakfast with his uncle for the first time, his uncle in bed, he himself sitting on a chair, the breakfast on a little table between them; perhaps that breakfast together would become a standing arrangement; perhaps as a result of such informal breakfasting, as was almost inevitable, they would meet oftener than simply once a day and so of course be able to speak more frankly to each other. After all, it was merely the lack of a frank interchange of confidences that had made him a little refractory, or better still, mulish, towards his uncle today. And even if he had to spend the night here on this occasion—and unfortunately it looked very like that, although they left him to stand by the window and amuse himself—perhaps this unlucky visit would become the turning-point in his relations with his uncle; perhaps his uncle was lying in bed and thinking the very same thing at that moment.

A little comforted, he turned round. Clara was standing beside him saying: "Don't you like being with us at all? Won't you try to make yourself a little more at home here? Come on, I'll make a last attempt."

She led him across the room towards the door. At a side table the two gentlemen were sitting, drinking out of tall glasses a light effervescent liquid which was unknown to Karl and which he would have liked to taste. Mr. Green had his elbows on the table and his face was pushed as close to Mr. Pollunder

as he could get it; if one had not known Mr. Pollunder, one might quite easily have suspected that some criminal plan was being discussed here and no legitimate business. While Mr. Pollunder's eyes followed Karl to the door with a friendly look, Mr. Green, though as a rule one's eyes involuntarily follow those of the man one is talking to, did not once glance round at Karl; and it seemed to Karl that in behaving like this Green was pointing his conviction that each of them, Karl on his part and Green on his, must fight for his own hand and that any obligatory social connection between them would be determined in time by the victory or destruction of one of them.

"If that's what he thinks," Karl told himself, "he's a fool. I really don't want anything from him and he should leave me in peace."

Hardly had he set foot in the corridor when it occurred to him that he had probably been discourteous, for his eyes had been so firmly fixed on Green that Clara had had almost to drag him from the room. He went all the more willingly with her now. As they passed along the corridors he could scarcely credit his eyes at first, when at every twenty paces he saw a servant in rich livery holding a huge candelabrum with a shaft so thick that both the man's hands were required to grasp it.

"The new electric wiring has been laid on only in the dining-room so far," explained Clara. "We've just newly bought this house and we're having it completely reconstructed, that is so far as an old house with all its odd peculiarities can be reconstructed."

"So you have actually old houses in America too," said Karl.

"Of course," said Clara with a laugh, pulling him along. "You have some queer ideas about America."

"You shouldn't laugh at me," he said in vexation. After all

66

he knew both Europe and America, while she knew only America.

In passing, Clara flung a door open with a light push of her hand and said without stopping: "That's where you're going to sleep."

Karl of course wanted to look at the room straight away, but Clara exclaimed with impatience, raising her voice almost to shouting pitch, that there was plenty of time for that later and that he must come with her first. They had a kind of tug-of-war in the corridor until it came into Karl's mind that he need not do everything Clara told him, and he wrested himself free and stepped into the room. The surprising darkness outside the window was explained by the spreading branches of a large tree swaying there. He could hear the twitter of birds. To be sure, in the room itself, which the moonlight had not yet reached, one could distinguish hardly anything. Karl felt sorry that he had not brought the electric torch which his uncle had given him. In this house an electric torch was absolutely indispensable; given a couple of torches, the servants could have been sent to their beds. He sat down on the window-ledge and stared out into the darkness, listening. A bird which he had disturbed seemed to be fluttering through the leafage of the old tree. The whistle of a suburban train sounded somewhere across the fields. Otherwise all was still.

But not for long, for Clara came rushing in. Visibly furious, she cried: "What's the meaning of this?" and beat her hand against her skirt. Karl decided not to answer her until she should show more politeness. But she advanced upon him with long strides, exclaiming: "Well, are you coming with me or are you not?" and either intentionally or in sheer agitation struck him so hard on the chest that he would have fallen out of the window if at the very last minute he had not launched himself from the window-ledge so that his feet touched the floor.

"I might have fallen out of the window," he said reproachfully.

"It's a pity you didn't. Why are you so uncivil? I'll push you right out next time."

And she actually seized him and carried him in her athletic arms almost as far as the window, since he was too surprised to remember to brace himself. But then he came to his senses, freed himself with a twist of the hips and caught hold of her instead.

"Oh, you're hurting me!" she said at once.

But now Karl felt that it was not safe to let her go. He gave her freedom to take any steps she liked, but followed her close, keeping hold of her. It was easy enough to grip her in her tight dress.

"Let me go," she whispered, her flushed face so close to his that he had to strain to see her. "Let me go; I'll give you something you don't expect."—"Why is she sighing like that?" thought Karl. "I can't hurt her, I'm not squeezing her," and he still did not let her go. But suddenly, after a moment of unguarded, silent immobility, he again felt her strength straining against his body and she had broken away from him, locked him in a well-applied wrestling hold, knocked his legs from under him by some foot-work in a technique strange to him and thrust him before her with amazing control, panting a little, to the wall. But there was a sofa by the wall on which she laid him down, keeping at a safe distance from him, and said: "Now move if you can."

"Cat, wild cat!" was all that Karl could shout in the confusion of rage and shame which he felt within him. "You must be crazy, you wild cat!"

"Take care what you say," she said and she slipped one hand to his throat, on which she began to press so strongly that Karl could only gasp for breath, while she swung the other fist against his cheek, touching it as if experimentally, and then again and again drew it back, farther and farther, ready to give him a buffet at any moment.

"What would you say," she asked, "if I punished you for your rudeness to a lady by sending you home with your ears well boxed? It might do you good for the rest of your life, although you wouldn't care to remember it. I'm really sorry about you, you're a passably good-looking boy, and if you'd learned jiu-jitsu you'd probably have beaten me. All the same, all the same—I feel enormously tempted to box your ears for you now that you're lying there. I'd probably regret it; but if I should do it, let me tell you that it'll be because I can't help it. And of course it won't be only one box on the ear I'll give you, but I'll let fly right and left till you're black and blue. And perhaps you're one of these men of honour—I could easily believe it—and couldn't survive the disgrace of having your ears boxed, and would have to do away with yourself. But why were you so horrid to me? Don't you like me? Isn't it worth while to come to my room? Ah, look out! I very nearly let fly at you by accident just now. And if I let you off tonight, see that you behave better next time. I'm not your uncle to put up with your tantrums. Anyhow, let me point out that if I let you off now, you needn't think that the disgrace is all the same whether your ears are boxed or not. I'd rather box your ears soundly for you than have you thinking that. I wonder what Mack will say when I tell him about all this?"

At the thought of Mack she loosened her grip; in his muzzy confusion Karl saw Mack as a deliverer. For a little while he

could still feel Clara's hand on his throat, and so he squirmed for a few minutes before lying still.

She urged him to get up; he neither answered nor stirred. She lit a candle somewhere, the room grew light, a blue zigzag pattern appeared on the ceiling, but Karl lay with his head on the sofa cushion exactly as Clara had placed it and did not move a finger's breadth. Clara walked round the room, her skirt rustling about her legs; she seemed to pause for a long time by the window.

"Got over your tantrums?" he heard her asking at last.

Karl thought it hard that in this room which Mr. Pollunder had assigned him for the night he could find no peace. The girl kept wandering about, stopping and talking now and then, and he was heartily sick of her. All he wanted to do was to fall asleep at once and get out of the place later. He did not even want to go to bed, he merely wanted to stay where he was on the sofa. He was only waiting for the girl to leave, so that he could spring to the door after her, bolt it, and then fling himself back on the sofa again. He felt an intense need to stretch and yawn, but he did not want to do that before Clara. And so he lay staring at the ceiling, feeling his face becoming more and more rigid, and a fly which was hovering about flitted before his eyes without his quite knowing what it was.

Clara stepped over to him again and leaned across his line of vision; and if he had not made an effort he would have had to look at her.

"I'm going now," she said. "Perhaps later on you'll feel like coming to see me. The door is the fourth from this one on the same side of the corridor. You pass the three next doors, that's to say, and the one after that is the right one. I'm not going downstairs again; I shall just stay in my room. You've made me thoroughly tired too. I shan't exactly expect you, but if

71

you want to come, then come. Remember that you promised to play the piano for me. But perhaps you're feeling quite prostrate and can't move; well then, stay here and have a good sleep. I shan't tell my father anything about our little scuffle, not for the present; I mention that merely in case you start worrying about it." And in spite of her ostensible tiredness she ran lightly out of the room.

Karl at once sat up; this lying down had already become unendurable. For the sake of using his limbs he went to the door and looked out into the corridor. But how dark it was! He felt glad when he had shut the door and bolted it and stood again by his table in the light of the candle. He made up his mind to stay no longer in this house, but to go down to Mr. Pollunder, tell him frankly how Clara had treated him—admitting his defeat did not matter a straw to him—and with that abundant justification ask leave to drive or to walk home. If Mr. Pollunder had any objecion to his immediate return, then Karl would at least ask him to instruct a servant to conduct him to the nearest hotel. As a rule, hosts were not treated in the way which Karl planned, but still more seldom were guests treated as Clara had treated him. She had actually regarded as a kindness her promise to say nothing to Mr. Pollunder about their scuffle, and that was really too outrageous. Had he been invited to a wrestling match, then, that he should be ashamed of being thrown by a girl who had apparently spent the greater part of her life·in learning wrestling holds? After all, she had probably been taking lessons from Mack. She could tell him everything if she liked; he was certainly intelligent, Karl felt sure of that, although he had never had occasion to prove it in any single instance. But Karl knew also that if he were to have lessons from Mack he would make much greater progress than Clara had done; then he could come here again one day, most likely without any invitation, would begin by studying the scene of action, an exact knowledge of which had been a great advantage to Clara, and then he would seize that same Clara and fling her down on the very sofa where she had flung him tonight.

Now he had merely to find his way back to the dining-room, where in his first embarrassment he had probably laid down his hat in some unsuitable place. Of course he would take the candle with him, but even with a light it was not easy to find one's bearings. For instance, he did not even know whether this room was on the same floor as the dining-room. On the way here Clara had kept pulling him, so that he had no chance to look around him. Mr. Green and the servants with the great candlesticks had also given him something to think about; in short, he actually could not remember whether they had climbed one or two flights of stairs or none at all. To judge from the view, the room was fairly high up, and so he tried to convince himself that they must have climbed stairs; yet at the front door there had been steps to climb, so why should not this side of the house be raised above ground-level too? If only there were a ray of light to be seen from some door in the corridor or a voice to be heard in the distance, no matter how faintly!

His watch, a present from his uncle, pointed to eleven; he took the candle and went out into the corridor. The door he left open, so that if his search should prove unsuccessful he might at least find his room again and in case of dire need the door of Clara's room. For safety he fixed the door open with a chair, so that it might not shut of itself. In the corridor he made the unwelcome discovery—naturally he turned to the left, away from Clara's room—that there was a draught blowing against his face, which though quite feeble might never-

73

theless easily blow out the candle, so that he had to guard the flame with his hand and often stop altogether to let the dying flame recover. It was a slow method of progress and it made the way seem doubly long. Karl had already passed great stretches of blank wall completely devoid of doors; one could not imagine what lay behind them. And then he came to one door after another; he tried to open several of them; they were locked and the rooms obviously unoccupied. It was an incredible squandering of space and Karl thought of the east end of New York which his uncle had promised to show him, where it was said that several families lived in one little room and the home of a whole family consisted of one corner where the children clustered round their parents. And here so many rooms stood empty and seemed to exist merely to make a hollow sound when you knocked on the door. Mr. Pollunder seemed to Karl to be misled by false friends and infatuated with his daughter, which was his ruin. Uncle Jacob had certainly judged him rightly, and only his axiom that it was not his business to influence Karl's judgment of other people was responsible for this visit and all this wandering through corridors. Tomorrow Karl would tell his uncle that quite frankly, for if he followed his own axiom his uncle should be glad to hear a nephew's judgment even on himself. Besides, that axiom was probably the only thing in his uncle which displeased Karl, and even that displeasure was not unqualified.

Suddenly the wall on one side of the corridor came to an end and an ice-cold, marble balustrade appeared in its place. Karl set the candle beside him and cautiously leaned over. A breath of dark emptiness met him. If this was the main hall of the house—in the glimmer of the candle a piece of vault-like ceiling could be seen—why had they not come in through it? What purpose could be served by this great, deep chamber?

74

One stood here as if in the gallery of a church. Karl almost regretted that he could not stay in the house till morning; he would have liked Mr. Pollunder to show him all round it by daylight and explain everything to him.

The balustrade was quite short and soon Karl was once more groping along a closed corridor. At a sudden turning he ran full tilt into the wall, and only the unswerving care with which he convulsively held the candle saved it from falling and going out. As the corridor seemed to have no end—no window appeared through which he could see where he was, nothing stirred either above him or below him—Karl began to think that he was going round in a circle and had a faint hope that he would come to the door of his room again; but neither it nor the balustrade re-appeared. Until now he had refrained from shouting, for he did not want to raise a noise in a strange house at such a late hour; but now he realised that it would not matter in this unlighted house, and he was just preparing to send a loud "halloo" echoing along the corridor in both directions when he noticed a little light approaching from behind him, the way that he had come. Now at last he could realise the length of that straight corridor. This house was a fortress, not a mansion. His joy on seeing that saving light was so great that he forgot all caution and ran towards it. At the first few steps he took, his candle blew out. But he paid no attention, for he did not need it any longer; here was an old servant with a lantern coming towards him and he would soon show him the right way.

"Who are you?" asked the servant, holding the lantern up to Karl's face and illumining his own as well. His face had a somewhat formal look because of a great white beard which ended on his breast in silken ringlets. "He must be a faithful servant if they let him wear a beard like that," thought Karl, gazing fixedly at the beard in all its length and breadth, without feeling any constraint because he himself was being observed in turn. He replied at once that he was a guest of Mr. Pollunder's, that he had left his room to go to the dining-room, but could not find it.

"Oh, yes," said the servant, "we haven't had the electric light laid on yet."

"I know," said Karl.

"Won't you light your candle at my lantern?" asked the servant.

"If you please," said Karl, doing so.

"There's such a draught here in the corridors," said the servant. "Candles easily get blown out; that's why I have a lantern."

"Yes, a lantern is much more practical," said Karl.

"Why, you're all covered with candle-drippings," said the servant, holding up the candle to Karl's suit.

"I never even noticed it!" cried Karl, feeling distressed, for it was his black suit, which his uncle said looked best of all upon him. His wrestling match with Clara could not have been very good for the suit either, it now occurred to him. The servant was obliging enough to clean the suit as well as could be done on the spot: Karl kept turning round and showing him another mark here and there, which the man obediently removed.

"But why should there be such a draught here?" asked Karl, as they went on again.

"Well, there's a great deal of building still to be done," said the servant. "The reconstruction work has been started, of course, but it's getting on very slowly. And now the builders' workmen have gone on strike, as perhaps you know. Building up a house like this gives lots of trouble. Several large breaches have been made in the walls, which nobody has filled in, and the draught blows through the whole house. If I didn't stuff my ears with cotton wool I couldn't stand it."

"Then shouldn't I speak louder?" asked Karl.

"No, you have a clear voice," said the servant. "But to come back to this building; especially in this part, near the chapel, which will certainly have to be shut off from the rest of the house later, the draught is simply unendurable."

"So the balustrade along this corridor gives on to a chapel?"

"Yes."

"I thought that at the time," said Karl.

"It is well worth seeing," said the servant. "If it hadn't been for that, Mr. Mack probably wouldn't have bought the house."

"Mr. Mack?" asked Karl. "I thought the house belonged to Mr. Pollunder."

"Yes, certainly," said the servant, "but it was Mr. Mack who decided the purchase. Don't you know Mr. Mack?"

"Oh, yes," said Karl. "But what connection does he have with Mr. Pollunder?"

"He is the young lady's fiancé," said the servant.

"I certainly didn't know that," said Karl, stopping short.

"Do you find that so surprising?" asked the servant.

"I'm only thinking it over. If you don't know about such connections, you can easily make the worst kind of mistakes," replied Karl.

"I'm only surprised that they haven't told you about it," said the servant.

"Yes, that's true," said Karl, feeling abashed.

"Probably they thought you knew," said the servant, "it's old news by this time. But here we are," and he opened a door behind which appeared a stair that led straight down to the

77

back door of the dining-room, which was still as brightly illumined as at Karl's arrival.

Before Karl went down to the dining-room, from which the voices of Mr. Pollunder and Mr. Green could be heard still talking as they had talked two hours before, the servant said: "If you like, I'll wait for you here and take you back to your room. It's always difficult to find one's way about here on the first evening."

"My room will never see me again," said Karl, without knowing why he felt sad as he gave this information.

"It won't be so bad as all that," said the servant, smiling in a slightly superior way and patting him on the arm. Probably he construed Karl's words as meaning that Karl intended to stay up all night in the dining-room, talking and drinking with the two gentlemen. Karl did not want to make any confessions just then, also he reflected that this servant, whom he liked better than the other servants in the house, would be able to direct him on his way to New York, and so he said: "If you would wait here, it would certainly be a great kindness and I gratefully accept it. I'll come up in a little while, in any case, and tell you what I'm going to do. I think that I may need your help yet." "Good," said the servant, setting his lantern on the floor and seating himself on a low pedestal, which was probably vacant on account of the reconstruction work. "I'll wait here, then. You can leave the candle with me too," he added, as Karl made to go downstairs with the lighted candle in his hand.

"I'm not noticing what I'm doing," said Karl, and he handed the candle to the servant, who merely nodded to him, though it was impossible to say whether the nod was deliberate or whether it was caused by his stroking his beard with his hand.

Karl opened the door, which through no fault of his rattled noisily, for it consisted of a single glass panel that almost jumped from the frame if the door were opened quickly and held fast only by the handle. Karl let the door swing back again in alarm, for he had wanted to enter the room as quietly as possible. Without turning round he was aware that behind him the servant, who had apparently descended from his pedestal, was now shutting the door carefully and without the slightest sound.

"Forgive me for disturbing you," he said to the two gentlemen, who stared at him with round, astonished faces. At the same time he flung a hasty glance round the room, to see if he could discover his hat somewhere. But it was nowhere to be seen; the dishes on the dining-table had all been cleared away; perhaps, he thought uncomfortably, the hat had been carried off to the kitchen along with them.

"But where have you left Clara?" asked Mr. Pollunder, to whom the intrusion, however, did not seem to be unwelcome, for he at once changed his position in the chair and turned his face full upon Karl. Mr. Green put on an air of indifference, pulled out a pocket-book, in size and thickness a giant of its kind, seemed to be searching in its many compartments for some particular paper, but during the search kept reading other papers which chanced to come his way.

"I have a request to make which you must not misunderstand," said Karl, walking up hastily to Mr. Pollunder and putting his hand on the arm of his chair, to get as near to him as he could.

"And what request can that be?" asked Mr. Pollunder, giving Karl a frank open look. "It is granted already." And he put his arm round Karl and drew him between his knees. Karl submitted willingly, though as a rule he felt much too grown up for such treatment. But of course it made the utterance of his request all the more difficult.

"And how do you really like being here?" asked Mr. Pollunder. "Don't you find that one gets a kind of free feeling on coming out of the town into the country? Usually"—and he looked askance at Mr. Green, a glance of unmistakable meaning, which was partly screened by Karl—"usually I get that feeling every evening."

"He talks," thought Karl, "as if he knew nothing about this huge house, the endless corridors, the chapel, the empty rooms, the darkness everywhere."

"Well," said Mr. Pollunder, "out with your request!" And he gave Karl, who stood silent, a friendly shake.

"Please," said Karl, and much as he lowered his voice he could not keep Green, sitting there, from hearing everything, though he would gladly have concealed from him this request, which might easily be construed as an insult to Pollunder—"Please let me go home now, late as it is."

And once he had put the worst into words, all the rest came pouring out after it, and he said without the slightest insincerity things of which he had never even thought before. "I want above all to get home. I'll be glad to come again, for wherever you are, Mr. Pollunder, I'll always be glad to stay. Only tonight I can't stay here. You know that my uncle was unwilling to give me permission for this visit. He must have had good reasons for that, as for everything that he does, and I had the presumption literally to force permission from him against his better judgment. I simply exploited his affection for me. It doesn't matter at all what his objections were; all that I know with absolute certainty is that there was nothing in these objections which could offend you, Mr. Pollunder, for you're the best, the very best friend that my uncle has. Nobody else can even remotely be compared with you among my uncle's friends. And that is the only excuse for my disobedience, though an insufficient one. You probably have no first-hand knowledge of the relations between my uncle and me, so I'll mention only the main points. Until my English studies are finished and while I am still insufficiently versed in practical things, I am entirely dependent on my uncle's kindness, which I can accept, of course, being a relation. You mustn't think that I'm in a position yet to earn my living decently—and God forbid that I should do it in any other way. I'm afraid my education has been too impractical for that. I managed to scrape through four classes of a European high school with moderate success, and for earning a livelihood that means less than nothing, for our schools are very much behind the times in their teaching methods. You would laugh if I were to tell you the kind of things I learned. If a boy can go on studying, finish his school course and enter the University, then, probably, it all straightens out in the long run and he finishes up with a proper education that lets him do something and gives him the confidence to set about earning a living. But unluckily I was torn right out of that systematic course of study. Sometimes I think I know nothing, and in any case the best of my knowledge wouldn't be adequate for America. Some of the high schools in my country have been reformed recently, teaching modern languages and perhaps even commercial subjects, but when I left my primary school there were none of these. My father certainly wanted me to learn English, but in the first place I couldn't foresee then that I would have such bad luck and that I would actually need English, and in the second place I had to learn a great deal of other things at school, so that I didn't have much time to spare—I mention all this to show you how dependent I am on my uncle, and how deeply I am bound to him in consequence. You must admit that in these circumstances I am not in a position to offend in the slightest against even his unexpressed wishes. And so if I am to make good even half of the offence which I have committed against him, I must go home at once."

During this long speech of Karl's, Mr. Pollunder had listened attentively, now and then tightening his arm round Karl, though imperceptibly, particularly when Uncle Jacob was mentioned, and several times gazing seriously and as if expectantly at Green, who was still occupied with his pocketbook. But Karl had felt more and more restless the more clearly he became aware of his relation to his uncle during his speech, and involuntarily he struggled to free himself from Pollunder's arm. Everything cramped him here; the road leading to his uncle through that glass door, down the steps, through the avenue, along the country roads, through the suburbs to the great main street where his uncle's house was, seemed to him a strictly ordered whole, which lay there empty smooth and prepared for him, and called to him with a strong voice. Mr. Pollunder's kindness and Mr. Green's loathsomeness ran into a blur together, and all that he asked from that smoky room was permission to leave. He felt cut off from Mr. Pollunder, prepared to do battle against Mr. Green, and yet all round him was a vague fear, whose impact troubled his sight.

He took a step back and now stood equally distant from Mr. Pollunder and Mr. Green.

"Hadn't you something to say to him?" asked Mr. Pollunder, turning to Mr. Green and seizing the man's hand imploringly.

"I don't know what I could have to say to him," said Mr. Green, who had taken a letter from his pocketbook at last and laid it before him on the table. "It is to his credit that he wants to go back to his uncle, and one might naturally assume that that would give his uncle great pleasure. Unless he has angered his uncle already too deeply by his disobedience, which is only too possible. In that case it would certainly be better for him to stay here. It's difficult to say anything definite; we're both friends of his uncle and it would be hard to say whether Mr. Pollunder's or my friendship ranks highest; but we can't see into his uncle's mind, especially at so many miles' distance from New York."

"Please, Mr. Green," said Karl, overcoming his distaste and approaching Mr. Green, "I can tell from what you say that you too think it would be best for me to go back at once."

"I said nothing of the kind," replied Mr. Green, and he once more returned to his contemplation of the letter, running his fingers over the edges of it. Apparently he wished to indicate that he had been asked a question by Mr. Pollunder and had answered it, while Karl was no concern of his at all.

Meanwhile Mr. Pollunder stepped over to Karl and gently led him away from Mr. Green to the big window.

"Dear Mr. Rossmann," he said, bending down to Karl's ear and as a preparation for what he had to say passing his handkerchief over his face until it encountered his nose, which he blew, "you must not think that I wish to keep you here against your will. There is no question of that. I can't put the car at your disposal, I admit, for it's parked in a public garage a good distance from here, since I haven't had the time yet to build a garage for myself here, where everything is still under construction. The chauffeur again doesn't sleep here but somewhere near the garage; I really don't know where, myself. Besides, he isn't supposed to be on duty just now; he's merely expected to appear at the right time in the morning. But all this would be no obstacle to your returning at once, for if you insist upon it I'll accompany you at once to the nearest railway station, though it's so far away that you wouldn't get home much sooner than if you came with me in my car tomorrow morning—we start at seven."

"Then, Mr. Pollunder, I would rather go by train all the same," said Karl. "I never thought of the train. You say yourself that I would arrive sooner by train than if I left tomorrow in your car."

"But it would make only a very little difference."

"All the same, all the same, Mr. Pollunder," said Karl, "I'll always be glad to come here again, remembering your kindness, that is, of course, if after my behaviour tonight you ever invite me again; and perhaps next time I'll be able to explain more clearly why every minute that keeps me away from my uncle now is so important to me." And as if he had already received permission to go away, he added: "But you mustn't come with me on any account. It's really quite unnecessary. There's a servant outside who'll be glad to show me the way to the station. Now, I have only to find my hat." And with these words he walked across the room to take a last hasty look, in case his hat were lying somewhere.

"Perhaps I could help you out with a cap?" said Mr. Green, drawing a cap from his pocket. "Maybe it will serve you for the time being?"

Karl stopped in amazement and said: "But I can't deprive you of your cap. I can go quite well with my head bare. I don't need anything."

"It isn't my cap. You just take it!"

"In that case, thanks," said Karl, so as not to delay any longer, taking the cap. He put it on and could not help laughing, for it fitted him perfectly; then he took it off again and examined it, but could not find the particular thing that he was looking for; it seemed a perfectly new cap. "It fits so well!" he said.

"So the cap fits!" cried Mr. Green, thumping the table.

Karl was already on his way to the door to fetch the servant, when Mr. Green got up, stretched himself after his ample meal and his long rest, struck himself resoundingly on the chest, and said in a voice between advice and command: "Before you go, you must say goodbye to Miss Clara."

"Yes, you must do that," agreed Mr. Pollunder, who had also got up. From the way in which he spoke one could tell that the words did not come from his heart; he kept flapping his hands feebly against the sides of his trousers and buttoning and re-buttoning his jacket, which after the fashion of the moment was quite short and scarcely reached his hips, an unbecoming garment for such a stout man as Mr. Pollunder. One also had the definite feeling as he stood there beside Mr. Green that Mr. Pollunder's fatness was not a healthy fatness. His massive back was somewhat bent, his paunch looked soft and flabby, an actual burden, and his face was pallid and worried. Mr. Green, on the other hand, was perhaps even fatter than Mr. Pollunder, but it was a homogeneous, balanced fatness; he stood with his heels together like a soldier, he bore his head with a jaunty erectness. He looked like a great athlete, a captain of athletes.

"You are to go first then," Mr. Green continued, "to Miss Clara. That is bound to be pleasant for you and it suits my time-table excellently as well. For before you leave here I have as a matter of fact something of interest to tell you, which will probably also decide whether you are to go back or not. But I am unfortunately bound by my orders to divulge nothing to you before midnight. You can imagine that I'm sorry for that myself, since it upsets my night's rest, but I shall stick to my instructions. It is a quarter-past eleven now, so that I can finish discussing my business with Mr. Pollunder, which you would only interrupt; besides, you can have a very pleasant time with Miss Clara. Then at twelve punctually you will report here, where you will learn what is necessary."

Could Karl reject his request, which demanded from him only the minimum of politeness and gratitude towards Mr. Pollunder and which, moreover, had been put by a man customarily rude and indifferent, while Mr. Pollunder, whom it really concerned, intervened neither by word nor glance? And what was the interesting news which he was not to learn until midnight? If it did not hasten his return by at least the forty-five minutes that it now made him waste, it would have little interest for him. But his greatest scruple was whether he dared visit Clara at all, seeing that she was his enemy. If only he had the stone-chisel with him which his uncle had given him as a letter weight! Clara's room might prove a really dangerous den. Yet it was quite impossible to say anything against Clara here, for she was Pollunder's daughter and, as he had just heard, Mack's fiancée as well. If she had only behaved a very little differently towards him, he would have frankly admired her for her connections. He was still considering all this when he perceived that no reflection was expected from him, for Green opened the door and said to the servant, who jumped up from his pedestal: "Conduct this young man to Miss Clara."

"This is how commands are executed," thought Karl, as the servant, almost running, groaning with infirmity, led him by a remarkably short cut to Clara's room. As Karl was passing his own room, whose door was still open, he asked leave to go in for a minute, hoping to compose himself. But the servant would not allow it.

"No," he said, "you must come along to Miss Clara. You heard that yourself."

"I only want to stay there a minute," said Karl, thinking what a relief it would be to lie on the sofa for a little, to quicken up the time between now and midnight.

"Don't obstruct me in the execution of my duty," said the servant.

"He seems to imagine it's a punishment to be taken to Miss Clara," thought Karl, and he went on a few steps, but then defiantly stopped again.

"Do come, young sir," said the servant, "since you're still here. I know that you wanted to leave this very night, but we don't always get what we want, and I told you already that it would hardly be possible."

"I do want to leave and I will leave too," said Karl, "and I'm merely going to say goodbye to Miss Clara."

"Is that so?" said the servant, and Karl could see that he did not believe a word of it. "Why are you so unwilling to say goodbye, then? Do come along."

"Who is that in the corridor?" said Clara's voice, and they saw her leaning out of a door near by, a big red-shaded table lamp in her hand. The servant hurried up to her and gave his message; Karl slowly followed him. "You're late in coming," said Clara.

Without answering her for the moment, Karl said to the servant softly, but in a tone of stern command, for he already knew the man's character: "You'll wait for me just outside this door!"

"I was just going to bed," said Clara, setting the lamp on

the table. As he had done in the dining-room, the servant carefully shut this door too from the outside. "It's after half-past eleven already."

"After half-past eleven?" said Karl interrogatively, as if alarmed at these figures. "But in that case I must say goodbye at once," he went on, "for at twelve punctually I must be down in the dining-room."

"What urgent business you seem to have!" said Clara, absently smoothing the folds of her loose night-dress. Her face was glowing and she kept on smiling. Karl decided that there was no danger of getting into another quarrel with Clara. "Couldn't you play the piano for a little after all, as Papa promised yesterday and you yourself promised tonight?"

"But isn't it too late now?" asked Karl. He would have liked to oblige her, for she was quite different now from what she had been before; it was as if she had somehow ascended into the Pollunder circle and into Mack's as well.

"Yes, it is late," she said, and her desire for music seemed already to have passed. "And every sound here echoes through the whole house; I'm afraid that if you play now it will waken up the very servants in the attics."

"Then I won't bother to play; you see, I hope to come back again another day; besides, if it isn't too great a bother, you might visit my uncle and have a look at my room while you are there. I have a marvellous piano. My uncle gave it to me. Then, if you like, I'll play all my pieces to you; there aren't many of them, unfortunately, and they don't suit such a fine instrument either, which needs a really great player to use it. But you may have the pleasure of hearing a good player if you tell me beforehand when you are coming, for my uncle means to engage a famous teacher for me—you can imagine how I look forward to it—and his playing would certainly make it worth your while to pay me a visit during one of my lessons. To be quite frank, I'm glad that it's too late to play, for I can't really play yet, you would be surprised how badly I play. And now allow me to take my leave; after all it must be your bed-time." And as Clara was looking at him with a kindly expression and seemed to bear him no ill-will because of the quarrel, he added with a smile, while he held out his hand: "In my country people say: 'Sleep well and sweet dreams'."

"Wait," she said, without taking his hand, "perhaps you might play after all." And she disappeared through a little side door, beside which the piano stood.

"What next?" thought Karl. "I can't wait long, even if she is nice to me." There was a knock at the corridor door and the servant, without daring quite to open it, whispered through a little chink: "Excuse me; I've just been called away and can't wait any longer."

"Then you can go," said Karl, who now felt confident that he could find his way alone to the dining-room. "But leave the lantern for me at the door. How late is it?"

"Almost a quarter to twelve," said the servant.

"How slowly the time passes," said Karl to himself. The servant was shutting the door when Karl remembered that he had not given him a tip, took a quarter from his trouser pocket —in the American fashion he now always carried his loose coins jingling in his trouser pocket, his bank notes, on the other hand, in his waistcoat pocket—and handed it to the servant with the words: "For your kindness."

Clara had already come back, patting her trim hair with her fingers, when it occurred to Karl that he should not have let the servant go after all, for who would now show him the way to the railway station? Well, Mr. Pollunder would surely manage to hunt up a servant somewhere, and perhaps the old servant had been summoned to the dining-room and so would be again at his disposal.

"Won't you really play a little for me? One hears music so seldom here that it's a pity to miss any opportunity of hearing it."

"It's high time I began then," said Karl without further consideration, sitting down at once at the piano.

"Do you want any special music?" asked Clara.

"No, thanks, I can't even read music correctly," replied Karl, and he began to play. It was a little air which, as he knew perfectly well, had to be played somewhat slowly to make it even comprehensible, especially to strangers; but he strummed it out in blatant march time. When he ended it the shattered silence of the house closed round them again, almost distressfully. They sat there as if frozen with embarrassment and did not move.

"Quite good," said Clara, but there was no formula of politeness which could have flattered Karl after that performance.

"How late is it?" he asked.

"A quarter to twelve."

"Then I still have a little time," he said and thought to himself: "Which is it to be? I needn't play through all the ten tunes I know, but I might play one at least as well as I can." And he began to play his beloved soldier's song. So slowly that the roused longing of his listener yearned for the next note, which Karl held back and yielded reluctantly. He had actually to pick out the keys first with his eyes as in playing all of his tunes, but he also felt rising within him a song which reached past the end of this song, seeking another end which it could not find.

"I'm no good," said Karl after he had finished, gazing at Clara with tears in his eyes.

Then from the next room came a sound of hand-clapping. "Someone has been listening!" cried Karl, taken back. "Mack," said Clara softly. And already he heard Mack shouting: "Karl Rossmann, Karl Rossmann!"

Karl swung both feet over the piano stool and opened the door. He saw Mack half sitting and half reclining in a huge double bed with the blankets loosely flung over his legs. A canopy of blue silk was the sole and somewhat school-girlish ornament of the bed, which was otherwise quite plain and roughly fashioned out of heavy wood. On the bedside table only a candle was burning, but the sheets and Mack's night-shirt were so white that the candle-light falling upon them was thrown off in an almost dazzling reflection; even the canopy shone, at least at the edges, with its slightly billowing silk tent, which was not stretched quite taut. But immediately behind Mack the bed and everything else sank into complete darkness. Clara leaned against the bed post and had eyes now only for Mack.

"Hallo," said Mack, reaching his hand to Karl. "You play very well; up to now I've only known your talent for riding." "I'm as bad at the one as at the other," said Karl. "If I'd known you were listening, I certainly wouldn't have played. But your young lady——" He stopped, he hesitated to say "fiancée," since Mack and Clara obviously shared the same bed already.

"But I guessed it," said Mack, "and so Clara had to lure you out here from New York, or else I would never have heard your playing. It's certainly amateurish enough, and even in these two airs, which have been set very simply and which you have practised a good deal, you made one or two mistakes; but all the same it pleased me greatly, quite apart from the fact that I never despise players of any kind. But won't you sit

91

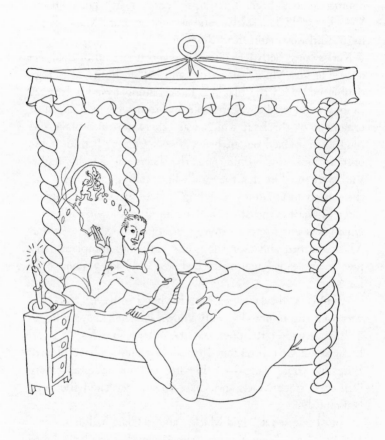

down and stay for a little while with us? Clara, give him a chair."

"Thanks," said Karl awkwardly. "I can't stay, glad as I would be to stay here. It's taken me too long to discover that there are such comfortable rooms in this house."

"I'm having everything reconstructed in this style," said Mack.

At that moment twelve strokes of a bell rang out in rapid succession, each breaking into the one before. Karl could feel on his cheeks the wind made by the swinging of that great bell. What sort of village could it be which had such bells!

"It's high time I was gone," said Karl, stretching out his hands to Mack and Clara without shaking theirs and rushing off into the corridor.

He found no lantern there and regretted having tipped the servant so soon.

He began to feel his way along the wall to his own room, but had hardly covered half the way when he saw Mr. Green hurriedly bobbing towards him with an upraised candle. In the hand holding the candle he was also clutching a letter.

"Rossmann, why didn't you come? Why have you kept me waiting? What on earth has kept you so long with Miss Clara?"

"How many questions!" thought Karl, "and now he's pushing me to the wall," for indeed Green was standing quite close to Karl, who had to lean his back against the wall. In this corridor Green took on an almost absurd size, and Karl wondered in jest if he could have eaten up good Mr. Pollunder.

"You certainly aren't a man of your word. You promised to come down at twelve and instead of that here you are prowling round Miss Clara's door. But I promised you some interesting news at midnight, and here it is." And with that he handed

93

Karl the letter. On the envelope was written: "To Karl Ross-mann, to be delivered personally at midnight, wherever he may be found."

"After all," said Mr. Green, while Karl opened the letter. "I think I am due some thanks for driving out here from New York on your account, so that you shouldn't expect me to chase after you through these corridors as well."

"From my uncle," said Karl, almost as soon as he glanced at the letter. "I have been expecting it," he said, turning to Mr. Green.

"Whether you were expecting it or not doesn't matter to me in the least. You just read it," said Green, holding up the candle to Karl.

Karl read by its light:

Dear Nephew,

As you will already have realised during our much too brief companionship, I am essentially a man of principle. That is unpleasant and depressing not only to those who come in contact with me, but also to myself as well. Yet it is my principles that have made me what I am, and no one can ask me to deny my fundamental self. Not even you, my dear nephew. Though you would be my first choice, if it ever occurred to me to permit such a general assault upon me. Then I would pick you up, of all people, with these two arms that are now holding this paper and set you above my head. But as for the moment nothing indicates that this could ever happen, I must, after the incident today, expressly send you away from me, and I urgently beg you neither to visit me in person, nor to try to get in touch with me either by writing or through intermediaries. Against my wishes you decided this evening to leave me; stick, then, to that decision all your life. Only then will it be a manly decision. As the bringer of this news I have chosen Mr. Green, my best friend, who no doubt will find indulgent words for you which at the moment are certainly not at my disposal. He is an influential man and, if only for my sake, will give you his advice and help in the first independent steps which you take. To explain our separation, which now as I end this letter once more seems incomprehensible to me, I have to keep telling myself again and again, Karl, that nothing good comes out of your family. If Mr. Green should forget to hand you your box and umbrella, remind him of them.

With best wishes for your further welfare,

Your faithful

Uncle Jacob.

"Are you finished?" asked Green.

"Yes," said Karl. "Have you brought the box and the umbrella with you?" he asked.

"Here it is," said Green, setting Karl's old travelling box, which until now he had held in his left hand concealed behind his back, beside Karl on the floor.

"And the umbrella?" Karl asked again.

"Everything here," said Green, bringing out the umbrella too, which had been hanging from one of his trouser pockets. "A man called Schubal, an engineer in the Hamburg-America Line, brought the things; he maintained that he found them on the ship. You can find an opportunity to thank him sometime."

"Now I have my old things back again at least," said Karl, laying the umbrella on the box.

"But you should take better care of them in future, the

95

Senator asked me to tell you," said Mr. Green and then asked, obviously out of private curiosity: "What queer kind of box is that?"

"It's the kind of box that soldiers in my country take with them when they join the army," replied Karl. "It's my father's old army chest. It's very useful too," he added with a smile, "provided you don't leave it behind you somewhere."

"After all, you've been taught your lesson," said Mr. Green, "and I bet you haven't a second uncle in America. Here is something else for you, a third-class ticket to San Francisco. I've decided on sending you there because in the first place your chances of earning a living are much better in the West, and in the second your uncle has got a finger in everything here that might suit you and a meeting between you must be strictly avoided. In 'Frisco you can tackle anything you like; just begin at the bottom and try gradually to work your way up."

Karl could not detect any malice in these words; the bad news which had lain sheathed in Green the whole evening was delivered, and now he seemed a harmless man with whom one could speak more frankly, perhaps, than with anybody else. The best of men, chosen through no fault of his own to be the bearer of such a secret and painful message, must appear a suspicious character so long as he had to keep it to himself. "I shall leave this house at once," said Karl, hoping that his resolution would be approved by Green's experience, "for I was invited as my uncle's nephew, while as a stranger I have no business here. Would you be so good as to show me the way out and tell me how I can get to the nearest inn?"

"As quick as you like," said Green, "you're not afraid of giving me trouble, are you?"

On seeing the huge strides which Green was taking, Karl at

once came to a stop; so much haste seemed highly suspicious, and he seized Green by the coat-tail, suddenly realising the true situation, and said: "There's one thing more you must explain: on the envelope you gave me it was merely stated that I was to receive it at midnight, wherever I might be found. Why, then, on the strength of that letter, did you keep me here when I wanted to leave at a quarter-past eleven? In doing that you exceeded your instructions."

Green accompanied his reply with a wave of the hand which indicated with melodramatic exaggeration the silliness of Karl's question, saying: "Was it stated on the envelope that I should run myself to death chasing about after you, and did the contents of the letter give any hint that the inscription was to be construed in such a way? If I had not kept you here, I should have had to hand you the letter precisely at midnight on the open road."

"No," said Karl, quite unmoved, "it isn't quite so. It says on the envelope: 'To be delivered at midnight'. You might have been too tired, perhaps, to follow me at all, or I might have reached my uncle's by midnight, though I grant you, Mr. Pollunder thought not, or as a last resort it might have been your duty to take me back to my uncle in your own car, which you so conveniently forgot to mention, since I was insisting on going back. Does not the inscription quite plainly convey that midnight was to be the final term for me? And it is you who are to blame that I missed it."

Karl looked at Green with shrewd eyes and clearly saw that shame over this exposure was conflicting in the man with joy at the success of his designs. At last he pulled himself together and said sharply, as if breaking into Karl's accusations, although Karl had been silent for a long time: "Not a word more!" And pushed Karl, who had once more picked up his box and his umbrella, out through a little door which he flung open before him.

To his astonishment Karl found himself in the open air. An outside stair without railings led downwards before him. He had simply to descend it and then turn to the right to reach the avenue which led to the road. In the bright moonlight he could not miss his way. Below him in the garden he could hear the manifold barking of dogs who had been let loose and were rushing about in the shadow of the trees. In the stillness he could distinctly hear them thudding on the grass as they landed after making their great bounds.

Without being molested by the dogs Karl safely got out of the garden. He could not tell with certainty in which direction New York lay. In coming here he had paid too little attention to details which might have been useful to him now. Finally he told himself that he need not of necessity go to New York, where nobody expected him and one man certainly did not expect him. So he chose a chance direction and set out on his way.

IN the small inn which Karl reached after a short walk and which was merely a last little eating-house for New York car and lorry drivers and so very seldom used as a night lodging, he asked for the cheapest bed that could be had, since he thought he had better begin to save at once. In keeping with his request, the landlord waved him up a stair as if he were a menial and at the top of the stair a dishevelled old hag, peevish at being roused from her sleep, received him almost without listening to him, warning him all the time to tread softly, and conducted him into a room whose door she shut on him, but not before giving him a whispered: "Hst!"

Karl could not make out at first whether the window curtains had merely been drawn or whether there was no window in the room at all, it was so dark; but in the end he noticed a skylight, whose covering he drew aside, whereupon a little light came in. There were two beds in the room, both of them already occupied. He saw two young men lying there in a heavy sleep; they did not look very trustworthy, chiefly because without any understandable reason they were sleeping in their clothes; one of them actually had his boots on.

At the moment when Karl uncovered the skylight one of the sleepers raised his arms and legs a little way in the air, which was such a curious sight that in spite of his cares Karl laughed to himself.

He soon realised that, quite apart from the absence of anything to sleep on, there being neither a couch nor a sofa, he would not be able to get any sleep here, since he could not risk losing his newly recovered box and the money he was carrying on him. But he did not want to go away either, for he did not know how he was to get past the old woman and the landlord if he left the house so soon. After all, he was perhaps just as safe here as on the open road. It was certainly strange that no sign of luggage was to be seen in the whole room, so far as he could make out in the half light. But perhaps, indeed very probably, the two young men were servants who had to get up early because of the boarders and for that reason slept with their clothes on. In that case it was no great honour, certainly, to sleep in their room, but it was all the less risky. Yet he must not fall asleep on any account until he was certain of this beyond all doubt.

Under the bed a candle was standing, along with matches; Karl softly crept over and fetched them. He had no scruples about lighting the candle, for on the landlord's authority the room belonged as much to him as to the other two men, who besides had already enjoyed half a night's sleep and being in possession of the beds held an immeasurable advantage over him. However, by moving about as quietly as possible, he naturally took every care not to waken them.

First of all he wanted to examine his box, so as to survey his things, of which by this time he had only a vague memory, and the most precious of which might well have disappeared. for once Schubal got his hands on anything there was little hope that you would get it back unscathed. Of course, he might have been counting on a big tip from Uncle Jacob, but on the other hand if anything were missing, he could easily shift the blame on to the original guardian of the box, Mr. Butterbaum.

Karl's first glance inside the box horrified him. How many hours had he spent during the voyage in arranging and re-arranging the things in this box, and now everything was in such wild confusion that as soon as he turned the key the lid sprang up of itself.

But soon he realised to his delight that the sole cause of the disorder was that someone had added the suit he had worn during the voyage, which the box, of course, was not intended to hold. Not the slightest thing was missing. In the secret pocket of his jacket he found not only his passport but also the money which his parents had given him, so that, including what he had upon him, he was amply furnished with money for the time being. Even the underclothes which he had worn on arriving were there, freshly washed and ironed. He at once put his watch and his money in the trusty secret pocket. The only regrettable thing was that the Veronese salami, which was still there too, had bestowed its smell upon everything else. If he could not find some way of eliminating that smell, he had every prospect of walking about for months enveloped in it.

As he was searching for some things at the very bottom—a pocket Bible, some letter paper and some photographs of his parents—the cap fell from his head into the box. In its old surroundings he recognised it at once; it was his own cap, the cap which his mother had given him to wear during the voyage. All the same, out of prudence he had not worn the cap on the boat, for he knew that in America everybody wore caps instead of hats, so that he did not want to wear his cap out before arriving. And Mr. Green had used it simply to make a fool of him. Could Uncle Jacob have instructed him to do that as well? And with an involuntary wrathful movement he gripped the lid of the box, which shut with a bang.

Now there was no help for it; the two sleepers were aroused. First one of them stretched and yawned, and then the other immediately followed suit. Almost all the contents of the box were lying in a heap on the table; if these men were thieves, they merely had to walk across the room and take what they fancied. Both to forestall this possibility and to know where he stood, Karl went over with the candle in his hand to the beds and explained how he happened to be there. They did not seem to have expected any explanation, for, still far too sleepy to talk, they merely gazed at him without any sign of surprise. They were both young men, but heavy work or poverty had prematurely sharpened the bones of their faces; unkempt beards hung from their chins; their hair, which had not been cut for a long time, lay matted on their heads; and they rubbed and knuckled their deep-set eyes, still heavy with sleep.

Karl resolved to take every advantage of their momentary weakness and so he said: "My name is Karl Rossmann and I am a German. Please tell me, as we are occupying the same room, what your names are and what country you come from. I may as well say that I don't expect a share of your beds, for I was late in arriving and in any case I have no intention of sleeping. And you mustn't draw the wrong conclusions from the good suit I have on; I am quite poor and without any prospects."

The smaller of the two men—the one with his boots on—indicating by his arms, legs and general demeanour that he was not interested in all this and had no time for such remarks, lay down again and immediately went to sleep; the other, a dark-skinned man, also lay down again, but before falling asleep said with a languid wave of the hand: "That chap there is called Robinson, and he's an Irishman, I'm called Delamarche and I'm a Frenchman, and now please be quiet." Scarcely had he said this when with a great puff he blew out Karl's candle and fell back on the pillow.

"Well, that danger is averted for the moment," Karl told himself, turning back to the table. If their sleepiness was not a pretext, everything was all right. The only disagreeable thing was that one of them was an Irishman. Karl could no longer remember in what book he had once read at home that if you went to America you must be on your guard against the Irish. While he was staying with his uncle he certainly had had an excellent opportunity to go thoroughly into the question of the Irish danger, but because he believed he was now well provided for to the end of his life he had completely neglected it. So he resolved that he would at least have a good look at this Irishman by the help of the candle, which he lit again, and found that the man really looked more bearable than the Frenchman. His cheeks had still a trace of roundness and he smiled in his sleep in quite a friendly way, so far as Karl could make out, standing at a distance on tiptoe.

Firmly resolved in spite of everything not to go to sleep, Karl sat down on the only chair in the room, postponed packing his box for the time being, since the whole night still lay before him in which to do it, and turned the leaves of his Bible for a little while, without reading anything. Then he took up a photograph of his parents, in which his small father stood very erect behind his mother, who sat in an easy-chair slightly sunk into herself. One of his father's hands lay on the back of the chair, the other, which was clenched to a fist, rested on a picture-book lying open on a fragile table beside him. There was another photograph in which Karl had been included together with his parents. In it his father and mother were eyeing him sharply, while he was staring at the camera, as the photographer bade him. But he had not taken this photograph with him on the voyage.

He gazed all the more attentively now at the one lying before him and tried to catch his father's eye from various angles. But his father refused to come to life, no matter how much his expression was modified by shifting the candle into different positions; nor did his thick, horizontal moustache look in the least real; it was not a good photograph. His mother, however, had come out better; her mouth was twisted as if she had been hurt and were forcing herself to smile. It seemed to Karl that anyone who saw the photograph must be so forcibly struck with this that he would begin immediately to think it an exaggerated, not to say foolish, interpretation. How could a photograph convey with such complete certainty the secret feelings of the person shown in it? And he looked away from the photograph for a little while. When he glanced at it again he noticed his mother's hand, which dropped from the arm of the chair in the foreground, near enough to kiss. He wondered if it might not be better to write to his parents, as both of them (and his father very strictly on leaving him at Hamburg) had enjoined him. On that terrible evening when his mother, standing by the window, had told him he was to go to America, he had made a fixed resolution never to write; but what did the resolve of an inexperienced boy matter here, in these new surroundings? He might as well have vowed then that two months in America would see him commanding the American Militia, instead of which here he was in a garret beside two vagrants, in an eating-house outside New York, the right place for him, too, as he could not but admit. And with a smile he scrutinised his parents' faces, as if to read in them whether they still wanted to hear news of their son.

Thus preoccupied, he soon became aware that he was very tired after all and would scarcely manage to keep awake all night. The photograph fell from his hands, and he laid his face on it, finding the coolness pleasant to his cheek; and with a comfortable feeling he fell asleep.

He was awakened early in the morning by someone tickling him under the armpit. It was the Frenchman who had taken that liberty. But the Irishman too was standing beside Karl's table, and both were staring at him with no less interest than he had shown in them during the night. Karl was not surprised that in getting up they had not wakened him; there was no need to impute evil intentions to their stealthy movements, for he had been sleeping heavily, and they had not had much to do in the way of dressing, or, from all appearances of washing either.

Now they introduced themselves properly, with a certain formality, and Karl learned that they were both mechanics who had been out of work for a long time in New York and so had come down in the world considerably. In proof of this Robinson unbuttoned his jacket to show that he had no shirt on, but one might have guessed that from the loose fit of the collar which was merely fastened to the neck of his jacket. They were making their way to the little town of Butterford, two days on foot from New York, where it was rumoured that work was to be had. They had no objection to Karl's accompanying them, and promised to take turns at carrying his box, and also, if they got work themselves, to find him a job as an apprentice, an easy matter when work was to be had at all. Karl had scarcely agreed to this when they advised him in a friendly manner to get out of his good suit, which would only be a hindrance to him in looking for a job. In that very house there was an excellent chance to dispose of the suit, for the old

woman dealt in old clothes. They helped Karl, who had not yet quite decided what to do about the suit, to take it off, and then they carried it away. Left to himself Karl, still heavy with sleep, slowly put on his old travelling suit, reproaching himself meanwhile for having sold the good one, which might perhaps hinder him from getting an apprentice's job but would be a good recommendation in looking for a better situation, and he had just opened the door to call the two men back when he met them face to face, furnished with half a dollar which they laid on the table as the proceeds of the sale, looking at the same time so gleeful that it was difficult to believe they had not raked off a profit for themselves—and a disgustingly big profit, too.

But there was no time to tell them off about that, for the old woman came in, just as sleepy as she had been the night before, and drove all three of them out into the passage with the explanation that the room had to be got ready for new occupants. There was no question of that, needless to say; she did it out of mere malice. Karl, who had started to pack his box, had to look on while she grabbed his things with both hands and flung them into the box with such violence that they might have been wild animals she was determined to master. The two mechanics kept dodging round her, tugging at her skirt, clapping her on the back, but if they fancied they were helping Karl at all they were quite mistaken. When the old woman had shut the box, she thrust the handle into Karl's fingers, shook off the mechanics, and drove all three from the room with the threat that if they did not get out there would be no coffee for them. Obviously she had quite forgotten that Karl had not been with the mechanics from the start, for she lumped the three of them together. After all, the mechanics had sold her Karl's suit, which argued a certain solidarity.

They had to walk up and down the passage for a long time, and the Frenchman, who had taken Karl by the arm, swore with great fluency, threatening to knock down the landlord if he dared to show himself and furiously beating his clenched fists together as if in preparation for the encounter. At last an innocent little boy appeared, who was so small that he had to stand on tiptoe to hand the coffee-can to the Frenchman. Unluckily there was nothing but a can, and they could not make the boy understand that glasses were also needed. So only one of them could drink at a time, while the other two stood by and waited. Karl could not bring himself to drink coffee in this way, but he did not want to offend the other two, and so, when his turn came, though he raised the can to his lips he drank nothing.

As a parting gesture the Irishman flung the can on the stone flags. Observed by no one, they left the house and stepped out into the thick, yellowish morning mist. They walked on in silence side by side at the edge of the road; Karl had to carry his box, since the others were not likely to relieve him unless he asked them. Now and then an automble shot out of the mist and all three turned their heads to gaze after the larger monsters, which were so remarkable to look at and passed so quickly that they never even noticed whether anyone was sitting inside. Later they began to meet columns of vehicles bringing provisions to New York, which streamed past in five rows taking up the whole breadth of the road and so continuously that no one could have got across to the other side. At intervals the road widened into a kind of a square, in the middle of which rose a structure like a tower, where a policeman was stationed to supervise everything, directing with a little staff the traffic of the main road and of the adjoining side roads, the only supervision the traffic received until it reached the next square and the next policeman, although meanwhile it was adequately and gratuitously controlled by the silent vigilance of the lorrymen and chauffeurs. Karl was surprised most of all by the general quiet. Had it not been for the bellowing of the careless cattle bound for the slaughter-house, you would probably have heard nothing but the clatter of hoofs and the whirring of motor vehicles. Of course the speed at which they went was not always the same. At some of the squares, because of a great rush of traffic from the side roads, large-scale adjustments had to be made and then whole rows of vehicles came to a stand-still, jerking forward by inches, but after that for a little while everything would fly past at lightning speed again until, as if governed by a single brake, the traffic slowed down once more. And yet no trace of dust rose from the road; all this speeding went on in perfectly limpid air. There were no pedestrians, no market-women straggling singly along the road towards the town, as in Karl's country, but every now and then appeared great, flat motor-trucks, on which stood some twenty women with baskets on their backs, perhaps market-women after all, craning their necks to oversee the traffic in their impatience for a quicker journey. There were also similar trucks on which a few men lounged about with their hands in their trouser pockets. These trucks all bore different inscriptions, and on one of them Karl read with an ejaculation of surprise: "Dock-labourers wanted by the Jacob Despatch Agency." The truck happened to be going rather slowly and a lively little stoop-shouldered man standing on the step invited the three wanderers to hop in. Karl dodged behind the mechanics, as if his uncle were on the truck and might catch sight of him. He was glad that his two companions refused the invitation, though he found some grounds for offence in the scornful way they did so. They had no business to think they were too good to work for his uncle. He immediately let them know it, though not of course in so many words. Delamarche turned on him and told him not to interfere in things which he did not understand; this way of taking on men was a scandalous fraud and the firm of Jacob was notorious throughout the whole United States. Karl made no reply, but from that moment kept close to the Irishman and begged him to carry the box for a little while, which he actually did, after Karl had asked him several times. But he kept grumbling about the weight of the box, until it turned out that all he wanted was to relieve it of the Veronese salami, to which it seemed he had taken a fancy before he left the inn. Karl had to unpack it, but the Frenchman grabbed it and with a knife somewhat like a dagger sliced it up and ate almost the whole of it himself. Robinson got only a piece now and then and Karl, who had been forced to carry the box again, seeing that he did not want to leave it standing on the road, got nothing at all, as if he had had his share beforehand. It seemed too silly to beg for a piece, but he began to feel bitter.

The mist had already vanished; in the distance gleamed a high mountain, which receded in wave-like ridges towards a still more distant summit, veiled in a sunlit haze. By the side of the road were badly tilled fields clustered round big factories which rose up blackened with smoke in the open country. Isolated blocks of tenements were set down at random, and their countless windows quivered with manifold movement and light, while on all the flimsy little balconies women and children were busy in numberless ways, half concealed and half revealed by washing of all kinds, hung up or spread out to dry, which fluttered around them in the morning wind and billowed mightily. If one's eyes strayed from the houses one saw larks high in the heavens and lower down the swallows, darting not very far above the heads of the wayfarers.

There was much that reminded Karl of his home, and he could not decide whether he was doing well in leaving New York and going into the interior. New York had the sea, which meant the opportunity to return at any moment to his own country. And so he came to a standstill and said to his two companions that he felt like going back to New York after all. And when Delamarche simply made as if to drive him on, he refused to be driven and protested that it was his business to decide for himself. The Irishman had to intervene and explain that Butterford was a much finer place than New York, and both had to coax him insistently for a while before he would go on again. And even then he would not have consented had he not told himself that it would probably be better for him to reach a place where it would not be so easy to think of returning home. He would certainly work and push his fortune all the better there, if he were not hindered by idle thoughts of home.

And now it was he who led the two others, and they were so delighted by his enthusiasm that, without even being asked, they carried the box in turns and Karl simply could not make out in what way he had caused them such happiness. They now came to rising country, and when they stopped here and there they could see on looking back the panorama of New York and its harbour, extending more and more spaciously below them. The bridge connecting New York with Brooklyn hung delicately over the East River, and if one half-shut one's eyes it seemed to tremble. It appeared to be quite bare of traffic, and beneath it stretched a smooth empty tongue of water. Both the huge cities seemed to stand there empty and purposeless. As for the houses, it was scarcely possible to distinguish the large ones from the small. In the invisible depths of the streets life probably went on after its own fashion, but above them nothing was discernible save a light fume, which though it never moved seemed the easiest thing in the world to dispel. Even to the harbour, the greatest in the world, peace had returned, and only now and then, probably influenced by some memory of an earlier view close at hand, did one fancy that one saw a ship cutting the water for a little distance. But one could not follow it for long; it escaped one's eyes and was no more to be found.

Delamarche and Robinson clearly saw much more; they pointed to right and to left and their outstretched hands gestured over squares and gardens which they named by their names. They could not understand how Karl could stay for two months in New York and yet see hardly anything of the city but one street. And they promised, when they had made enough money in Butterford, to take him to New York with them and show him all the sights worth seeing, above all, of course, the places where you could enjoy yourself to your heart's content. Thinking of that, Robinson began to sing at the top of his voice a song which Delamarche accompanied by clapping his hands; Karl recognised it as an operatic melody of his own country, which pleased him more in the English version than it had ever pleased him at home. So there followed a little open-air concert, in which all took part; though the city at their feet, which was supposed to enjoy that melody so much, remained apparently indifferent.

Once Karl asked where Jacob's Despatch Agency lay, and Delamarche and Robinson at once stabbed the air with their forefingers, indicating perhaps the same point and perhaps points miles asunder. When they went on again, Karl asked how soon they would be able to return to New York if they got good jobs? Delamarche said they could easily do it in a month, for there was a scarcity of labour in Butterford and wages were high. Of course they would put their money into a common fund, so that chance differences in their earnings might be equalised as among friends. The common fund did not appeal to Karl, although as an apprentice he would naturally earn less than a skilled worker. In any case, Robinson went on, if there was no work in Butterford they would of course have to wander farther and either get jobs as workers on the land, or perhaps try panning for gold in California, which, to judge from Robinson's circumstantial tales, was the plan that appealed to him most.

"But why did you turn mechanic if you want to go looking for gold?" asked Karl, who was reluctant to admit the necessity for more distant and uncertain journeys.

"Why a mechanic?" said Robinson. "Certainly not to let my mother's son die of hunger. There's big money in the gold-fields."

"Was at one time," said Delamarche.

"Still is," said Robinson, and he told of countless people he knew who had grown rich there, who were still there, but of course did not need to lift a finger now, yet for old friendship's sake would help him to wealth and any friends of his too, naturally.

"We'll squeeze jobs out of Butterford all right," said Delamarche, and in saying this he uttered Karl's dearest wish; yet it could hardly be called a confident statement.

During the day they stopped only once at an eating-house and in front of it in the open air, at a table which to Karl's eyes seemed to be made of iron, ate almost raw flesh which could not be cut but only hacked with their knives and forks. The bread was baked in a cylindrical shape and in each of the loaves was stuck a long knife. With this meal a black liquor was supplied, which burnt one's throat. But Delamarche and Robinson liked it; they kept raising their glasses to the fulfilment of various toasts, clinking them together high in the air for a minute at a time. At a neighbouring table workmen in lime-stained blouses were sitting, all drinking the same liquor. Cars passing in great numbers flung swathes of dust over the table. Enormous newspapers were being handed round and there was excited talk of a strike among the building workers: the name Mack was often mentioned. Karl enquired regarding him and learned that he was the father of the Mack he knew, and the greatest building contractor in New York. The strike was supposed to be costing him millions and possibly endangering his financial position. Karl did not believe a word of what was said by these badly informed and spiteful people.

The meal was spoiled even more for Karl by the doubt in his mind how it was going to be paid for. The natural thing would have been for each to pay his shot, but both Delamarche and Robinson casually remarked that the price of their last night's lodging had emptied their pockets. Watch, ring or anything else that could be sold, was to be seen on neither of them. And Karl could hardly point out that they had lined their pockets over the sale of his suit; that would be an insult, and goodbye for ever. But the astonishing thing was that neither Delamarche nor Robinson bothered themselves about the payment; on the contrary they were in such good spirits that they kept trying to make up to the waitress, who moved with heavy stateliness from table to table. Her hair was loosened at the sides and tumbled over her brow and cheeks; she kept putting it back by pushing it up with her hand. At last, just when they thought they were going to get a friendly word from her, she came up to their table, planted both hands on it and asked: "Who is paying?" Never did hands shoot out more quickly than those of Delamarche and Robinson as they pointed at Karl. Karl was not taken aback, for he had foreseen this, and he saw no harm in paying a trifling bill for his comrades, from whom he expected assistance in turn, although it would certainly have been more decent of them to discuss the matter frankly before the crucial moment. All that troubled him was that he would first have to fish the money out of the secret pocket. His original intention had been to save up his money in case of extreme need and for the time being to put himself, as it were, on a level with his friends. The advantage which he held over them through possessing that money and above all through concealing it was easily outweighed by the fact that they had lived in America since their childhood, that they had ample skill and experience for wage-earning, and finally that they were not accustomed to anything better than their present circumstances. Karl's original intention to save his money, then, need not be affected by his paying the bill now, since after all he could spare a quarter of a dollar; he could simply lay a quarter on the table and tell them that that was all he had, and that he was willing to part with it to get them all to Butterford. For a journey on foot a quarter should be ample. But he did not know whether he had enough small change, and anyhow his change was beside the wad of banknotes in the recesses of his secret pocket, where it was difficult to get hold of anything without emptying the whole lot on to the table. Besides, it was quite unnecessary for his companions to know anything about the secret pocket at all. By good luck, however, his friends seemed to be much more interested in the waitress than in how Karl was to produce the money for the bill. Delamarche, under cover of asking her to make out the bill, had lured her in between himself and Robinson, and the only way in which she could repel their familiarities was by pushing their faces away with the flat of her hand. Meanwhile, sweating with the effort, Karl gathered in one hand under the table the money he felt for and extracted, coin by coin, from the secret pocket with the other. At long last, although he was not yet familiar with American money, he judged that he had enough small coins to make up the sum and laid them all on the table. The clink of money at once put an end to all by-play. To Karl's annoyance and to the general surprise it turned out that almost a whole dollar was lying there. No one asked why Karl had said nothing about this money, which would have been suffi-cient for a comfortable railway journey to Butterford; yet Karl felt deeply embarrassed all the same. After paying the bill, he slowly pocketed the coins again, but from his very fingers Delamarche snatched one of them, as a special tip for the waitress, whom he embraced ardently with one hand while giving her the coin with the other.

Karl felt grateful to them for not saying anything about his money as they walked away together, and for a while he actually considered confessing his whole wealth to them, but then refrained, as he could not find a suitable opportunity. Towards evening they came to a more rustic, fertile neighbour-hood. All around they could see endless fields stretching across gentle hills in their first green; rich country villas bordered the road on either side, and for hours they walked between gilded garden railings; several times they crossed the same slow stream, and often they heard above them trains thundering over the lofty viaducts.

The sun was just setting behind the level edge of distant woods when they mounted a gentle rise crowned with a clump of trees and flung themselves on the grass so as to rest from their travels. Delamarche and Robinson lay flat and stretched themselves mightily. Karl sat up and gazed at the road a few yards below, on which motor-cars flew lightly past one another as they had done the whole day, as if a certain number of them were always being despatched from some distant place and the same number were being awaited in another place equally distant. During the whole day since early morning Karl had seen not a single car stopping, not a single passenger getting out.

Robinson proposed that they should spend the night here, since they were all very tired and would be able to start all the earlier in the morning; besides, they would scarcely find a cheaper and more suitable place to spend the night before complete darkness fell. Delamarche was of the same mind, but Karl felt obliged to remark that he had enough money to pay for a night's lodgings for them all in some hotel. Delamarche replied that they might still need the money; better to save it for the present. He made no concealment of the fact that they were counting on Karl's money. As his first proposal had been accepted, Robinson went on to suggest that before going to sleep they should have a good meal to strengthen them for the morning, and that one of them should fetch food for all three from the hotel close by on the main road, which bore the lighted sign: "Hotel Occidental." As he was the youngest and nobody else offered to go, Karl had no hesitation in volunteering for the job, and after the others had announced that they wanted bacon, bread and beer, he went across to the hotel.

It seemed that they must be near a big town, for the very first room of the hotel that Karl entered was filled with a noisy crowd, and at the buffet, which ran along the whole length and two sides of the room, a host of waiters with white aprons kept rushing about yet could not satisfy their impatient customers, for loud cursing and the pounding of fists on tables sounded unceasingly from all quarters. No one paid any attention to Karl; in the body of the saloon itself there was no service; the customers, crowded at tiny tables scarcely big enough for three people, had to fetch everything they wanted from the buffet. On each table stood a big bottle of oil, vinegar or something of the kind, and all the food that was brought from the buffet was liberally dosed from the bottle before being eaten. If Karl was to reach the buffet at all, where his real difficulties would probably begin because of the huge crowd standing at it, he would have to squeeze his way between the countless tables, and this of course, in spite of every care, could not be done without rudely disturbing the customers, who, however, accepted every inconvenience apathetically, even when Karl cannoned violently into a table—through no fault of his own, certainly—and almost knocked it over. He apologised, but obviously without being understood; nor could he for his part make out any of the remarks that were shouted at him. At the buffet he found with difficulty a few inches of free space, where his view was obscured for a long time by the elbows of the men standing on either side of him. It seemed a universal custom here to plant your elbow on the counter and rest your head on your hand. Karl could not help remembering how his Latin teacher Doctor Krumpal had hated that posture, and how he would steal up silently and unexpectedly and knock your elbow off the desk with a playful rap of a ruler which suddenly appeared from nowhere.

Karl was squeezed close against the counter, for scarcely had he reached it when a table was set up behind him, and a wide hat kept brushing against his back whenever the customer sitting there leaned backwards a little in talking. Also there seemed to be little hope of his getting anything out of the waiters, even after his two unmannerly neighbours had gone away satisfied. Once or twice Karl snatched at a waiter's apron across the counter, but the waiter always tore himself away with a grimace. Not one of them would stop; they did nothing but rush to and fro. If there had even been anything suitable to eat near at hand Karl would have grabbed it, enquired what the price was, laid down the money and taken himself off with relief. But in front of him there were only dishes of fish which looked like herring, with dark scales gleaming golden at the edges. They might be very dear and would probably sate nobody's hunger. There were also small casks of rum within reach, but he did not want to bring his friends rum; as it was, whenever they had the chance they seemed to drink only concentrated alcohol, and he had no wish to encourage them in that.

So nothing remained for Karl but to find another point of vantage and start all over again. But by now the hour had considerably advanced. The clock at the other end of the room, whose hands could still just be discerned through the smoke if one looked very intently, showed that it was after nine. Yet the rest of the counter was even more crowded than the first place he had found, which was in a retired corner. Also the room was filling up more and more, as the evening went on. New customers kept pushing through the main door with loud halloos. At several places customers had autocratically cleared the counter and seated themselves upon it and were drinking to one another; that was the best position of all, you could overlook the whole room.

Karl still pressed forward, but any real hope of achieving anything had vanished. He blamed himself for having volunteered to run this errand without knowing anything of the local conditions. His friends would swear at him, with perfect right, and might perhaps even think that he had brought nothing back simply in order to save his money. He had now reached a part of the room where hot meat-dishes and fine yellow potatoes were being devoured at all tables; it was incomprehensible to him how the customers had got hold of them.

Then a few steps in front of him he saw an elderly woman who clearly belonged to the hotel staff and was talking and laughing with a customer. As she talked she kept poking at her hair with a hair-pin. Karl at once decided to confide his wants to this woman, mainly because as the only woman in the room she stood out as an exception in the general hubbub, and also for the simple reason that she was the only hotel employee he could get hold of, that is to say, if she did not rush away on her own business at the first word he addressed to her. But quite the opposite happened. Karl had not even spoken to her, he had only dodged round her for a little while, when, as often happens in the middle of a conversation, she looked aside and caught sight of him and, interrupting what she was saying, asked him kindly and in English as clear as the grammar-book if he wanted anything.

"Yes, indeed," said Karl, "I can't get a single thing anywhere in the place."

"Then come with me, my boy," she said, and she said goodbye to her acquaintance, who raised his hat, which in this room seemed an incredible mark of politeness; then taking Karl by the hand she went up to the counter, pushed a customer aside, lifted a flap-door, went along a passage behind the counter, where they had to side-step the tirelessly rushing waiters, and opened a double-door concealed in the wall, which led straight into a large, cool store-room. "You have to know the workings of these places," Karl said to himself.

"Well now, what do you want?" she asked, bending down to him kindly. She was very fat, so that her body quivered, but

by comparison her face was almost delicately modelled. Karl felt almost tempted, gazing at the great variety of eatables neatly set out on shelves and tables, to invent a more elegant supper on the spur of the moment and order that instead, especially as he might get it more cheaply from this influential lady; but in the end he mentioned nothing but bacon, bread and beer after all, as he could not think of anything more suitable.

"Nothing more?" asked the woman.

"No, thanks," said Karl, "but enough for three people."

When the woman enquired who the two others were, Karl told her in a few brief words about his companions; he felt glad to be asked some questions.

"But that's prison fare," said the woman, obviously expecting Karl to order something else. But Karl was now afraid that she might bestow the food on him as a gift and refuse to accept any money, and so he kept silent. "That won't take long to get ready," said the woman, and she walked over to a table with an agility wonderful in one so fat, cut with a long, thin, saw-edged knife a great piece of bacon richly streaked with lean, took a loaf from a shelf, lifted three bottles of beer from the floor, and put them all in a light straw basket, which she handed to Karl. As she was doing this she explained to him that she had brought him here because the food in the buffet, though it was quickly replenished, always lost its freshness in the smoke and all the steam. Still, for the people out there anything was good enough. This struck Karl quite dumb, for he could not see how he had earned such special treatment. He thought of his companions who, in spite of all their American experience, would probably never have reached this store-room, but would have had to be content with the stale food in the buffet. No sound from the saloon could be heard here;

the walls must be very thick to keep this vaulted chamber so cool. Karl had already been holding the straw basket in his hand for some time, yet he thought neither of paying nor of going away. Not until the woman made to put in the basket, as an extra, a bottle similar to those standing on the table outside, did he make a move, refusing it with a shiver.

"Have you much farther to go?" asked the woman.

"To Butterford," replied Karl.

"That's a long way still," said the woman.

"Another day's journey," said Karl.

"Isn't it more than that?" asked the woman.

"Oh no," said Karl.

The woman re-arranged some things on the tables; a waiter came in, looked round interrogatively, and was directed by her to a huge platter, on which lay a large heap of sardines lightly strewn with parsley, which he then bore in his raised hands into the saloon.

"Why should you spend the night in the open air?" asked the woman. "We have room enough here. Come and sleep here with us in the hotel."

The thought was very tempting to Karl, particularly as he had slept so badly the previous night.

"I have my luggage out there," he said hesitatingly and not without a certain pride.

"Then just bring it here," said the woman, "that's no hindrance."

"But what about my friends?" said Karl, realising at once that they were certainly a hindrance.

"They can spend the night here too, of course," said the woman. "Do come! Don't be so difficult."

"My friends are first-rate comrades," said Karl, "but they're not exactly clean."

"Haven't you seen the dirt in the saloon?" asked the woman with a grimace. "We can well take in the hardest cases. All right, I'll have three beds got ready at once. Only in an attic, I'm afraid, for the hotel is full; I've had to move into an attic myself, but at any rate it's better than sleeping out."

"I can't bring my friends here," said Karl. He pictured to himself the row the two of them would make in the passages of this fine hotel; Robinson would dirty everything and Delamarche would not fail to molest the woman herself.

"I don't see why that should be impossible," said she, "but if you insist on it, then leave your friends behind and come without them."

"That wouldn't do," said Karl. "They're my friends and I must stick to them."

"You're very obstinate," said the woman, turning her eyes away, "when people mean well by you and try to do you a good turn, you do your best to hinder them."

Karl realised all this, but he saw no way out, so he merely said: "My best thanks to you for your kindness." Then he remembered that he had not paid her yet, and he asked what he owed.

"You can pay me when you bring the basket back," said the woman. "I must have it tomorrow morning at the latest."

"Thank you," said Karl. She opened a door which led straight into the open air and said, as he stepped out with a bow: "Goodnight. But you're not doing the right thing." He was already a few yards away when she cried after him again: "Till tomorrow morning!"

Hardly was he outside when he heard again the undiminished roar of the saloon, with which was now mingled the blare of wind instruments. He was glad that he had not to go out through the saloon. All five floors of the hotel were now illuminated and made the road in front of it bright from one side to the other. Automobiles were still careering along the road, although more intermittently, looming into sight more rapidly than by day, feeling for the road before them with the white beams of their headlights, which paled as they crossed the lighted zone of the hotel only to blaze out again as they rushed into the farther darkness.

Karl found his friends sleeping soundly; but then he had been far too long away. He was just preparing to set out temptingly on paper the food he had brought, making all ready before waking his companions, when to his horror he saw his box, which he had left securely locked and whose key he had in his pocket, standing wide open and half its contents scattered about on the grass.

"Get up!" he cried. "There have been thieves here, and you lying sleeping!"

"Why, is anything missing?" asked Delamarche. Robinson was not quite awake, yet his hand was already reaching towards the beer.

"I don't know," cried Karl, "but the box is open. It was very careless of you to go to sleep and leave the box here at anybody's mercy."

Delamarche and Robinson laughed, and Delamarche said: "Then you'd better not stay away so long next time. It's only a step or two to the hotel and yet you take three hours to go there and come back again. We were hungry, we thought that you might have something to eat in your box, so we just tickled the lock until it opened. But there was nothing in it after all and your stuff can easily go back again."

"I see," said Karl, staring at the quickly emptying basket and listening to the curious noise which Robinson made in drinking, for the beer seemed first to plunge right down into his throat and gurgle up again with a sort of whistle before finally pouring its flood into the deep.

"Have you had enough now?" he asked, when the two of them paused to take breath for a moment.

"Why, didn't you have your supper in the hotel?" asked Delamarche, who thought that Karl was putting in a claim for his share.

"If you want any more, then hurry up," said Karl, going over to his box.

"He seems to be in a huff," said Delamarche to Robinson.

"I'm not in a huff," said Karl, "but do you think it's right to break open my box and fling out my things while I'm away? I know that one must put up with a lot from friends and I've been prepared to do that; but this is too much. I'm going to spend the night in the hotel, and I'm not going with you to Butterford. Finish your supper quickly; I've got to take back the basket."

"Just listen to him, Robinson," said Delamarche. "That's a fine way of talking. He's a German all right. You did warn me against him at the beginning, but I'm a kind-hearted fool and so I let him come with us all the same. We've given him our confidence, we've dragged him with us all day and lost half a day at least on his account, and now—just because he's chummed up with somebody in the hotel—he gives us the go-by, simply gives us the go-by. But because he's a lying German he doesn't do it frankly but makes his box a pretext, and being an ill-mannered German he can't leave us without insulting our honour and calling us thieves, just because we had a little fun with his box."

Karl, who was packing his things, said without turning round: "The more you say, the easier you make it for me to leave you. I know quite well what friendship is. I have had friends in Europe too and none of them can accuse me of ever behaving falsely or meanly to him. I'm not in touch with them now, naturally, but if I ever go back to Europe again they'll all be glad to see me, and they'll welcome me at once as a friend. As for you, Delamarche and Robinson, I'm supposed to have betrayed you, am I, after you were so kind—and I'll never forget that—as to let me join up with you and have a chance of an apprentice's job in Butterford? But that isn't how it is at all. I think none the less of you because you own nothing, but you grudge me my few possessions and try to humiliate me because of them, and that I cannot endure. And you break open my box and offer no word of excuse, but abuse me instead and my people as well—and that simply makes it impossible for me to stay with you. All the same, this doesn't really apply to you, Robinson. I have nothing against you except that you are far too dependent on Delamarche."

"So now we see," said Delamarche, stepping over to Karl and giving him a slight push, as if to insist on his attention, "so now we see you at last in your true colours. All day you've trotted behind me, hanging on to my coat-tails and doing whatever I did and keeping as quiet as a mouse. But now that somebody in the hotel's backing you up, you begin to throw your weight about. You're a little twister, and I'm not so sure that we're going to put up with that kind of thing. I'm not so sure that we aren't going to make you pay for what you've learned by watching us today. We envy him, Robinson—envy him, says he—because of his possessions. One day's work in Butterford—not to mention California—and we'll have ten times as much as anything you've showed us yet, or anything you've still got hidden in the lining of that coat. So keep your tongue quiet!"

Karl had risen from his box and saw Robinson also advancing upon him, still sleepy but a little enlivened by the beer. "If I stay here longer," he said, "I'll maybe get some more surprises. It seems to me you want to beat me up."

"Nobody's patience lasts for ever," said Robinson.

"You'd better keep out of it, Robinson," said Karl, without taking his eyes from Delamarche, "in your heart you know that I'm right, but you've got to make a show of agreeing with Delamarche!"

"Are you maybe thinking of bribing him?" asked Delamarche.

"Never occurred to me," said Karl. "I'm glad to be going and I want to have nothing more to do with either of you. There's only one thing more I want to say: you reproached me for having money and concealing it from you. Granted that's true, wasn't it the right thing to do with people that I had known only for a few hours, and isn't the way you're carrying on now a proof of how right I was?"

"Keep quiet," said Delamarche to Robinson, though Robinson had not moved. Then he said to Karl: "Seeing that you're making such a parade of honesty, why not stretch your honesty a little farther, now that we're having a friendly heart-to-heart, and tell us why you really want to go to the hotel?" Karl had to take a step back over the box, Delamarche had pushed up so close to him. But Delamarche was not to be deflected, he kicked the box aside, took another step forward, planting his foot on a white dickey that had been left lying on the grass, and repeated his question.

As if in answer a man with a powerful flash-lamp climbed up from the road towards the group. It was one of the waiters from the hotel. As soon as he caught sight of Karl he said: "I've been looking for you for nearly half an hour. I've been hunting through all the bushes on both sides of the road. The

Manageress sent me to tell you that she needs that straw basket she lent you."

"Here it is," said Karl in a voice trembling with agitation. Delamarche and Robinson had drawn aside in pretended humility, as they always did when decent looking strangers appeared. The waiter picked up the basket and said: "The Manageress also told me to ask you whether you haven't changed your mind and would like to sleep in the hotel after all. The other two gentlemen would be welcome too, if you care to bring them with you. The beds are all ready for you. It's warm enough tonight, but it's far from safe to sleep in this place; you often come across snakes."

"Since the Manageress is so kind, I'll accept her invitation after all," said Karl, and waited for his companions to say something. But Robinson stood there quite dumb and Delamarche was looking up at the stars with his hands in his trouser pockets. Both were obviously expecting Karl to take them with him without further ado.

"In that case," said the waiter, "I have orders to take you to the hotel and carry your luggage there."

"Then please just wait a moment," said Karl, bending down to put in his box the few things which were still lying about.

Suddenly he straightened himself. The photograph, which had been lying on the very top, was missing and nowhere to be found. Everything else was there, except the photograph. "I can't find the photograph," he said to Delamarche imploringly.

"What photograph?" asked Delamarche.

"The photograph of my parents," said Karl.

"We haven't seen any photograph in the box, Mr. Rossmann," said Robinson.

"But that's quite impossible," said Karl, and his beseeching glances brought the waiter nearer. "It was lying on the top and now it's gone. I do wish you hadn't played about with my box."

"We're not making any mistake," said Delamarche, "there was no photograph in the box."

"It was more important to me than all the other things in the box," said Karl to the waiter, who was walking about looking in the grass. "For it's irreplaceable; I can't get another one." And when the waiter gave up the hopeless search, Karl added: "It was the only photograph of my parents that I possessed."

Then the waiter said aloud, without any attempt to mitigate his words: "Maybe we could run through these gentlemen's pockets."

"Yes," said Karl at once, "I must find the photograph. But before searching their pockets, let me say this, that whoever gives me the photograph of his own accord can have my box and everything in it." After a moment of general silence Karl said to the waiter: "It seems my friends prefer to have their pockets searched. But even now I promise the box and everything in it to anyone in whose pocket the photograph is found. More I can't do."

The waiter immediately set about searching Delamarche, who seemed to him more difficult to handle than Robinson, whom he left to Karl. He impressed upon Karl that they must both be searched simultaneously, otherwise one of them might get rid of the photograph unobserved. As soon as he put his hand into Robinson's pocket, Karl found a scarf belonging to himself, but he refrained from taking it and called to the waiter: "Whatever you find on Delamarche, let him keep it. I want nothing but the photograph, only the photograph."

In searching the breast pocket of Robinson's coat Karl's hand came in contact with the man's hot, flabby chest and he became aware that he might be doing his companions a great injustice. That made him hurry as fast as he could. But all was in vain; no photograph was to be found either on Robinson of on Delamarche.

"It's no good," said the waiter.

"They've probably torn up the photograph and flung the pieces away," said Karl. "I thought they were friends, but in their hearts they only wished me ill. Not so much Robinson; it would never have occurred to him that I set such store on the photograph; that's more like Delamarche." Karl could now see only the waiter, whose flash-lamp lit up a tiny circle, while everything else, including Delamarche and Robinson, lay in deep darkness.

There was naturally no question now of the two men going to the hotel with Karl. The waiter swung the box on to his shoulder, Karl picked up the straw basket, and they set off. Karl had already reached the road when, starting out of his thoughts, he stopped and shouted up into the darkness: "Listen to me. If either of you has the photograph and will bring it to me at the hotel, he can still have the box, and I swear that I won't make any charge against him." No actual answer came, only a stifled word could be heard, the beginning of a shout from Robinson, whose mouth was obviously stopped at once by Delamarche. Karl waited for a long time, in case the men above him might change their minds. He shouted twice, at intervals: "I'm still here!" But no sound came in reply, except that a stone rolled down the slope, perhaps a chance stone, perhaps a badly-aimed throw.

On reaching the hotel Karl was at once conducted to a sort of office, in which the Manageress, with a notebook in her hand, was dictating a letter to a young stenographer sitting at a typewriter. The consummately precise dictation, the controlled and buoyant tapping of the keys raced on to the ticking, noticeable only now and then, of a clock standing against the wall, whose hands pointed to almost half-past eleven. "There!" said the Manageress, shutting the notebook; the stenographer jumped up and put the lid on the typewriter without taking her eyes from Karl during these mechanical actions. She looked like a schoolgirl still, her overall was neatly ironed, even pleated at the shoulders; her hair was piled up high; and it was a little surprising, after noting these details, to see the gravity of her face. After making a bow, first to the Manageress, then to Karl, she left the room and Karl involuntarily flung a questioning glance at the Manageress.

"It's splendid that you've come after all," said the Manageress. "And what about your friends?"

"I haven't brought them with me," said Karl.

"They'll be moving on very early in the morning, I suppose," said the Manageress, as if to explain the matter to herself.

"But mustn't she think in that case that I'll have to start early too?" Karl asked himself, and so he said to put an end to all misunderstanding: "We parted on bad terms."

The Manageress seemed to construe this as excellent news. "So then you're free?" she said.

"Yes, I'm free," said Karl, and nothing seemed more worthless than his freedom.

"Listen, wouldn't you like to take a job here in the hotel?" asked the Manageress.

"Very much," said Karl, "but I have terribly little experience. For instance, I can't even use a typewriter."

"That's not very important," said the Manageress. "You'd be given only a small job to begin with, and it would be your business to work your way up by diligence and attentiveness. But in any case I think it would be better and wiser for you to settle down somewhere, instead of wandering about like this. I don't think you're made for that kind of thing."

"My uncle would subscribe to that too," Karl told himself, nodding in agreement. At the same time he reminded himself that though the Manageress had shown such concern for him, he had not yet introduced himself. "Please forgive me," he said, "for not having introduced myself before. My name is Karl Rossmann."

"You're a German, aren't you?"

"Yes," said Karl, "I haven't been long in America."

"Where do you come from?"

"From Prague, in Bohemia," said Karl.

"Just think of that!" cried the Manageress in English with a strong German inflexion, almost flinging her hands in the air. "Then we're compatriots, for my name is Grete Mitzelbach and I come from Vienna. And I know Prague quite well; I worked for half a year in the 'Golden Goose' in Wenceslaus Square. Only think of that!"

"When was that?" asked Karl.

"Many, many years ago now."

133

"The old 'Golden Goose'," said Karl, "was pulled down two years ago."

"Well, well," said the Manageress, quite absorbed in her thoughts of past days.

But all at once, becoming animated again, she seized both Karl's hands and cried: "Now that you turn out to be a country-man of mine, you mustn't go away on any account. You mustn't offend me by doing that. How would you like, for instance, to be a lift-boy? Just say the word and it's done. If you've seen something of this country, you'll realise that it isn't very easy to get such posts, for they're the best start in life that you can think of. You come in contact with all the hotel guests, people are always seeing you and giving you little errands to do; in short, every day you have the chance to better yourself. I'll fix everything up for you; leave it to me."

"I should like quite well to be a lift-boy," said Karl after a slight pause. It would be very foolish to have any scruples about accepting a post as lift-boy because of his High School education. Here in America he had much more cause to be ashamed of his High School. Besides, Karl had always admired lift-boys; he thought them very ornamental.

"Isn't a knowledge of languages required?" he asked next.

"You speak German and perfectly good English; that's quite enough."

"I've learned English only in the last two and a half months in America," said Karl, for he thought he had better not conceal his one merit. "That's a sufficient recommendation in itself," said the Manageress. "When I think of the difficulties I had with my English! Of course, that's thirty years ago now. I was talking about it only yesterday. For yesterday was my fiftieth birthday." And she smilingly tried to read in Karl's face the impression which such a dignified age made upon him.

"Then I wish you much happiness," said Karl.

"Well, it always comes in useful," said she, shaking Karl's hand and looking a little melancholy over the old German phrase which had come quite naturally to the tip of her tongue.

"But I am keeping you here," she cried all at once. "And you must be tired, and we can talk over everything much better tomorrow. My pleasure in meeting a countryman has made me forget everything else. Come, I'll show you your room."

"I have one more favour to beg," said Karl, glancing at the telephone which stood on the table. "It's possible that tomorrow morning these one-time friends of mine may bring me a photograph which I urgently need. Would you be so kind as to telephone to the porter to send the men up to me, or else call me down?"

"Certainly," said the Manageress, "but wouldn't it do if they gave him the photograph? What photograph is it, if I may ask?"

"It's a photograph of my parents," said Karl. "No, I must speak to the men myself." The Manageress said nothing further and telephoned the order to the porter's office, giving 536 as the number of Karl's room.

They went then through a door facing the entrance door and along a short passage, where a small lift-boy was leaning against the railing of a lift, fast asleep. "We can work it ourselves," said the Manageress softly, ushering Karl into the lift. "A working day of from ten to twelve hours is really rather much for a boy like that," she added, while they ascended. "But America's a strange country. Take this boy, for instance; he came here only half a year ago with his parents; he's an Italian. At the moment it looks as if he simply wouldn't be able to stand the work, his face has fallen away to nothing and he goes to sleep on the job, although he's naturally a very willing lad—but let him only go on working here or anywhere else in America for another six months and he'll be able to take it all in his stride, and in another five years he'll be a strong man. I could spend hours telling you about such cases. You're not one of them, for you're a strong lad already; you're seventeen, aren't you?"

"I'll be sixteen next month," replied Karl.

"Not even sixteen!" said the Manageress. "Then you don't need to worry!"

At the top of the building she led Karl to a room which, being a garret, had a sloping wall, but was lit by two electric lamps and looked most inviting. "Don't be surprised at the furnishings," said the Manageress, "for this isn't a hotel room, but one of my rooms; I have three of them, so that you won't disturb me in the least. I'll lock the connecting doors and you'll be quite private. Tomorrow, as a new hotel employee, you will of course be given your own room. If your friends had come with you, I would have put you all in the large attic where the hotel servants sleep; but as you are alone I think you would be better here, though you'll have nothing but a sofa to lie on. And now sleep well and gather strength for your work. Tomorrow it won't be so very hard."

"Thank you very much indeed for your kindness."

"Wait," she said, stopping by the door, "I'll have to keep you from being wakened up too early." And she went to a side door opening out of the room, knocked on it and cried: "Therese!"

"Yes, madam," replied the voice of the typist.

"When you waken me in the morning go round by the passage; there's a guest sleeping in this room. He's dead tired." She smiled at Karl while saying this. "Do you understand?"

"Yes, madam."

"Well then, goodnight."

"Goodnight."

"I have slept," said the Manageress in explanation, "very badly for several years. I have every right to be satisfied with my present position and don't really need to worry. But all my earlier worries must be taking it out of me now and keeping me from sleeping. If I fall asleep by three in the morning, I can count myself lucky. But as I have to be at my post by five, or half-past five at the latest, I have to be wakened and very gently wakened, to prevent me from turning more nervous than I am already. And so Therese wakens me. But now I've really told you everything there is to tell and I'm not away yet. Goodnight." And in spite of her bulk she almost flitted out of the room.

Karl was looking forward to his sleep, for the day had taken a great deal out of him. And more comfortable quarters for a long, unbroken sleep he could not wish for. The room was certainly not intended for a bedroom, it was rather the Manageress's living-room, or more exactly reception-room, and a washstand had been specially put in it for his use that night; yet he did not feel like an intruder, but only that he was being well looked after. His box was there all right, waiting for him, and certainly had not been so safe for a long time. On a low chest of drawers, over which a large-meshed woollen cover had been flung, several framed photographs were standing; in making his round of the room Karl stopped to look at them. They were nearly all old photographs, mostly of girls in old-fashioned, uncomfortable clothes, a small, high-crowned hat insecurely perched on each head and the right hand resting on the handle of a sun-shade; girls who stood facing the spectator and yet refused to meet his eyes. Among the photographs of the men

Karl was particularly struck by a young soldier who had laid his cap on a table and was standing erect with a thatch of wild black hair and a look of suppressed but arrogant amusement. Someone had retouched the buttons of his uniform with dots of gold paint. All these photographs probably came from Europe, and by turning them over it would be possible to make sure, yet Karl did not want to lay a finger upon them. He would have liked to set up the photograph of his parents in the room he was going to have, just like these photographs here.

He was just stretching himself on the sofa and looking forward to his sleep after washing himself thoroughly from head to foot, which he had taken care to do as quietly as possible on account of the girl next door, when he thought he heard a low knock at a door. He could not make out at once which door it was; it might well have been only some random noise. Nor was it repeated at once, and he was half-asleep by the time it came again. But now it was unmistakably a knock and it came from the door of the typist's room. Karl tiptoed to the door and asked so softly that, even if the girl in the next room were sleeping after all, it could not waken her: "Do you want anything?"

At once the reply came in an equally soft voice: "Won't you open the door? The key is on your side."

"Certainly," said Karl, "only I must put on some clothes first."

There was a slight pause, then the girl said: "You don't need to do that. Unlock the door and go back to bed again; I'll wait for a little."

"Good," said Karl and did as she had suggested, except that he switched on the electric light as well. "I'm in bed now," he said then, somewhat more loudly. Then the typist emerged from her dark room fully dressed as she had left the office; apparently she had not even thought of going to bed.

"Please excuse me," she said, drooping a little before Karl's sofa, "and please don't tell on me. And I won't disturb you for long; I know you're dead tired."

"I'm not so tired as all that," said Karl, "but maybe it might have been better if I had put on some clothes." He had to lie quite flat to keep himself covered to the neck, for he had no nightshirt.

"I'll only stay a minute," she said, looking about for a chair. "May I sit beside the sofa?" Karl nodded. She set her chair so close to the sofa that Karl had to squeeze against the wall to look up at her. She had a round, regularly formed face, except that the brow looked unusually high, but that might have been an effect of the way her hair was done, which did not quite suit her. Her dress was very clean and neat. In her left hand she was crushing a handkerchief.

"Are you going to stay here long?" she asked.

"It isn't quite settled yet," replied Karl, "but I think I'm going to stay."

"That would be splendid," she said, passing the handkerchief over her face, "for I feel so lonely here."

"I'm surprised at that," said Karl. "The Manageress is very kind to you, isn't she? She doesn't treat you like an employee at all. I actually thought you were a relation of hers."

"Oh, no," she said, "my name is Therese Berchtold; I come from Pomerania."

Karl also introduced himself. At that, she looked him full in the face for the first time, as if he had become a little more strange to her by mentioning his name. They were both silent for a while. Then she said: "You mustn't think that I'm ungrateful. If it weren't for the Manageress I'd be in a much worse state. I used to be a kitchen-maid here in the hotel and in great danger of being dismissed too, for I wasn't equal to the heavy work. They expect a lot from you here. A month ago a kitchen-maid simply fainted under the strain and had to lie up in hospital for fourteen days. And I'm not very strong, I was often ill as a child, and so I've been slow in catching up; you would never think, would you, that I'm eighteen? But I'm getting stronger now."

"The work here must really be very tiring," said Karl. "I saw a lift-boy downstairs standing sleeping on his feet."

"The lift-boys have the best of it, all the same," she said. "They make quite a lot in tips and in spite of that they don't have to work nearly so hard as the girls in the kitchen. But for once in my life I really was lucky, for one day the Manageress needed a girl to arrange the table napkins for a banquet and she sent down for a kitchen-maid; now there are about fifty kitchen-maids here and I just happened to be handy; well, I gave her great satisfaction, for I have always been very good at arranging table napkins. And so from that day she kept me with her and trained me by stages till I became her secretary. And I've learned a great deal."

"Is there so much writing to be done here, then?" asked Karl.

"Oh, a great deal," she replied, "more than you would imagine. You saw yourself that I was working up to half-past eleven tonight, and that's quite usual. Of course, I don't type all the time, for I do lots of errands in the town as well."

"What's the name of this town?" asked Karl.

"Don't you know?" she said. "Rameses."

"Is it a big town?" asked Karl.

"Very big," she replied. "I don't enjoy visiting it. But wouldn't you really like to go to sleep now?"

"No, no," said Karl, "you haven't told me yet why you came to see me."

"Because I have no one to talk to. I'm not complaining, but there's really no one, and it makes me happy to find someone at last who will let me talk. I saw you below in the saloon, I was just coming to fetch the Manageress when she took you off to the store-room."

"That saloon is a terrible place," said Karl.

"I don't even notice it these days," she replied. "But I only wanted to say that the Manageress is as kind to me as if she were my mother. Yet there's too great a difference between our positions for me to speak freely to her. I used to have good friends among the kitchen-maids, but they've all left here long ago and I scarcely know the new girls. And besides, it often seems to me that the work I'm doing now is a greater strain than what I did before, that I don't even do it so well as the other, and that the Manageress keeps me on merely out of charity. After all, it really needs a better education than I have had to be a secretary. It's a sin to say it, but often and often I feel it's driving me out of my mind. For God's sake," she burst out, speaking much more rapidly and hastily touching Karl's shoulder, since he kept his hands below the blankets, "don't tell the Manageress a word of this, or else I'm really done for. If besides worrying her by my work, I were to cause her actual pain as well, that would really be too much."

"Of course I won't tell her anything," replied Karl.

"Then that's all right," she said, "and you must go on staying here. I'd be glad if you would, and if you like we could be friends. As soon as I saw you, I felt I could trust you. And yet—you see how wicked I am—I was afraid too that the Manageress might make you her secretary in my place and dismiss me. It took me a long time, sitting by myself next door, while you were below in the office, to straighten it all out in my mind until I saw that it might actually be a very good thing if you were to take over my work, for you certainly would understand it better. If you didn't want to do the errands in the town, I could keep that job for myself. But apart from that, I would certainly be of much more use in the kitchen, especially as I'm stronger now than I used to be."

"It's all settled already," said Karl, "I'm to be a lift-boy and you're to go on being secretary. But if you even hint at these plans of yours to the Manageress, I'll tell her all you've told me tonight, sorry as I would be to do it."

Karl's tone alarmed Therese so greatly that she flung herself down beside the sofa weeping and hiding her face in the bed-clothes.

"Oh, I shan't tell," said Karl, "but you mustn't say anything either."

Now he could not help coming a little out from under his coverings, and stroked her arm softly, but he did not find the right words to say and could only reflect that this girl's life was a bitter one. Finally he comforted her so far that she grew ashamed of her weeping, looked at him gratefully, advised him to sleep long next morning, and promised, if she could find time, to come up at eight o'clock and waken him.

"You are so clever at wakening people," said Karl.

"Yes, some things I can do," she said, ran her hand softly over the bed-clothes in farewell, and rushed off to her room.

Next day Karl insisted on beginning work at once, although the Manageress wanted him to take the day off and have a look round the town. He told her frankly that he would have plenty of opportunities for sight-seeing later, but that for the moment the most important thing for him was to make a start with his job, for he had already broken off one career in Europe to no purpose and was now beginning again as a lift-boy at an age when his contemporaries, if they were ambitious, had every expectation of being promoted to more responsible work. It was right and needful for him to begin as a lift-boy, but equally needful for him to advance with extra rapidity. In these circumstances he would take no pleasure at all in strolling idly through Rameses. He would not even consent to go for a short walk with Therese, when she suggested it. He could not rid his mind of the idea that if he did not work hard he might sink as low as Delamarche and Robinson.

The hotel tailor fitted him for a lift-boy's uniform, which was resplendent enough with gold buttons and gold braid, but made him shudder a little when he put it on, for under the arms particularly the short jacket was cold, stiff and incurably damp with the sweat of the many boys who had worn it before him. The jacket had to be altered for Karl, especially over the chest, since not one of the ten spare jackets would even meet upon him. Yet in spite of the stitching that needed to be done, and although the master-tailor seemed to be exacting in his standards—twice he pitched the uniform back into the work-shop after it was apparently finished—the fitting was completed in barely five minutes, and Karl left the tailor's room already clad in closely fitting trousers and a jacket which, in spite of the master tailor's categorical assurances to the contrary, was very tight indeed and tempted Karl to indulge in breathing exercises, for he wanted to see if it was still possible to breathe at all.

Then he reported to the Head Waiter, under whose direction he was to be, a slender, handsome man with a big nose, who might well have been in the forties. The Head Waiter had no time to exchange even a word with him and simply rang

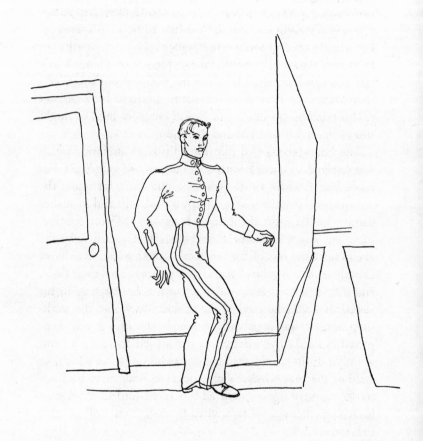

for a lift-boy, who chanced to be the very one that Karl had
seen yesterday. The Head Waiter called him only by his first
name, Giacomo, but it took Karl some time to identify the
name, for in the English pronunciation it was unrecognisable.
The boy was instructed to show Karl all the duties of a lift-boy,
but he was so shy and hasty that, little as there was actually to
be shown, Karl could scarcely make out that little from him.
No doubt Giacomo was annoyed too because he had been removed from the lift service, apparently on Karl's account, and
had been assigned to help the chamber-maids, which seemed
degrading in his eyes because of certain experiences, which,
however, he did not divulge. Karl's deepest disappointment
was the discovery that a lift-boy had nothing to do with the
machinery of the lift but to set it in motion by simply pressing
a button, while all repairs were done exclusively by the mechanics belonging to the hotel; for example, in spite of half
a year's service on the lift, Giacomo had never seen with his
own eyes either the dynamo in the cellar or the inner mechanism of the lift, although, as he said himself, that would have
delighted him. Indeed the work was monotonous, and the
twelve-hour shifts, alternately by day and night, were so exhausting that according to Giacomo one simply could not
bear it if one did not sleep on one's feet for a few minutes now
and then. Karl made no comment, but he was perfectly aware
that that very trick had cost Giacomo his post.

Karl was very pleased that the lift he had to attend to was
reserved for the upper floors, since he would not have to deal
with the wealthy guests, who were the most exacting. Still, he
would not learn so much as at the other lifts, and it was good
only for a beginning.

After the very first week he realised that he was quite equal
to the job. The brasswork in his lift was the most brightly

polished of all; none of the thirty other lifts had anything to compare with it, and it might have been still brighter if the other boy who partnered him had come anywhere near him in thoroughness and had not felt confirmed in his negligence by Karl's strict attention to duty. He was a native American of the name of Rennell, a conceited youth with dark eyes and smooth, somewhat hollow cheeks. He had an elegant suit of his own which he wore on his free evenings, when he hurried off to the town faintly smelling of perfume; now and then he would even ask Karl to take his duty of an evening, saying that he had been called away on family business and paying little heed to the contradiction between such pretexts and his festive appearance. All the same, Karl liked him quite well and was pleased to see Rennell stopping beside the lift in his fine suit before going out on one of these evenings, making his excuses again while he pulled on his gloves, and then stalking off along the corridor. Besides, Karl thought it only natural that he should oblige an older colleague in this way at the start; he had no intention of making it a permanent arrangement. For running the lift up and down was tiring enough in itself, and especially during the evening; there was almost no respite from it.

Soon Karl also learned how to make the quick, low bow which was expected of lift-boys, and to accept tips with lightning speed. They vanished into his waistcoat pocket, and no one could have told from his expression whether they were big or small. For ladies he opened the door with a little air of gallantry and swung himself into the lift slowly after them, since in their anxiety about their hats, dresses and fal-lals they took a longer time than men to get inside. While working the lift he stood close beside the door, since that seemed the most unobtrusive place, with his back to the passengers, holding the door-lever in his hand so that he was ready the instant they arrived to slide the door sideways without delaying or startling them. Only seldom did anyone tap him on the shoulder during a journey to ask some little piece of information; then he would turn round smartly as if he had been expecting the request and give the answer in a loud voice. Often, particularly after the theatres or the arrival of certain express trains, there was such a rush, in spite of the numerous lifts, that as soon as he had deposited one set of passengers on the top floor he had to fly back again for those who were waiting below. It was possible, by pulling on a wire cable which passed through the lift, to increase its ordinary speed, though this was forbidden by the regulations and was also supposed to be dangerous. So Karl never did it while he was carrying passengers, but as soon as he had unloaded them upstairs and was returning for more, he had no scruples at all and hauled on the cable with strong, rhythmical heaves like a sailor. Besides, he knew that the other lift-boys did it as well, and he did not want to lose his passengers to them. Individual guests who had been staying in the hotel for quite a long time—a common habit here—showed occasionally by a smile that they recognised Karl as their lift-boy. These marks of kindness Karl accepted gravely but with gratitude. Sometimes, if he were not so rushed as usual, he could take on little errands as well, fetching some trifle or other which a guest had forgotten in his room and did not want the trouble of going up for; then Karl would soar aloft all by himself in the lift, which seemed peculiarly his own at such times, enter the strange room, where curious things which he had never seen before were lying about or hanging on clothes pegs, smell the characteristic odour of some unfamiliar soap or perfume or toothpaste and hurry back, not lingering even a moment, with the required object, though he usually got the vaguest instructions for finding it. He often regretted that he could not go on longer errands, which were reserved for special attendants and message-boys equipped with bicycles, even with motor-bicycles. The utmost he could do was to undertake commissions to the dining-room or the gambling-rooms.

After a twelve-hour shift, coming off duty at six o'clock in the evening for three days and for the next three at six o'clock in the morning, he was so weary that he went straight to bed without heeding anyone. His bed was in the lift-boys' dormitory; the Manageress, who turned out to be not quite so influential as he had thought on the first evening, had indeed tried to get him a room for himself, and might even have succeeded in doing so, but when Karl saw what difficulties it caused and that she had to keep ringing up his immediate superior, the busy Head Waiter, on his account, he refused it and convinced her of the sincerity of his refusal by telling her that he did not want to make the other boys jealous through receiving a privilege which he had not really earned.

As a quiet place to sleep in, the dormitory certainly left much to be desired. For each boy had his own time-table for eating, sleeping, recreation and incidental services during his free twelve hours; so that the place was always in a turmoil. Some would be lying asleep with blankets pulled over their ears to deaden noises, and if one of them were roused he would yell with such fury about the din made by the rest that all the other sleepers, no matter how soundly they slept, were bound to waken up. Almost every boy had a pipe, which was indulged in as a sort of luxury, and Karl got himself one too and soon acquired a taste for it. Now smoking was of course forbidden on duty, and the consequence was that in the dormitory everyone smoked if he was not actually asleep. As a result, each bed stood in its own smoke cloud and the whole room was enveloped in a general haze. Although the majority agreed in principle that lights should be kept burning only at one end of the room during the night, it was impossible to enforce this. Had the suggestion been carried out, those who wanted to sleep could have done so in peace in the half of the room which lay in darkness—it was a huge room with forty beds—while the others in the lighted part could have played at dice or cards and done all the other things for which light was needed. A boy whose bed was in the lighted half of the room and who wanted to sleep could have lain down in one of the vacant beds in the dark half; for there were always enough beds vacant, and no boy objected to another's making a temporary use of his bed. But it was impossible to stick to this arrangement for even a single night. There would always be a couple of boys, for instance, who had taken advantage of the darkness to snatch some sleep and then felt inclined for a game of cards on a board stretched between their beds; naturally enough they switched on the nearest electric light, which wakened up those who were sleeping with their faces turned towards its glare. Of course, one could squirm away from the light for a while, but in the end the only thing to do was to start a game of cards with one's own wakeful neighbour and switch on another light. And that meant pipes going too, all round. Here and there, to be sure, some determined sleepers—among whom Karl was usually to be counted—burrowed their heads under the pillows instead of lying on top of them; but how was one to go on sleeping if the boy in the next bed got up in the very middle of the night for a few hours' roistering in the town before going on duty and washed his face with a clatter and much scattering of water at the wash-basin fixed at the head of one's own bed, if he not only put on his boots noisily but even stamped them on the floor to get his feet thoroughly into them—most of the boys' boots were too narrow, in spite of the shape of American footwear—and if he finally, not being able to find some trifle or other to complete his toilet, simply lifted one's pillow off one's face, the pillow beneath which one had of course long given up trying to sleep and was waiting merely to let fly at him? Now the boys were also great lovers of sport, and most of them young, strong lads who wanted to miss no chance of training their bodies. So if you were startled out of your sleep in the night by an uproar, you were sure to find a boxing-match in full career on the floor beside your bed, while expert spectators in shirts and drawers stood on all the beds round about, with every light turned on. It happened once that in such a midnight boxing-match one of the combatants fell over Karl as he was sleeping, and the first thing that he saw on opening his eyes was a stream of blood from the boy's nose which, before anything could be done about it, bespattered all the bed-clothes. Karl often spent nearly the whole of his twelve hours in trying to get a few hours' sleep. He was strongly enough tempted to take part in the general fun; but then it always came into his mind that the others had gained a better start in life and that he must catch up on them by harder work and a little renunciation. So, although he was eager to get sufficient sleep, chiefly on account of his work, he complained neither to the Manageress nor to Therese about the conditions in the dormitory; for all the other boys suffered in the same way without really grumbling about it, and besides, the tribulations of the dormitory were a necessary part of the job which he had gratefully accepted from the hands of the Manageress.

Once a week, on changing from day to night duty, he had a free period of twenty-four hours, part of which he devoted to seeing the Manageress once or twice and exchanging a few words with Therese, usually in some corner or other, or in a corridor, very rarely indeed in her room, whenever he caught her off duty for a moment or two. Sometimes too he escorted her on her errands to the town, which had all to be executed at top speed. They would rush to the nearest underground station almost at a run, Karl carrying the basket; the journey flashed past in a second, as if the train were being pulled through a vacuum, and they were already getting out and clattering up the stairs at the other end without waiting for the lift, which was too slow for them; then the great squares appeared, from which the streets rayed out star-fashion, bringing a tumult of steadily streaming traffic from every side; but Karl and Therese stuck close together and hurried to the different offices, laundries, warehouses and shops to do the errands which could not easily be attended to by telephone, mostly purchases of a minor nature or trifling complaints. Therese soon noticed that Karl's assistance was not to be despised; indeed, that in many cases it greatly expedited matters. In his company she had never to stand waiting, as at other times, for the overdriven shopkeepers to attend to her. He marched up to the counter and rapped on it with his knuckles until someone came; in his newly acquired and still somewhat pedantic English, easy to distinguish from a hundred other accents, he shouted across high walls of human beings; he went up to people without hesitation, even if they were haughtily withdrawn into the recesses of the longest shops. He did all this not out of arrogance, nor from any lack of respect for difficulties, but because he felt himself in a secure position which gave him certain rights; the Hotel Occidental was not to be despised as a customer, and after all, Therese sorely needed help in spite of her business experience.

"You should always come with me," she often said, laughing happily, when they returned from a particularly successful expedition.

During the month and a half that Karl stayed at Rameses, he was only thrice in Therese's room for long visits of a few hours at a time. It was naturally smaller than the Manageress's rooms; the few things in it were crowded round the window; but after his experiences in the dormitory Karl could appreciate the value of a private, relatively quiet room, and though he never expressly said so, Therese could see how much he liked being there. She had no secrets from him, and indeed it would not have been very easy to keep secrets from him after that visit of hers on the first night. She was an illegitimate child; her father was a foreman mason who had sent for her and her mother from Pomerania; but as if that had been his whole duty, or as if the work-worn woman and the sickly child whom he met at the landing stage had disappointed his expectations, he had gone off to Canada without much explanation shortly after their arrival, and they had received neither a letter nor any other word from him, which indeed was not wholly surprising, for they were lost beyond discovery among the tenements in the east end of New York.

On one occasion Therese told Karl—he was standing beside her at the window looking down at the street—of her mother's death. How her mother and she one winter evening—she must have been about five then—were hurrying through the streets, each carrying a bundle, to find some shelter for the night. How her mother had at first taken her hand—there was a snow-storm and it was not easy to make headway—until her own hand grew numb and she let Therese go without even looking to see what had become of her, so that the child had to make shift to hang on by herself to her mother's skirts. Often Therese stumbled and even fell, but her mother seemed to be beyond herself and went on without stopping. And what snowstorms you got in the long, straight streets of New York! Karl had no experience of what winter in New York was like. If you walked against the wind, which kept whirling round and round, you could not open your eyes even for a minute, the wind lashed the snow into your face all the time, you walked and walked but got no farther forward; it was enough to make you desperate. A child naturally was at an advantage compared with a grown-up; it could duck under the wind and get through and even find a little pleasure in the struggle. So that night Therese was hardly able to understand her mother's situation, and she was now firmly convinced that if she had only acted then more wisely towards her mother,—of course, she was such a very little girl—her mother might not have had to die such a wretched death. Her mother had had no work at all for two days; her last coin was gone; they had passed the day in the open without a bite, and the bundles they carried contained nothing but useless odds and ends which, perhaps out of superstition, they did not dare to throw away. There was a prospect of work the very next morning at a new building, but Therese's mother was afraid, as she had tried to explain the whole day, that she might not be able to take advantage of the chance, for she felt dead tired and that very morning had coughed up a great deal of blood in the street to the alarm of passers-by; her only wish was to get into some place where she could be warm and rest. And just that evening it was impossible to find even a corner. Sometimes a janitor would not let them inside the doorway of a building, where they might at least have sheltered a little from the cold; but if they did get past the janitor they scurried through oppressive, icy corridors, climbed countless stairs, circled narrow balconies overlooking courtyards, beating upon doors at random, at one moment not daring to speak to anyone and at another imploring everyone they met; and once or twice her mother sat down breathlessly on a step in some quiet stairway, drew Therese, who was almost reluctant, to her breast and kissed her with painful insistence on the lips. When Therese realised afterwards that these were her mother's last kisses, she could not understand how she could have been so blind as not to know it, small creature though she was. Some of the doors they passed by stood open to let out a stifling fug; in the smoky reek which filled these rooms, as if they were on fire, nothing could be discerned but some figure looming in the doorway who discouraged them, either by stolid silence or by a curt word, from expecting accommodation within. On looking back, Therese thought it was only in the first few hours that her mother was really seeking for a place of shelter, for after about midnight she spoke to no one at all, although she was on her feet, with brief interruptions, until dawn, and although these tenements never locked their doors all night and there was a constant traffic of people whom she could not help meeting. Of course, they were not actually running about from place to place, but they were moving as fast as their strength would permit, perhaps in reality at a kind of crawling shuffle. And Therese could not tell whether between midnight and five o'clock in the morning they had been in twenty buildings, or in two, or only in one. The corridors of these tenements were cunningly contrived to save space, but not to make it easy to find one's way about; likely enough they had trailed again and again through the same corridor. Therese had a dim recollection of emerging from the door of a house which they had been traversing endlessly, only to turn back, or so it seemed to her, when they had reached the street, and plunge again into it. For a child like her it was of course an incomprehensible torture to be dragged along, sometimes holding her mother's hand, sometimes clinging to her skirts, without a single word of comfort, and in her bewilderment the only explanation she could find was that her mother wanted to run away from her. So for safety's sake Therese clutched all the more firmly at her mother's skirts with one hand even when her mother was holding her by the other hand, and sobbed at intervals. She did not want to be left behind among these people who went stamping up the stairs before them or came behind them, invisibly, round the next turn of the stairway below, people who stood quarrelling in the corridors before a door and pushed each other into it by turns. Drunk men wandered about the place dolefully singing, and Therese's mother was lucky to slip with her through their hands, which almost barred the way. At such a late hour of night, when no one was paying much attention to anything and rights were no longer insisted on, she could certainly have cadged a place in one of the common doss-houses run by private owners, several of which they passed, but Therese was unaware of this and her mother was past all thought of resting. Morning found them, at the dawn of a fine winter day, both leaning against a house wall; perhaps they had slept for a little while there, perhaps only stared about them with open eyes. It appeared that Therese had lost her bundle, and her mother made to beat her as a punishment for her negligence; but Therese neither heard nor felt any blow. Then they went on again through the wakening streets, Therese's mother next to the wall; they crossed a bridge, where her mother's hand brushed rime from the railing, and at length—Therese accepted it as a matter of course at the time but now she could not understand it—they fetched up at the very building where her mother had been asked to report that morning. She did not tell Therese whether to wait or go away, and Therese took this as a command to wait, since that was what she preferred to do. So she sat down on a heap of bricks and looked on while her mother undid her bundle, took out a gay scrap of material, and bound it round the head-cloth which she had been wearing all night. Therese was too tired even to think of helping her mother. Without giving in her name at the foreman's office, as was customary, and without enquiring of anyone, her mother began to climb a ladder, as if she already knew the task that was allotted to her. Therese was surprised at this, since the hod-women usually worked on ground level, mixing the lime, carrying the bricks and performing other simple duties. So she thought that her mother was going to do some better-paid kind of work today, and sleepily smiled up to her. The building was not very high yet, it had hardly reached the first storey, though the tall scaffolding for the rest of the structure, still without its connecting boards, rose up into the blue sky. Reaching the top of the wall, her mother skilfully skirted round the brick-layers, who went on stolidly setting brick on brick and for some incomprehensible reason paid no attention to her; with gentle fingers she felt her way cautiously along a wooden partition which served as a railing, and Therese, dozing below, was amazed at such skill and fancied that her mother glanced at her kindly. But in her course her mother now came to a little heap of bricks, beyond which the railing and obviously also the wall came to an end; yet she did not stop for that but walked straight on to the heap of bricks, and there her skill seemed to desert her, for she knocked down the bricks and fell sheer over them to the ground. A shower of bricks came after her and then, a good few minutes later, a heavy plank detached itself from somewhere and crashed down upon her. Therese's last memory of her mother was seeing her lying there in her checked skirt, which had come all the way from Pomerania, her legs thrown wide, almost covered by the rough plank atop of her, while people came running up from every side and a man shouted down angrily from the top of the wall.

It was late when Therese finished her story. She had told it with a wealth of detail unusual for her, and notably at quite unimportant passages, such as when she described the scaffolding poles each rising to heaven by itself, she had been compelled to stop now and then with tears in her eyes. The most trifling circumstance of that morning was still stamped exactly on her memory after more than ten years, and because the sight of her mother on the half-finished house-wall was the last living memory of her mother, and she wanted to bring it still more vividly before her friend, she tried to return to it again after she had ended her story, but then she faltered, put her face in her hands and said not another word.

Still, they had merry hours too in Therese's room. On his first visit Karl had seen a text-book of commercial correspondence lying there and had asked leave to borrow it. They arranged at the same time that Karl should write out the exercises in the book and bring them to Therese, who had already studied them as far as her own work required, for correction. Now Karl lay for whole nights in his bed in the dormitory with cotton wool in his ears, shifting into every conceivable posture to relax himself, and read the book and scribbled the exercises in a little notebook with a fountain pen which the Manageress had given him in reward for drawing up methodically and writing out neatly a long inventory of hers. He managed to turn to his advantage most of the distracting interruptions of the other boys by perpetually asking them for advice on small points of the English language, so that they grew tired of it and left him in peace. Often he was amazed that the others were so reconciled to their present lot, that they did not feel its provisional character, nor even realise the need to come to a decision about their future occupations, and in spite of Karl's example read nothing at all except tattered and filthy copies of detective stories which were passed from bed to bed.

At their conferences Therese now corrected Karl's exercises, perhaps rather too painstakingly. Differences of opinion arose. Karl adduced his great New York professor in his support, but that gentleman counted for as little with Therese as the grammatical theories of the lift-boys. She would take the fountain pen from Karl's hand and score out the passages which she was convinced were erroneous. But in such dubious cases, although the matter could hardly be brought before a higher authority than Therese, Karl would score out, for the sake of accuracy, the strokes which Therese had made against him. Sometimes the Manageress would turn up and give the decision in Therese's favour, yet that was not definitive, as Therese was her secretary. At the same time, however, she would establish a general amnesty, for tea would be made, cakes sent for and Karl urged to tell stories about Europe, with many interruptions from the Manageress, who kept inquiring and exclaiming, so that he realised how many things had been radically changed in a relatively short time, and how much had probably changed since his own departure and would always go on changing.

Karl might have been about a month in Rameses when one evening Rennell said to him in passing that a man called Delamarche had stopped him in front of the hotel and questioned him about Karl. Having no cause to make a secret of it, Rennell had replied truthfully that Karl was a lift-boy but had prospects of getting a much better post because of the interest the Manageress took in him. Karl noted how carefully Delamarche had handled Rennell, for he had actually invited him to a meal that evening.

"I want nothing more to do with Delamarche," said Karl, "and you'd better be on your guard against him too!"

"Me?" said Rennell, stretching himself and hurrying off. He was the best-looking youngster in the hotel, and it was rumoured among the other boys, though no one knew who had started the story, that a fashionable lady who had been staying in the hotel for some time had kissed him, to say the least of it, in the lift. Those who knew this rumour found it very titillating to watch the self-possessed lady passing by with her calm, light step, her filmy veil and tightly-laced figure, for her external appearance gave not the slightest indication that such behaviour was possible on her part. She stayed on the first floor, which was not served by Rennell's lift, but one could not of course forbid guests to enter another lift if their own lifts were engaged at the moment. So now and then it happened that she used Karl's and Rennell's lift, yet only when Rennell was on duty. This might have been chance, but nobody believed it, and when the lift started off with the two of them, there was an almost uncontrollable excitement among the lift-boys which actually made it necessary once for the Head Waiter to intervene. Now, whether the lady or the rumour was the cause, the fact remained that Rennell was changing, he had become much more self-confident, he left the polishing of the lift entirely to Karl, who was only waiting for the chance of a radical explanation on this point, and no longer was to be seen in the dormitory. No other boy had so completely deserted the community of the lift-boys, for, at least in questions concerning their work, they generally held strictly together and had an organisation of their own which was recognised by the hotel management.

All this flashed through Karl's mind, together with reflections on Delamarche, but he went on with his work as usual. Towards midnight he had a little diversion, for Therese, who often surprised him with small gifts, brought him a big apple and a bar of chocolate. They talked together for a while, scarcely conscious of the interruptions caused by the lift journeys. They came to speak of Delamarche, and Karl realised that he must really have let himself be influenced by Therese in coming to the conclusion that he was a dangerous man, for after what Karl had told her that was Therese's opinion of him. Karl himself believed that he was only a shiftless creature who had let himself be demoralised by ill-luck and would be easy enough to get on with. But Therese contradicted him violently, and in a long harangue insisted that he should promise never to speak to Delamarche again. Instead of giving the promise, Karl kept urging her to go to bed, for midnight was long since past, and when she refused, he threatened to leave his post and take her to her room. When at last she was ready to go, he said: "Why bother yourself so needlessly, Therese? If it will make you sleep any better, I'm ready to promise that I won't speak to Delamarche unless I can't avoid it." Then came a crowd of passengers, for the boy in the neighbouring lift had been withdrawn for some other duty and Karl had to attend to both lifts. Some of the guests grumbled at the dislocation, and a gentleman who was escorting a lady actually tapped Karl lightly with his walking cane to make him hurry, an admonition which was quite unnecessary. It would not have been so bad if the guests, when they saw that one lift was unattended, had made directly for Karl's lift; but instead of that they drifted to the next lift and stood there holding the handle of the door or even walked right into the lift, an act which the lift-boys were expressly forbidden by the regulations to permit in any circumstances. So Karl had to rush up and down until he was quite exhausted, without earning the consciousness that he was efficiently fulfilling his duty. On top of this, towards three o'clock in the morning a luggage porter, an old man with whom he was on fairly friendly terms, asked some slight help from him which he could not give, for guests were standing before both his lifts and it required all his presence of mind to decide immediately which group to take first. He was consequently relieved when the other boy came back, and he called out a few words of reproach to him because he had stayed away so long, although it was probably no fault of his.

After four o'clock a lull set in which Karl badly needed. He leant wearily against the balustrade beside his lift, slowly eating the apple, which gave out a strong fragrance as soon as he bit into it, and gazed down into a lighted shaft surrounded by the great windows of the store-rooms, behind which hanging masses of bananas gleamed faintly in the darkness.

THEN someone tapped him on the shoulder. Karl, who naturally thought it was a guest, hastily stuck the apple in his pocket
and hurried to the lift almost without glancing at the man.

"Good evening, Mr. Rossmann," said the man, "it's me,
Robinson."

"But you look quite different," said Karl, shaking his head.

"Yes, I'm doing well," said Robinson, contemplating his
clothes, which consisted of garments that might have been fine
enough separately but were so ill-assorted that they looked posi-
tively shabby. What struck the eye most was a white waistcoat, obviously worn for the first time, with four little black-
bordered pockets, to which Robinson tried to draw attention
by expanding his chest.

"These things of yours are expensive," said Karl, and he
thought in passing of his good simple suit, in which he could
have held his own even with Rennell, but which his two bad
friends had sold.

"Yes," said Robinson, "I buy myself something nearly every
day. How do you like the waistcoat?"

"Quite well," said Karl.

"But these aren't real pockets, they're just made to look like
pockets," said Robinson, taking Karl's hand so that he might
prove it for himself. But Karl recoiled, for an unendurable reek
of brandy came from Robinson's mouth.

"You've started drinking again," said Karl, going back to the balustrade.

"No," said Robinson, "not very much," and he added, contradicting his first complacency: "What else can a man do in this world?" A lift journey interrupted their talk, and scarcely had Karl reached the bottom again when a telephone message came asking him to fetch the hotel doctor, for a lady on the seventh floor had fainted. During this errand Karl secretly hoped that Robinson would have disappeared before he returned, for he did not want to be seen with him and, thinking of Therese's warning, did not want to hear about Delamarche either. But Robinson was still waiting with the wooden gravity of a very drunk man just as a high official in frock-coat and top hat went past, fortunately, as it seemed, without paying any attention to the intruder.

"Wouldn't you like to come and see us, Rossmann. We're living in great style now," said Robinson, leering seductively at Karl.

"Does the invitation come from you or from Delamarche?" asked Karl.

"From me and Delamarche. Both of us together," said Robinson.

"Then let me tell you, and you can pass it on to Delamarche: that break between us, if it wasn't obvious enough to you at the time, was final. You two have done me more harm than anyone else has ever done. Can you have taken it into your heads not to leave me in peace even now?"

"But we're your friends," said Robinson disgustingly, maudlin tears rising to his eyes. "Delamarche asked me to tell you that he'll make it all up to you. We're living now with Brunelda, a lovely singer." And at the name he started to sing in a high quavering voice, but Karl silenced him in time, hissing at him: "Shut your mouth this minute; don't you know where you are?"

"Rossmann," said Robinson, intimidated as far as singing was concerned, "I'm a friend of yours, I am; say what you like. And now you've got such a fine job here, couldn't you lend me something?"

"You would only drink it," said Karl. "Why, I can see a brandy bottle in your pocket, and you must have been drinking out of it while I was away, for you were fairly sober at the start."

"That's only to strengthen me when I'm out on a journey," said Robinson apologetically.

"Well, I'm not going to bother about you any more," said Karl.

"But what about the money?" said Robinson, opening his eyes wide.

"I suppose Delamarche told you to bring money back. All right, I'll give you some money, but only on condition that you go away at once and never come here again. If you want to get in touch with me, you can write me a letter; Karl Rossmann, Lift Boy, Hotel Occidental, will always find me. But I tell you again, you must never come looking for me here. I'm in service here and I have no time for visitors. Well, will you have the money on these conditions?" asked Karl, putting his hand into his waistcoat pocket, for he had made up his mind to sacrifice the tips he had received that night. Robinson merely nodded in answer to the question, breathing heavily. Karl interpreted this wrongly and asked again: "Yes or no?"

Then Robinson beckoned him nearer and with writhings which told their own story whispered: "Rossmann, I feel awfully sick."

"What the devil!" cried Karl, and with both hands he

dragged him to the stair railings. And a stream poured from Robinson's mouth into the deep. In the pauses of his sickness he felt helplessly and blindly for Karl.

"You're a good lad," he would say then, or: "It's stopped now," which however was far short of being the case, or: "The swine, what sort of stuff is this they have poured into me!" In his agitation and loathing Karl could not bear to stay beside him any longer and began to walk up and down. Here, in this corner beside the lift, Robinson was not likely to be seen, but what if someone should notice him, one of these rich and fussy guests who were always waiting to complain to the first hotel official they saw, who would revenge himself for it on the whole staff in his fury; or what if he were seen by one of these hotel detectives, who were always being changed and consequently were known only to the hotel management, so that one suspected a detective in every man who peered at things, though he might be merely short-sighted? And some waiter down below only needed to go to the store-rooms to fetch something—for the restaurant buffet went on all night—to be shocked at the sight of the disgusting mess at the foot of the shaft and telephone to Karl asking in God's name what was wrong up there. Could Karl refuse to acknowledge Robinson in that case? And if he did refuse, was not Robinson stupid and desperate enough simply to cling to Karl instead of apologising? And would not Karl be dismissed at once, since it was unheard of for a lift-boy, the lowest and most easily replaced member of the stupendous hierarchy of the hotel staff, to allow a friend of his to defile the hotel and perhaps even drive away guests? Could a lift-boy be tolerated who had such friends, and who allowed them actually to visit him during working hours? Did it not look as if such a lift-boy must himself be a drunkard or even worse, for what assumption was more natural than that he stuffed his friends with food from the hotel stores until they could not help defiling, as Robinson had done, any part of this scrupulously clean hotel they happened to be in? And why should such a boy restrict himself to stealing food and drink, since he had literally innumerable opportunities for theft because of the notorious negligence of the guests, the wardrobes standing open everywhere, the valuables lying about on tables, the caskets flung wide open, the keys thrown down at random?

Just then Karl spied in the distance a number of guests coming upstairs from a beer-cellar, in which a variety performance had newly finished. He stationed himself beside his lift and did not dare even to look round at Robinson for fear of what he might see. It gave him little comfort that no sound, not even a groan, was to be heard from that direction. He attended to his guests and kept going up and down with them, but he could not quite conceal his distraction and on every downward journey was prepared to encounter some catastrophic surprise.

At last he had time to look after Robinson, who was cowering abjectly in his corner with his face pressed against his knees. He had pushed his hard round hat far back off his brow.

"You must really go now," said Karl softly but firmly. "Here is the money. If you're quick I can find time to show you the shortest way."

"I'll never be able to move," said Robinson, wiping his forehead with a minute handkerchief, "I'll just die here. You can't imagine how bad I feel. Delamarche takes me into all his expensive drinking dens; but I can't stand the silly stuff you get there; I tell him that every day."

"Well, you simply can't stay here," said Karl. "Remember

where you are. If you're discovered here you'll get into trouble and I'll lose my job. Do you want that?"

"I can't get up," said Robinson. "I'd rather jump down there," and he pointed between the stair railings down into the air-shaft. "As long as I sit here like this, I can bear it, but I can't get up; I tried it once while you were away."

"Then I'll fetch a taxi to take you to the hospital," said Karl, tugging a little at Robinson's legs, for he seemed in danger of subsiding into complete lethargy at any moment. But as soon as he heard the word hospital, which seemed to rouse horrible associations, he began to weep loudly and held out his hands to Karl, as if begging for mercy.

"Be quiet," said Karl, and he struck down Robinson's hands, ran across to the lift-boy whose work he had taken on that night, begged him to oblige him in return for a little while, hurried back to Robinson, who was still sobbing, jerked him violently to his feet and whispered to him; "Robinson, if you want me to help you, you must pull yourself together and try to hold yourself straight for a short distance. I'm going to take you to my bed, where you can stay till you feel better again. You'll be surprised how quickly you'll recover. But now you must really behave sensibly, for there are all sorts of people in the passages and my bed is in a big dormitory. If you attract even the slightest attention, I can do nothing more for you. And you must keep your eyes open; I can't cart you about if you look as if you were on the point of death."

"I'll do everything you tell me," said Robinson, "but you won't manage to hold me up by yourself. Can't you get Rennell too?"

"Rennell isn't here," said Karl.

"Oh, of course," said Robinson, "Rennell's with Delamarche. The two of them sent me to see you. I've got all mixed up." Karl took advantage of these and other incomprehensible monologues of Robinson to push him along, and without accident managed to get him as far as a corner, from which a more dimly-lit passage led to the lift-boys' dormitory. A lift-boy came running towards them and passed them at full speed just at that moment. Until now they had had only harmless encounters; between four and five was the quietest time; and Karl was well aware that if he could not get rid of Robinson now, there was no hope of doing so in the early morning, after the day's work had begun.

At the far end of the dormitory a big fight or an entertainment of some kind was going on; he could hear the rhythmical clapping of hands, the agitated stamping of feet, and shouts of encouragement. In the part of the dormitory near the door a very few sound sleepers were to be seen in the beds; the majority lay on their backs staring at the roof, while here and there a boy, clothed or unclothed as he chanced to be, sprang out of bed to see how things were going at the other end of the room. So Karl managed to guide Robinson, who had now become somewhat used to walking, as far as Rennell's bed without rousing much attention, for the bed was quite near the door and luckily unoccupied; in his own bed, as he could see from the distance, a strange boy whom he did not know was quietly sleeping. As soon as Robinson felt the bed under him he went to sleep at once, with one leg hanging outside.

Karl drew the blankets quite over Robinson's face and thought there was no need to worry for the time being, as the man was not likely to waken before six at the earliest, and by then he would be here himself and perhaps with Rennell's help would find some means of smuggling him out of the hotel. The dormitory was never inspected by the higher authorities of the hotel, except on extraordinary occasions; several years previously the lift-boys had succeeded in abolishing the routine inspections which had been customary before then; so from that side there was nothing to be feared either.

When Karl got back to his lift again, he saw that both his own lift and its neighbour were vanishing upwards. He waited in some trepidation for this to explain itself. His own lift came down first, and out of it stepped the boy who had run past him in the passage a little while before.

"Here, where have you been, Rossmann?" he asked. "Why did you go away? Why didn't you report your absence?"

"But I asked him to attend to my lift for a minute," said Karl, indicating the boy in the next lift, which had just arrived. "I did as much for him for two whole hours when the traffic was at its worst."

"That's all very well," said the boy in question, "but it won't do. Don't you know that you must report even the shortest absence from duty to the Head Waiter's office? That's what the telephone's there for. I'd have been glad to do your work, but you know yourself that it isn't so easy. There was a crowd of new arrivals off the 4:30 express standing at both the lifts. I couldn't take your lift first and leave my own guests waiting, could I, so I just went up first in my own lift!"

"Well?" asked Karl tensely, as both boys fell silent.

"Well," said the boy from the next lift, "that was the very moment the Head Waiter came along and saw the people waiting before your lift and no one attending to it; he flew off into a rage and asked me, for I was on the spot in no time, where you were; of course I had no idea, for you didn't even tell me where you were going; and so he telephoned straight off to the dormitory for another boy to come at once."

"I met you in the passage, didn't I?" asked the new boy. Karl nodded.

"Of course," the other boy assured him, "I told him at once that you had asked me to take your place, but would he listen to excuses? You don't seem to know him yet. And we were to tell you that you're to go to the office at once. So you'd better not wait any longer, but just leg it. Perhaps he'll let you off after all; you weren't away for more than two minutes really. You just stick to it that you asked me to take your place. Better not mention that you took mine though, that's my advice; nothing can happen to me, for I had leave of absence; but there isn't any good in mentioning that and mixing it up with this business, since it has nothing to do with it."

"It's the first time I have ever left my post," said Karl.

"It always happens like that, but nobody believes it," said the boy, running to his lift, for there were people coming.

Karl's deputy, a boy of about fourteen, who obviously felt sorry for Karl, said: "They've let boys off this kind of thing often enough already. Usually they shift you to a different job. As far as I know, they've only once made it the sack. You must think up a good excuse. But don't try to tell him that you suddenly felt sick; that'll only make him laugh. Much better say that a guest sent you on an urgent errand to another guest, but you can't remember who the first guest was and you weren't able to find the other one."

"Well," said Karl, "it won't be so very bad." After all he had heard, he could not believe that the affair would end well. Even if this act of negligence were condoned, Robinson was lying there in the dormitory as a living offence, and it was only too probable that the Head Waiter, vindictive as he was, would not be content with a superficial investigation and would light on Robinson at last. It was true that there was no express prohibition against taking strangers into the dormitory, but that prohibition did not exist simply because there was no point in mentioning what was unthinkable.

When Karl entered the office the Head Waiter was sitting over his morning coffee, taking an occasional sip and studying a list which had apparently been brought him by the Head Porter, who was also there. The latter was a tall bulky man, whose splendid and richly-ornamented uniform—even its shoulders and sleeves were heavy with gold chains and braid—made him look still more broad-shouldered than he actually was. His gleaming black moustache drawn out to two points in the Hungarian fashion never stirred even at the most abrupt movement of his head. Also, because of his stiff, heavy clothing, the man could move only with difficulty and always stood with his legs planted wide apart, so that his weight might be evenly distributed.

Karl entered boldly and quickly, as he was used to do in the hotel; for that slowness and circumstance which passes for politeness among private persons is looked upon as laziness in lift-boys. Besides, he must not appear to be conscious of guilt on his very entrance. The Head Waiter glanced up fleetingly when the door opened, but then immediately returned to his coffee and his reading without paying any further attention to Karl. But the porter seemed to be annoyed at Karl's presence; perhaps he had some secret information or request to impart; at any rate he glared angrily at Karl every few minutes with his head stiffly inclined, and whenever his eyes met Karl's, which was clearly what he wanted, he turned away at once to the Head Waiter again. Yet Karl thought he would be ill-advised to quit the office, now that he was here, without an express order to do so from the Head Waiter. But the Head

Waiter was still studying his list and meanwhile eating a piece of cake, from which he now and then shook the sugar, without interrupting his reading. Once a sheet of the list fell to the floor; the porter did not even make any attempt to pick it up, for he knew that he could not, nor was it at all necessary, since Karl pounced on the paper and reached it to the Head Waiter, who accepted it with a casual movement of his hand, as if it had flown of its own accord from the floor. The little service had availed nothing, for the porter went on darting his angry looks at Karl.

In spite of that, Karl now felt more composed. The very fact that his offence seemed to have so little importance for the Head Waiter might be taken as a good sign. After all, it was perfectly understandable. A lift-boy was of no importance and so could not take any liberties, but just because he was of no importance, any offence he committed could not be taken very seriously. After all, the Head Waiter himself had begun as a lift-boy—indeed his career was the boast of the present generation of lift-boys—it was he who had first organised the lift-boys, and certainly he too must have left his post occasionally without permission, though nobody could force him now to remember that, and though it must not be forgotten that his having been a lift-boy made him all the more severe and unrelenting in keeping the lift-boys in order. But Karl also drew hope from the steadily passing minutes. According to the office clock it was now more than a quarter-past five; Rennell might come back at any moment, perhaps he was back already, for he must have noticed that Robinson did not return, and in any case Delamarche and Rennell could not have been very far from the Hotel Occidental, it occurred to Karl, for otherwise Robinson, in his wretched condition, would never have reached it. Now, if Rennell found Robinson in his bed, which was bound to happen, then everything would be all right. For practical as Rennell was, especially where his own interests were concerned, he would soon get Robinson out of the hotel in some way or other, which would be all the easier as Robinson must have recovered somewhat by now, and Delamarche was probably waiting outside the hotel to take charge of him. But once Robinson was got rid of, Karl could encounter the Head Waiter with a much quieter mind and for this time perhaps escape with a reprimand, though a severe one. Then he would consult with Therese whether he should tell the Manageress the whole truth—for his part he could see nothing against it— and if that could be done, then the matter could be finally disposed of without much harm done.

Karl had just reassured himself somewhat by these reflections and was beginning unobtrusively to count over the tips he had taken that night, since he had a feeling that they were heavier than usual, when the Head Waiter laid the list on the table, saying: "Just wait a minute longer, will you, Feodor," sprang at one bound to his feet and yelled so loudly at Karl that the boy could only stare terror-stricken into the black cavern of his mouth.

"You were absent from duty without leave. Do you know what that means? It means dismissal. I'll listen to no excuses, you can keep your lying apologies to yourself; the fact that you were not there is quite enough for me. If I once pass that over and let you off, all my forty lift-boys will soon be taking to their heels during working hours, and I'll be left to carry my five thousand guests up the stairs on my own shoulders."

Karl said nothing. The porter came nearer and gave a downward tug to Karl's jacket, which was slightly creased, doubtless intending in this way to draw the Head Waiter's special attention to the slight disorder of the uniform.

"Perhaps you were suddenly taken sick?" asked the Head Waiter craftily.

Karl gave him a scrutinising look and answered: "No."

"So you weren't even sick?" shouted the Head Waiter all the more loudly. "Then you must have hit on some remarkable new lie. What excuse are you going to offer? Out with it."

"I didn't know that I had to telephone for permission to leave."

"That's really priceless," said the Head Waiter, and he seized Karl by the collar and almost slung him across the room till they were both facing the lift regulations, which were pinned to the wall. The porter came on their heels. "There! Read it!" said the Head Waiter, pointing at one of the paragraphs. Karl thought that he was to read it to himself. But the Head Waiter shouted: "Aloud!"

Instead of reading the paragraph aloud, Karl said to the Head Waiter, hoping that this would appease him: "I know the paragraphs, for I got a copy of the regulations and read them carefully. But it's just the regulation one never needs that one forgets about. I have been working for two months now and I've never left my post once."

"Well, you'll leave it now," said the Head Waiter, and he went over to the table, took up the list again, as if to go on reading it, but instead smacked it down on the table again as if it were of no account, and with a deep flush on his brow and cheeks began to stride up and down the room. "All this trouble over a silly fool of a boy! All this disturbance on night duty!" he exclaimed several times. "Do you know who was left stranded down below when this fellow here ran away from his lift?" he asked, turning to the porter. And he mentioned a name at which the porter, who certainly knew all the hotel clients and their standing, was so horror-stricken that he had to give a fleeting look at Karl to assure himself that the boy did exist who had deserted a lift and left the bearer of that name to wait a while unattended.

"That's awful!" said the porter, slowly shaking his head in stupefaction over Karl, who watched him gloomily and reflected that this man's shocked stupidity was another item for which he would have to pay. "Besides, I know you already," said the porter, stretching out his great, thick, rigid first finger. "You're the only boy who simply refuses to give me a greeting. Who do you think you are? Every boy that passes the porter's office has to give me a greeting. With the other porters you can do as you like, but I insist on manners. Sometimes I pretend not to notice, but you can take it from me that I know perfectly well who says good-day to me and who doesn't, you lout!" And he turned away from Karl and stalked grandly up to the Head Waiter, who, however, instead of commenting on this new accusation, sat down to finish his breakfast, glancing over the morning paper which an attendant had just brought him.

"Sir," said Karl, thinking that at least he had better put himself right with the Head Porter while the Head Waiter was ignoring him, since he realised that though the porter's reproaches could not do him any harm, his enmity could, "I most certainly do not pass you without a greeting. I haven't been long in America yet and I have just come from Europe, where people are in the habit of greeting each other excessively, as is well known. And of course I haven't been quite able to get over the habit yet; why, only two months ago in New York, where I happened to be taken into good society, I was always being told that I was too profuse in my salutations. And now you say that I don't greet you of all people! I have greeted you every day several times a day. But of course not every time I saw you, for I pass you hundreds of times daily."

"You have to greet me every time, every single time, without exception; you have to stand with your cap in your hand all the time you're speaking to me; and you must always say 'sir' when you are speaking to me, and not simply 'you.' And you must do all that every time, every single time."

"Every time?" repeated Karl softly, in a questioning tone, for he remembered now that during the whole of his stay in the hotel the Head Porter had seemed to regard him with a severe and reproachful expression, from the very first morning when, being still new to his work and somewhat too free and easy, he had gone up to the man without thinking and had enquired of him insistently and in detail whether two men had not asked for him or maybe left a photograph for him.

"Now you see what such behaviour brings you to," said the porter, again coming quite close to Karl and pointing at the Head Waiter, still deep in his papers, as if that gentleman were the instrument of his vengeance. "In your next job you'll remember to be polite to the porter, even if it's only in some stinking tavern."

Karl understood now that he had really lost his post, for the Head Waiter had already told him so and here was the Head Porter repeating it as an accomplished fact, and in the case of a lift-boy there was probably no need for the hotel management to confirm a dismissal. Yet it had happened with a rapidity he had not expected, for after all he had worked here for two months as well as he could, and certainly better than many of the other boys. But obviously such considerations were taken into account at the decisive moment in no part of the world, neither in Europe, nor in America; the verdict was determined by the first words that happened to fall from the judge's lips in an impulse of fury. Perhaps it would be best to take his leave at once and go away; the Manageress and Therese were probably still asleep and he could say goodbye to them by letter, so as to spare them at least the disappointment and sorrow which they would feel if he said goodbye to them in person; he could hastily pack his box and quietly steal away. If he were to stay even a day longer—and he could certainly have done with a little sleep—all he could expect was the magnifying of the incident into a scandal, reproaches from every side, the unendurable sight of Therese and perhaps the Manageress herself in tears, and possibly on top of all that some punishment as well. But it also confused him to be confronted by two enemies, to have every word that he said quibbled at, if not by the one then by the other, and misconstrued. So he remained silent and for the time being enjoyed the quietness of the room, for the Head Waiter was still reading the newspaper and the Head Porter stood at the table arranging the scattered pages of his list according to their numbers, a task which he found very difficult, being obviously short-sighted.

At last the Head Waiter laid the newspaper aside with a yawn, assured himself with a glance that Karl was still there, and turned the indicator of his table telephone. He shouted: "Hallo" several times, but nobody answered. "There's no answer," he said to the Head Porter. The Head Porter who, it seemed to Karl, was following the telephoning with great interest, said: "It's a quarter to six already. She must be awake by now. Ring harder." But at that moment, without further summons, the telephone rang in answer. "This is Isbary speaking," the Head Waiter began. "Good morning. I hope I haven't wakened you? I'm so sorry. Yes, yes, it's a quarter to six. But I'm really very sorry if I gave you a shock. You should take the telephone off the hook while you're asleep. No, no, there's really no excuse for me, especially as it's only a trivial matter I want to discuss with you. But of course I have plenty of time, of course; I'll wait and hold on if you want me to."

"She must have rushed to the telephone in her nightdress," the Head Waiter said smilingly to the Head Porter, who all the time had been bending over the instrument with an intent expression. "I must really have disturbed her, for she's usually wakened by the girl who does her typewriting, but this morning she must have missed doing it for some reason or other. I'm sorry if I startled her; she's nervous enough as it is."

"Why has she gone away from the telephone?"

"To see what has happened to the girl," replied the Head Waiter, lifting the receiver again, for it had started to ring. "She'll turn up all right," he went on, speaking into the telephone. "You mustn't be so easily alarmed by everything. You really do need a thorough rest. Well now, to come to my little affair. There's a lift boy here called"—he turned round with a questioning look at Karl who, listening with close attention, at once provided his name—"called Karl Rossmann. If I remember rightly, you have shown some interest in him; I am sorry to say that he has ill repaid your kindness, he left his work without permission and has brought me into serious difficulties; I can't even tell yet what the consequences may be; and so I have just dismissed him. I hope you won't take it too badly. What did you say? Dismissed, yes, dismissed. But I've just told you that he deserted his lift. No, there I really cannot agree with you, my dear lady. It's a matter of authority, there's too much at stake, a boy like this might corrupt the whole lot of them. With lift-boys particularly you must be devilish strict. No, no, in this case I can't oblige you, much as

I like to stand in your good graces. And even if I were to let him stay in spite of everything, simply to keep my temper in exercise, it wouldn't be fair for your sake, yes, for your sake, to have him here. You take an interest in him which he doesn't at all deserve, and I know him, and I know you too, and I'm certain that he'll bring you nothing but severe disappointment which you must be saved from at all costs. I say this quite openly in the boy's own hearing, for he's standing only a step away, as bold as brass. He is to be dismissed; no, no, he is to be dismissed once and for all; no, no, he's not to be given some other kind of work, I have no use for him at all. Besides, there are other people complaining about him. The Head Porter, for instance, yes, Feodor, of course, yes, Feodor has been complaining about his impoliteness and insolence. What, that shouldn't be enough? My dear lady, you go against your own character in supporting this boy. No, you really shouldn't press me like this."

At that moment the porter bent down and whispered something into the Head Waiter's ear. The Head Waiter first looked at him in astonishment and then spoke so rapidly into the telephone that for a moment Karl could not quite make him out and came a little nearer on tiptoe.

"My dear Manageress," he said, "to be quite frank, I wouldn't have believed that you were such a bad judge of character. I've just learned something about your angel boy which will radically alter your opinion of him, and I almost feel sorry that it is from me it has to come to your ears. This fine pet of yours, this pattern of all the virtues, rushes off to the town on every single free night he has and never comes back till morning. Yes, yes, I have evidence of it, unimpeachable evidence, yes. Now can you tell me, perhaps, where he gets hold of the money for these nocturnal adventures? Or how he can be expected to attend properly to his work? And do you want me to go the length of telling you what he does in the town? A boy like that is to be got rid of as quickly as possible. And please let this be a warning to you how careful you should be with boys who turn up from nowhere."

"But sir," cried Karl, actually relieved by the gross mistake which seemed to have occurred, for it might well bring about an unlooked-for improvement of the whole situation, "there must certainly be some mistake. I understand the Head Porter has told you that I am out every night. But that simply isn't true; I spend every night in the dormitory; all the other boys can confirm that. When I'm not sleeping I study commercial correspondence; but I have never left the dormitory a single night. That's quite easy to prove. The Head Porter has evidently mistaken me for someone else, and I see now, too, why he thinks I pass him without a greeting."

"Will you hold your tongue?" shouted the Head Porter, shaking his fist, where anyone else would have shaken his finger. "So I've mistaken you for someone else, have I? How could I go on being the Head Porter here if I mistook one person for another? I ask you, Mr. Isbary, how could I be the Head Porter here if I mistook people? In all my thirty years' service I've never mistaken anyone yet, as hundreds of waiters who have been here in my time could tell you, and is it likely that I would make a beginning with you, you wretched boy? With that smooth face of yours that nobody could mistake? What have mistakes got to do with it, anyway; you could sneak off to the town every night behind my back, and it only needs one look at your face to see that you're a good-for-nothing lout."

"Enough, Feodor," said the Head Waiter, whose conversation with the Manageress seemed suddenly to have broken off.

"It's quite a simple matter. We're not particularly concerned about how he spends his nights. No doubt he would like us to undertake a full-dress enquiry into his night-life before he leaves us. I can well imagine that that would delight his heart. Every one of our forty lift-boys would have to be trotted out, if he had his will, to give evidence; they would naturally have mistaken him for someone else too, and so bit by bit the whole staff would have to be dragged in as witnesses; the hotel, of course, would stop working altogether for a time; and though he would be flung out in the end he would at least have had his fun. So we'll leave that out of account. He has already made a fool of the Manageress, that kind-hearted woman, and we'll let it stop there. I won't listen to another word; you're dismissed on the spot for neglecting your duties. I'll give you a note to the cashier, and your wages will be paid up till today. And let me tell you that after the way you have behaved, it's sheer charity to give you wages, and I'm only doing it out of consideration for the Manageress."

Another ring of the telephone interrupted the Head Waiter before he could sign the note. After listening to the first few words he exclaimed: "There's nothing but trouble from these lift-boys today!" Then after a while he cried: "This is unheard-of!" And turning from the telephone, he said to the Head Porter: "Please, Feodor, hold that boy for a while; we'll have more to say to him yet." Then he shouted into the telephone: "Come up at once!"

Now the Head Porter could at least vent his rage, which he had not succeeded in doing verbally. He grabbed Karl firmly by the upper arm, yet not with a steady grip which could have been borne; every now and then he loosened his hold and then bit by bit tightened it so cruelly, for he was immensely strong and the pressure seemed as if it would never stop, that every-

thing went dark before Karl's eyes. Moreover, he not merely
held Karl, but as if he had been ordered to stretch him as well,
jerked him now and then almost off his feet and shook him,
saying all the time half interrogatively to the Head Waiter:
"Maybe I'm mistaking him for someone else now, maybe I'm
mistaking him for someone else now."

It was a great relief for Karl when the head lift-boy, a fat,
panting lad called Best, appeared and distracted the Head
Porter's attention for a while. Karl was so exhausted that when
to his astonishment Therese came slipping in behind the boy,
pale as death, her clothes in disorder, her hair loosely put up,
he could hardly summon a smile for her. In a moment she was
beside him and had whispered: "Does the Manageress know?"

"The Head Waiter has told her over the telephone," replied Karl.

"Then it's all right, then it's all right," she said quickly, her
eyes lighting up.

"No," said Karl. "You don't know what they have against
me. I must go away, the Manageress is already convinced of
that herself. Please don't stay here; go upstairs again; I'll come
to say goodbye to you later."

"But, Rossmann, what are you thinking of? You can stay
with us as long as you like. The Head Waiter does anything
the Manageress asks him; he's in love with her; I found that
out a little time ago. So don't worry."

"Please, Therese, do go away now. I can't defend myself
so well if you are here. And I must defend myself thoroughly,
for they're telling lies about me. And the better I can pin them
down and defend myself, the more chance I have of staying
here. So, Therese——" But then unluckily, in a sudden spasm
of pain, he added these words, though in a low tone: "If only
the Head Porter would let me go! I had no idea he was my

enemy. But he keeps on crushing and twisting me."—"Why did I say that?" he thought simultaneously. "No woman could listen to it unmoved," and actually, before he could prevent her with his free arm, Therese had turned to the Head Porter and said: "Please, sir, let Rossmann go at once. You're hurting him. The Manageress will be here herself in a minute, and then you'll see that this is all a mistake. Let him go; what pleasure can it give you to torture him!" And she actually tugged at the Head Porter's arm. "Orders, little girl, orders," said the Head Porter, affectionately pulling Therese to him with his free hand, while with the other he squeezed Karl with all his might, as if he not merely wished to hurt him, but had some particular and, so far, unfulfilled design upon the arm he was holding.

It took Therese some time to disengage herself from the Head Porter's embrace, and she was just about to make an appeal to the Head Waiter, who was still listening to the slow and circumstantial Best, when the Manageress hastily entered.

"Thank God!" cried Therese, and for a moment nothing could be heard in the room but that loud exclamation. The Head Waiter jumped up at once and pushed Best aside.

"So you have come yourself, my dear madam? Because of this trifling matter? After our talk on the telephone I half feared it, but I couldn't actually believe it. And since then your protégé's case has grown worse and worse. I'm afraid I won't merely have to dismiss him, but send him to prison as well. Hear for yourself." And he gave a sign to Best.

"I would like to have a few words with Rossmann first," said the Manageress, sitting down on a chair which the Head Waiter insisted on setting out for her.

"Please, Karl, come nearer," she said. Karl obeyed, or rather was dragged nearer by the Head Porter. "Let him go, can't

183

you?" said the Manageress in exasperation. "He isn't a murderer!" The Head Porter actually let him go, but before doing so crushed his arm in a final grip so violently that tears came to his own eyes with the effort.

"Karl," said the Manageress, folding her hands calmly in her lap and looking at Karl with her head bent—it was not in the least like an interrogation—"first of all I want to tell you that I still have complete confidence in you. Also the Head Waiter is a just man; I can vouch for that. Both of us at bottom would be glad to keep you here"—here she glanced briefly at the Head Waiter, as if begging him not to interrupt. Nor did he do so. "So forget everything that may have been said to you here till now. Above all, you mustn't take too seriously anything the Head Porter may have said. He's an irritable man, which is no wonder considering his work; but he has a wife and children too, and he knows that a boy who has to fend for himself needs no extra torments, since the rest of the world will see that he gets his fair share of them."

It was quite still in the room. The Head Porter looked at the Head Waiter as if expecting support, the Head Waiter looked at the Manageress and shook his head. Best, the lift boy, grinned idiotically behind the Head Waiter's back. Therese was quietly sobbing with grief and joy and doing her best to keep the others from remarking it.

Yet, although it could only be construed as a bad sign, Karl did not look at the Manageress, who certainly wished him to do so, but in front of him at the floor. The pain in his arm was still shooting in all directions, his shirt-sleeve was sticking to the bruises, and he should really have taken off his jacket to attend to them. What the Manageress said was of course very kindly meant, yet it seemed to him that simply because of the way in which she was acting, the others must think that her kindness was foolish, that he had been enjoying her friendship on false pretences for two months, and that he actually deserved nothing better than to fall into the Head Porter's hands. "I say this," went on the Manageress, "so that you can give me a straight answer which it's likely you would have done in any case, if I know you."

"Please, may I go for the doctor in the meantime; the man may be bleeding to death," the lift boy Best suddenly put in, very politely, but very disconcertingly.

"Go," the Head Waiter said to Best, who at once rushed off. And then to the Manageress: "The case is this. The Head Porter wasn't holding the boy as a joke. Down in the lift-boys' dormitory an utter stranger, completely drunk, was discovered carefully tucked up in one of the beds. The boys naturally wakened him and tried to get rid of him. But then the fellow began to make a great row, shouting that this was Karl Rossmann's bedroom and that he was Rossmann's guest, that Rossmann had brought him there, and would thrash anyone who dared to touch him. Besides, he simply had to wait until Karl Rossmann came back, for Rossmann had promised him money and had gone to fetch it. Please note that, my dear madam: had promised him money and gone to fetch it. You note that too, Rossmann," the Head Waiter said over his shoulder to Karl, who had just glanced round at Therese, who in turn was staring at the Head Waiter as if spell-bound and continually pushing a strand of hair from her forehead or else mechanically lifting her hand to her brow for the sake of something to do. "Perhaps you need reminding of your engagements. For the man below also said that on your return you were going to spend the night with some female singer, whose name nobody could make out, I grant you, since the fellow always burst into song whenever he came to it."

Here the Head Waiter paused, for the Manageress, grown visibly paler, rose from her chair, pushing it back a little.

"I'll spare you the rest," said the Head Waiter.

"No, please, no," said the Manageress, seizing his arm. "Please go on; I must know everything; that's why I'm here."

The Head Porter, who now stepped forward and struck himself loudly on the chest to advertise that he had seen through everything from the very beginning, was simultaneously appeased and put in his place by the Head Waiter with the words: "Yes, you were quite right, Feodor."

"There isn't much more to tell," went on the Head Waiter. "The boys, being what they are, laughed at the man first, then got into a fight with him, and as there are plenty of good boxers among them, he was simply knocked out; and I haven't dared to ask even where he is bleeding and in how many places, for these boys are punishing boxers and a drunk man is of course easy game to them."

"I see," said the Manageress, laying her hand on the arm of the chair and looking down at the seat which she had just left.

"Please do say something, Rossmann!" she said then. Therese had rushed across the room and was clinging to her mistress, a thing which Karl had never seen her do before. The Head Waiter was standing close behind the Manageress, slowly smoothing her modest little lace collar, which had slipped somewhat awry. The Head Porter standing beside Karl said: "Speak up!" but merely used the words to cover the punch which he gave him in the back.

"It's true," said Karl, more uncertainly than he intended, because of the blow, "that I put the man in the dormitory."

"That's all we need to know," said the porter, speaking for everyone present. The Manageress turned dumbly to the Head Waiter and then to Therese.

"I couldn't help myself," Karl went on. "The man is someone I used to know; he came here to pay me a visit after not seeing me for two months; but he was so drunk that he couldn't go away again by himself."

The Head Waiter, standing beside the Manageress, said softly as if to himself: "So he came to pay you a visit and later got so drunk that he couldn't leave." The Manageress whispered something over her shoulder to the Head Waiter, who seemed to raise objections but smiled at her in a way that obviously had nothing to do with Karl. Therese—Karl kept his eyes fixed on her—pressed her face in complete despair against the Manageress and refused to look at anything. The only one who was completely satisfied with Karl's explanation was the Head Porter, who repeated several times: "That's quite right, you must stand by a pal when he's drunk," and tried to emphasise this explanation by looking at the others and waving his hands.

"I'm to blame, therefore," said Karl, and paused as if waiting for a kind word from his judges to give him courage for continuing his defence, but none came. "I am to blame, therefore, only for taking the man to the dormitory—he's called Robinson and he's an Irishman. Everything else he said because he was drunk, and it isn't true."

"So you didn't promise him money?" asked the Head Waiter.

"Yes," said Karl, and he felt sorry at having forgotten that; in his haste and confusion he had been too peremptory in declaring himself innocent. "I did promise him money because he begged me for it. But I had no intention of fetching it, but merely of giving him the tips I got tonight." And in proof he pulled the money out of his pocket and held out his hand with the few small coins.

"You're tying yourself up more and more," said the Head Waiter. "If we're to believe you, we've got to keep forgetting what you said before. First you only took the man to the dormitory—and I don't even believe that his name is Robinson, for no Irishman was ever called that since Ireland was Ireland—first you only took him to the dormitory—and for that alone you could be flung out on your neck, I may tell you—but you didn't promise him money, yet when the question is sprung on you, it seems you did promise him money. This isn't a game of question and answer, let me remind you; you're supposed to be giving an explanation of yourself. And at first you had no intention of fetching the money, you merely meant to give him the tips you got tonight, and now it turns out that you still have this money on you, and so you must have intended to get some more money, a supposition which is strengthened by your long absence. After all, it wouldn't be strange if you wanted to get some money from your box for him; but it certainly is strange that you deny it so violently, and that you keep on hiding the fact that you made the man drunk here in the hotel, of which there can be no possible doubt, for you yourself admit that he came here by himself but could not leave by himself, and he has told everybody in the dormitory that he is your guest. So now only two things remain in doubt, which you can tell us yourself if you wish to save trouble, but which can be perfectly well established without your help: first, how you managed to get into the storerooms, and second, how you got your hands on enough money to give away?"

"It's impossible to defend oneself where there is no good will," Karl told himself, and he made no further answer to the Head Waiter, deeply as that seemed to afflict Therese. He knew that all he could say would appear quite different to the others, and that whether a good or a bad construction was to

188

be put on his actions depended alone on the spirit in which he was judged.

"He makes no answer," said the Manageress.

"It is the best thing he can do," said the Head Waiter.

"He'll soon think out something else," said the Head Porter, caressing his whiskers with a hand now gentle, though lately so terrible.

"Be quiet," said the Manageress to Therese, who had begun to sob, standing beside her, "you see that he has no answer to make, so how can I do anything for him? After all, it is I who am put in the wrong in the Head Waiter's eyes. Tell me, Therese, in your opinion have I omitted anything I could have done for him?" How could Therese know that, and what point was there in giving away so much before these two men by this public question and appeal to the girl?

"Madam," said Karl, once more pulling himself together, for no other purpose than simply to spare Therese the effort of answering, "I think that I haven't brought any discredit on you, and if a proper investigation were made, everyone else would have to agree with me."

"Everyone else," said the Head Porter, pointing his finger at the Head Waiter, "that's meant for you, Mr. Isbary."

"Now, madam," said Mr. Isbary, "it's half-past six, and it's high time this was settled. I think you had better leave me the last word in this matter, which we have handled far too patiently."

Little Giacomo came in and made to go up to Karl, but, daunted by the general silence, checked himself and waited.

Since the last words he had said, the Manageress had never taken her eyes off Karl, nor was there any indication that she had heard the Head Waiter's remark. Her eyes looked straight at Karl; they were large and blue, but a little dimmed by age and many troubles. As she stood there gently tilting the chair before her, she looked as if she would say next minute: "Well, Karl, when I think it over, this business isn't at all clear yet and needs, as you rightly say, a thorough investigation. And we'll proceed to make that now, whether anyone agrees or not, for justice must be done."

But instead of this, the Manageress said after a short pause which no one dared to interrupt—except that the clock struck half-past six in confirmation of the Head Waiter's words and with it, as everyone knew, all the other clocks in the whole hotel; it rang forbodingly in the ear, like the double beat of a universal great impatience: "No, Karl, no, no! We won't listen to any more of this. When things are right they look right, and I must confess that your actions don't. I am entitled to say so and I am bound to say so; I am bound to admit it, for it was I who came here with every prepossession in your favour. You see that Therese is silent too." (But she was not silent, she was crying.)

The Manageress stopped as if suddenly coming to a decision and said: "Karl, come over here," and when he went over to her,—the Head Waiter and the Head Porter immediately began an animated conversation behind his back—she put her left arm round him and led him, followed by the passive Therese, to the other end of the room, where she began to walk up and down with the two of them, and said: "It's possible, Karl, and you seem to put faith in it, otherwise I really wouldn't know what to make of you, that an investigation might justify you on separate small points. Why shouldn't it? Maybe you did give a greeting to the Head Porter. I feel certain you did, and I have my own opinion of the Head Porter; you see I am still quite frank with you. But such small justifications won't help you in the least. The Head Waiter, whose knowledge of people I have learned to prize in the course of many years, and who is the most trustworthy man I know, has clearly pronounced your guilt, and I must say it seems undeniable to me. Perhaps you merely acted without thinking, but perhaps too you aren't the boy I thought you were. And yet," with that she interrupted herself and cast a fleeting glance over her shoulder at the two men, "I can't help still thinking of you as a fundamentally decent lad."

"Madam! Madam!" said the Head Waiter, warningly, for he had caught her glance.

"We'll be finished in a minute," said the Manageress, beginning to admonish Karl more hurriedly: "Listen, Karl, from what I can make out of this business, I am actually glad that the Head Waiter doesn't want to start an enquiry; for if he were to do it, I should have to prevent it in your own interest. No one must know how or where you got drink for that man, who couldn't have been one of your former friends, as you give out, for you quarrelled violently with them when you left them, so that you wouldn't be so friendly with either of them now. Therefore it must have been an acquaintance you just picked up one night in some drinking den in the town. How could you hide all these things from me, Karl? If you really couldn't bear the dormitory and began to rake about at night for an innocent reason like that, why did you never say a word about it? You know that I wanted to get you a room of your own and only gave up the idea at your own request. It looks now as if you preferred the general dormitory because you felt that you had more liberty there. And you always put by your money in my safe and brought me the tips you got every week; where in heaven's name, boy, did you get the money for these excursions and where did you intend to find the money for your friend? Of course, these are things that I can't mention to the Head Waiter, for the moment at least, or else perhaps an enquiry might be unavoidable. So you must simply leave the hotel, and as soon as possible too. Go straight to the Pension Brenner—you've been there several times with Therese already—they'll take you in for nothing if you show them this—" and she wrote a few lines on a card with a gold pencil which she pulled out of her blouse, but without interrupting what she was saying—"I'll send your box after you at once. Therese, run up to the lift-boys' cloakroom and pack his box!" (But Therese did not stir, for as she had endured all the grief, she wanted also to share to the full this turn for the better which Karl's fortunes had taken, thanks to the kindness of the Manageress.)

Someone opened the door a little without showing himself and shut it again at once. It must have been a reminder to Giacomo, for he stepped forward and said: "Rossmann, I must speak to you."

"In a minute," said the Manageress, sticking the card in Karl's pocket as he stood listening with drooping head, "I'll keep your money for the time being; you know that it's safe in my hands. Stay in your room today and consider your position; tomorrow—I have no time today, and I've been kept far too long here too—I'll come to the Brenner and we'll see what more can be done for you. I won't forsake you, you must know that quite well already. You needn't worry about your future, but rather about these last few weeks." She patted him on the shoulder and then went over to the Head Waiter. Karl raised his head and gazed after the tall stately woman, as she walked away from him with her light step and easy bearing.

"Well, aren't you glad," said Therese, who had stayed beside him, "that everything has turned out so well?"

"Oh yes," said Karl, and he smiled at her, yet could not see

192

why he should be glad because he had been dismissed as a thief. Therese's eyes shone with the purest joy, as if it were a matter of complete indifference to her whether Karl had committed a crime or not, whether he had been justly sentenced or not, if he were only permitted to escape, in shame or in honour. And it was Therese who behaved like this, Therese who was so scrupulous in everything relating to herself that she would turn over in her mind and examine for weeks any half-doubtful word of the Manageress. With deliberate design he said: "Will you pack my box for me and send it off at once?" In spite of himself he had to shake his head in astonishment, so quickly did Therese catch the implications of the question, and in her conviction that there were things in the box which no one must see, she did not take time even to glance at Karl, even to shake his hand, but merely whispered: "Certainly, Karl, at once, I'll pack the box this minute." And she was gone.

But now Giacomo could not restrain himself any longer and, agitated by his long wait, cried: "Rossmann, the man is kicking up a row in the passage and won't go away. They want to take him to hospital, but he's objecting and saying that you'll never let him be taken to a hospital. He says we must call a taxi and drive him home and that you'll pay the fare. Will you?"

"The man seems to rely on you," said the Head Waiter. Karl shrugged his shoulders and counted his money into Giacomo's hand. "That's all I have," he said.

"I was to ask too if you're going in the taxi with him," added Giacomo, jingling the money.

"No, he isn't going," said the Manageress.

"Well, Rossmann," said the Head Waiter quickly, without even waiting until Giacomo was out of the room, "you are dismissed here and now." The Head Porter nodded several times, as if these were his own words and the Head Waiter merely his mouthpiece. "The reasons for your dismissal I simply can't mention publicly, for in that case I would have to send you to jail." The Head Porter looked very severely at the Manageress, for he knew perfectly well that she was the cause of such excessively mild treatment. "Now go to Best, change your clothes, hand over your uniform to Best and leave the hotel at once, but at once."

The Manageress closed her eyes, wishing by this to reassure Karl. As he bowed himself out, he saw the Head Waiter surreptitiously seizing her hand and fondling it. With heavy steps the Head Porter escorted Karl to the door, which he would not let him shut, but held open with his own hands so as to shout after him: "In a quarter of a minute you will pass my office and leave by the main door. See to that!"

Karl made what haste he could, so as to avoid any molestation on leaving, but everything went much more slowly than he wanted. First of all, Best could not be found immediately, and at this time during the breakfast hour a great many people were about; then it appeared that another boy had borrowed Karl's old trousers, and Karl had to search the clothes pegs beside almost all the beds before he found them; so that five minutes at least had elapsed before he reached the main door. Just in front of him a lady was walking accompanied by four gentlemen. They all went over to a big car which was waiting for them; a lackey was holding open the door while he stretched out his free arm sideways at shoulder level, very stiffly, which looked highly impressive. But Karl's hope of getting away unobserved behind this fashionable group was a vain one. For the Head Porter caught him by the hand and dragged him back between two of the gentlemen, with a word of excuse to them.

"Do you call this a quarter of a minute?" he asked, looking askance at Karl, as if he were examining a clock that did not keep time. "Come in here," he went on, propelling him into the huge porter's office, which Karl had once been eager enough to inspect but now that he was thrust into it viewed with suspicion. Just inside the door he squirmed round and tried to push the Head Porter away and escape.

"No, no, this way in," said the Head Porter, turning him round again.

"But I've been thrown out," said Karl, meaning that nobody in the hotel had a right to give him orders now.

"As long as I keep hold of you, you're not thrown out," said the porter, which was also true enough.

Besides, Karl could see no actual reason for resisting the porter. After all, what more could happen to him now? Also, the walls of the office consisted entirely of enormous panes of glass, through which you could see the incoming and outgoing streams of guests in the vestibule as clearly as if you were among them. Yes, there seemed to be no nook or corner in the whole office where you could be hidden from their eyes. No matter in how great a hurry the people outside seemed to be, as with outstretched arms, bent heads and peering eyes, holding their luggage high, they sought their way, hardly one of them omitted to cast a glance into the porter's office, for behind the panes announcements and news were always hanging which were intended both for the guests and the hotel staff. Moreover, the porter's office and the vestibule were in direct communication with each other, for at two great sliding windows sat two under-porters perpetually occupied in giving information on the most diverse subjects. These men were indeed over-burdened, and Karl had a shrewd guess that the Head Porter, from what he knew of him, had circumvented this stage in the course of his advancement. These two providers of information—from outside you could not really imagine what it looked like—had always at least ten enquiring faces before them in the window opening. Among these ten, who were continually changing, there was often a perfect babel of tongues, as if each were an emissary from a different country. There were always several making enquiries at the same time, while others again carried on a conversation with each other. The majority wanted to deposit something in the porter's office or take something away, so that wildly gesticulating hands could also be seen rising from the crowd. Or a man was impatient to look at a newspaper, which suddenly unfolded in the air and for a moment blotted out all the faces. All this the two under-porters had to deal with. Mere talking would not have sufficed for their work; they gabbled, and one in particular, a gloomy man with a dark beard almost hiding his whole face, poured out information without even taking breath. He neither looked at the counter, where he was perpetually handing things out, nor at the face of this or that questioner, but straight in front of him, obviously to economise and conserve his strength. His beard too must have somewhat interfered with the clearness of his enunciation, and in the short time that he was standing there Karl could make out very little of what was said, though possibly, in spite of the English intonation, it was in some foreign language which was required at the moment. Additionally confusing was the fact that one answer came so quickly on the heels of another as to be indistinguishable from it, so that often an enquirer went on listening intently, in the belief that his question was still being answered, without noticing for some time that his turn was past. You had also to get used to the under-porter's habit of never asking a question to be repeated; even if it was vague only in wording and quite sensible on the whole, he merely gave an almost imperceptible shake of the head to indicate that he did not intend to answer that question and it was the questioner's business to recognise his own error and formulate the question more correctly. This in particular kept many people for a long time in front of the counter. To help the under-porters, each of them was allotted a messenger boy, who had to rush to and fro bringing from a bookcase and various cupboards whatever the under-porter might need. These were the best paid if also the hardest posts that young boys could get in the hotel; in a sense these boys were still harder put to it than the under-porters, who had merely to think and speak, while the boys had to think and run about at the same time. If they ever brought the wrong thing, the under-porter was too pressed, of course, to give them a long lecture; with one flip of the hand he simply knocked to the floor whatever they had laid on the counter. Very interesting was the changing of the under-porters, which took place shortly after Karl came in. These changes had of course to happen frequently, at least during the day, for probably no man alive could have held out for more than an hour at the counter. At the relief hour a bell rang, and simultaneously there emerged from a side door the two under-porters whose turn had now come, each followed by his messenger boy. For the time being they posted themselves idly by the window and contemplated for a while the people outside, so as to discover exactly what questions were being dealt with. When the moment seemed suitable for intervention, the new-comer would tap on the shoulder the under-porter he was to relieve, who, although until now he had paid no attention to what was going on behind his back, at once responded and left his place. It all happened so quickly that it often surprised the people standing outside, and they almost jumped in alarm when a strange face popped up before them. The two men who were relieved stretched themselves and then poured water over their hot heads at two wash-basins standing ready for them. But the messenger-boys could not stretch themselves so soon, being kept busy for a little longer picking up and returning to their places the various objects which had been flung on the floor during their shift.

All this Karl had taken in with the closest attention in a few minutes, and then with a slight headache he quietly followed the Head Porter, who led him farther on. The Head Porter had obviously noticed the deep impression which this method of answering enquiries had made on Karl, for he gave his arm a sudden jerk and said: "You see that's the way we work here." Karl had certainly not been idle in the hotel, but he had had no conception of such work as this and he looked up, forgetting almost completely that the Head Porter was his mortal enemy, and nodded with silent appreciation. But this again seemed to the Head Porter an over-valuation of the under-porters and perhaps a piece of presumption towards himself, for he exclaimed, without caring that everyone heard him, and quite as if he had just been making a fool of Karl: "Of course this work here is the stupidest in the whole hotel; you need only listen for an hour to know pretty well all the questions that will be asked, and the rest you don't have to answer at all. If you weren't so impudent and ill-mannered, if you hadn't lied, lazed, boozed and thieved, perhaps I might have managed to put you at one of these windows, since it's only a job for dunderheads." Karl ignored the insult to himself, so indignant was he that the hard and honourable work of the under-porters should be jeered at instead of being recognised, and jeered at moveover by a man who, if he ever ventured to sit down at one of these windows, would certainly cover himself with ridicule in a few minutes and have to abandon the job.

"Let me go," said Karl, his curiosity concerning the porter's office more than satiated, "I don't want to have anything more to do with you."

"That's no reason for letting you go," said the Head Porter, crushing Karl's arm until it was numb and literally dragging him to the other end of the office. Couldn't the people outside see this bullying? Or, if they saw it, what did they think it meant, since none of them objected to it or even tapped on the glass to show the Head Porter that he was being watched and could not deal with Karl just as he liked?

But Karl soon gave up all hope of getting help from the vestibule, for the Head Porter seized a cord, and over the glass panes of one-half of the office black curtains reaching from the roof to the floor were drawn in a twinkling. In this part of the office, too, there were people, but all working at top speed and without an ear or an eye for anything unconnected with their work. Also they were completely dependent on the Head Porter, and instead of helping Karl would rather have helped to conceal anything that the Head Porter took it into his head to do. For instance, there were six under-porters attending to six telephones. Their method of working was obvious at a glance; out of each couple one did nothing but note down conversations, passing on these notes to his neighbour, who despatched the messages by another telephone. The instruments were of the new-fashioned kind which do not need a telephone box, for the ringing of the bell was no louder than a twitter, and a mere whisper into the mouthpiece was electrically amplified until it reached its destination in a voice of thunder. For this reason the three men who were speaking into the telephones were scarcely audible, and one might have thought they were muttering to themselves about something happening in the mouthpiece, while the other three, as if deafened by the thunder coming from their ear-pieces, although no one else could hear a sound, drooped their heads over the sheets of paper on which they had to make their notes. Here too a boy assistant stood beside each of the three whisperers; these three boys did nothing but alternately lean their heads towards their masters in a listening posture and then hastily, as if stung, search for telephone numbers in huge, yellow books: the rustling of so many massed pages easily drowned any noise from the telephones.

Karl simply could not keep himself from watching all this, although the Head Porter, who had sat down, clutched him in a sort of hug.

"It is my duty," said the Head Porter, shaking Karl as if he only wanted to make him turn his face towards him, "it is my duty, if the Head Waiter has left anything undone, for whatever reason, to repair his omission in the name of the hotel management, as best I can. We always do our best here to help one another out. If it weren't for that, such a great organisation would be unthinkable. You may say that I'm not your immediate superior; well, it's all the more to my credit if I attend to things that other people neglect. Besides, as Head Porter I am in a sense placed over everyone, for I'm in charge of all the doors of the hotel, this main door, the three middle and the ten side doors, not to mention innumerable little doors and doorless exits. Naturally all the service staff who come in contact with me have to obey me absolutely. In return for this great honour, of course, I have myself an obligation to the hotel management to let no one out of the hotel who is in the slightest degree suspicious. And you are just the person who strikes my fancy as being a highly suspicious character." He was so pleased with himself that he lifted his hands and brought them down again with a heavy smack that hurt. "It is possible," he added, enjoying himself royally, "that you could have slipped out of the hotel by some other door; of course I shouldn't trouble to give out special instructions on your account. But since you're here, I'm going to make the most of you. Besides, I never really doubted that you would keep our rendezvous by the front door, for it is a general rule that impudent and disobedient creatures take to being virtuous just when they're likely to suffer from the consequences. You'll certainly be able to notice that often enough from your own experience."

"Don't imagine," said Karl, inhaling the curiously depressing odour given out by the Head Porter, which he had not noticed until he had stood so close to him for so long, "don't imagine," he said, "that I am completely in your power, for I can scream."

"And I can stop your mouth," said the Head Porter as calmly and quickly as he probably would have done it in case of need. "And do you really think, if you brought anyone in, that you could find a single person who would take your word against mine, the word of the Head Porter? So you can see how foolish your hopes are. Let me tell you, when you were still in uniform you actually looked a fairly respectable character, but in that suit of yours, which could only have been made in Europe!—" And he tugged at the most diverse parts of the suit, which now, although it had been almost new five months ago, was certainly shabby, creased, and above all spotty, chiefly because of the heedlessness of the lift-boys, who were supposed to keep the dormitory floor polished and free from dust according to the general regulation, but in their laziness, instead of giving it a real cleaning, sprinkled the floor every day with some oil or other and at the same time spattered all the clothes on the clothes-stands. One could stow one's clothes where one liked, there was always someone who could not lay his hands on his own clothes, but never failed to find his neighbour's hidden garments and promptly borrow them. And almost invariably it was the boy who had to clean the dormitory that day, so that one's clothes were not only spattered with oil but dripping with it from head to foot. Rennell was the only boy who had found a secret place to hide his expensive clothes in; they were hardly ever discovered, since it was not malice or stinginess that prompted the boys to borrow clothes, but sheer haste and carelessness; they simply picked up garments wherever they found them. Yet even Rennell's suit had a round, reddish splash of oil in the midde of the back, and in the town an expert might have detected, from the evidence of that splash, that the stylish young dandy was a lift-boy after all.

Remembering these things, Karl told himself that he had suffered enough as a lift-boy and yet it had all been in vain, for his job had not proved, as he had hoped, a step to something higher, but had rather pushed him farther down, and even brought him very near prison. On top of this, he was still in the clutches of the Head Porter, who was no doubt considering ways and means of putting him to greater shame. And quite forgetting that the Head Porter was the last man to listen to reason, Karl exclaimed, striking his brow several times with the hand that happened to be free: "Even if I actually did pass you without a greeting, how can a grown man be so vindictive about such an omission!"

"I am not vindictive," said the Head Porter, "I only want to search your pockets. I am convinced, to be sure, that I'll find nothing, for you've probably been careful and slipped every-

202

thing to your friend bit by bit, a little every day. But searched you must be." And he thrust his hand into one of Karl's coat pockets with such violence that the side-stitches burst. "So there's nothing here," he said, turning over in his hand the contents of the pocket, a calendar issued by the hotel, a sheet of paper containing an exercise in commercial correspondence, a few coat and trouser buttons, the Manageress's card, a nail-file which a guest had once tossed to him as he was packing his trunk, an old pocket mirror which Rennell had once given him as a reward for taking over his work ten times or so, and a few more trifles. "So there's nothing here," said the Head Porter again, flinging everything under the bench, as if that were the proper place for any of Karl's possessions which happened not to be stolen property.

"But this is the last straw," said Karl to himself—his face must have been flaming red—and as the Head Porter, rendered incautious by greed, was rummaging in his second pocket, Karl slipped out of the sleeves with a jerk, cannoned into an under-porter with his first blind spring, knocking the man violently against his telephone, ran through the stuffy room to the door, actually not so fast as he had intended, but fast enough to get outside before the Head Porter in his heavy coat was able even to rise up. The organisation of the hotel could not be so perfect after all; some bells were ringing, it was true, but heaven only knew to what purpose! Members of the hotel staff were careering about the entrance this way and that, in such numbers that one might almost have thought they wanted unobtrusively to make it impossible for anyone to get out, since it was hard to find much sense in all the coming and going; however, Karl was soon in the open air, but had still to keep along the front of the hotel, for an unbroken line of cars was slowly moving past the entrance and he could not reach the road.

These cars, in their eagerness to get to their owners as quickly as possible, were actually touching each other, nosing each other forward. A pedestrian here and there, in a particular hurry to cross the road, would climb through the nearest car as if it were a public passage, not caring at all whether there was only a chauffeur in it and a couple of servants, or the most fashionable company. But that kind of behaviour seemed rather high-handed to Karl, and he reflected that one must be very sure of oneself to venture on it; he might easily hit upon a car whose occupants resented it, threw him out and raised a row, and as a runaway suspect lift-boy in his shirt-sleeves there was nothing that he could fear more. After all, the line of cars could not go on for ever, and so long as he stuck close to the hotel there was the less reason to suspect him. Actually he reached a point at last where the line of cars was not exactly broken, but curved away towards the street and loosened out a little. He was just on the point of slipping through into the traffic of the street, where far more suspicious-looking people than himself were probably at large, when he heard his name being called near by. He turned round and saw in a small, low doorway, which looked like the entrance to a vault, a couple of lift-boys whom he knew well, straining and tugging at a stretcher on which, as he now perceived, Robinson was actually lying, his head, face and arms swathed in manifold bandages. It was horrible to see him lift his arms to his eyes to wipe away his tears with the bandages, tears of pain or grief or perhaps even of joy at seeing Karl again.

"Rossmann," he cried reproachfully, "why have you kept me waiting so long? For a whole hour I've been struggling to keep myself from being carted away before you came. These fellows"—and he gave one of the lift-boys a clout on the head, as if his bandages secured him from retaliation—"are absolute

devils. Ah, Rossmann, I've had to pay dearly for this visit to you."

"Why, what have they been doing to you?" said Karl, stepping over to the stretcher, which the lift-boys laughingly set down so as to have a rest.

"You ask that," groaned Robinson, "and yet you can see what I look like. Just think of it, they've very likely made me a cripple for life. I have frightful pains from here right down to here"—and he pointed first to his head and then to his toes—"I only wish you had seen how much my nose bled. My waistcoat is completely ruined, and I had to leave it behind me too; my trousers are in tatters, I'm in my drawers"—and he lifted the blanket a little and invited Karl to look under it. "What on earth is to become of me? I'll have to lie in bed for months at least, and I may tell you at once there's nobody but you to nurse me; Delamarche is far too impatient. Rossmann, don't leave me!" And Robinson stretched out one hand towards the reluctant Karl, seeking to win him over by caresses. "Why had I to come and call on you!" he repeated several times, to keep Karl from forgetting that he was partly responsible for his misfortunes.—Now it did not take Karl a minute to see that Robinson's lamentations were caused not by his wounds but by the colossal hang-over he was suffering from, since just after falling asleep dead-drunk he had been wakened up and to his surprise violently assaulted until he had lost all sense of reality. The trivial nature of his wounds could be seen from the old rags of bandages with which the lift-boys, obviously in jest, had swathed him round and round. And the two boys at either end of the stretcher kept going into fits of laughter. But this was hardly the place to bring Robinson to his senses, for people were streaming past without paying any attention to the group beside the stretcher, often enough taking a flying leap clean over Robinson, while the taxi-driver who had been paid with Karl's money kept crying: "Come on! Come on!" The lift-boys put out all their strength and raised the stretcher, and Robinson seized Karl's hand, saying coaxingly: "Come along, do come." Considering the figure he cut, would not Karl be best provided for in the sheltering darkness of the taxi? And so he settled himself beside Robinson, who leaned his head against him. The two lift-boys heartily shook hands with him through the window, taking leave of their one-time colleague, and the taxi made a sharp turn into the thoroughfare. It looked as if an accident were inevitable, but the all-embracing stream of traffic quietly swept into itself even the arrowy thrust of their vehicle.

I⊤ seemed to be an outlying suburban street where the taxi stopped, for everything was quiet and children were sitting playing on the edge of the pavement. A man with a pile of old clothes slung over his shoulder kept a watchful eye on the house-windows above him as he cried his wares. Karl was so weary that he felt out of place when he stepped out of the car on to the asphalt, which lay warm and bright in the morning sunshine.

"Is this really where you live?" he called into the taxi.

Robinson, who had slept peacefully during the whole journey, growled an indistinct affirmative and seemed to be waiting for Karl to carry him out.

"Then you don't need me any more. Goodbye," said Karl, and started to walk away down the slight slope of the street.

"But Karl, what on earth are you thinking of?" cried Robinson, and his anxiety was so great that he stood up in the car fairly straight, except that his knees were somewhat shaky.

"I've got to go now," said Karl, who had observed Robinson's speedy recovery.

"In your shirt-sleeves?" asked Robinson.

"I'll soon earn myself another jacket," replied Karl, and he nodded confidently to Robinson, raised his hand in farewell and would have departed in earnest had not the taxi-driver called out: "Just a moment, sir!"

Unfortunately it appeared that the man laid claim to a supplementary payment, to cover the extra time he had waited in front of the hotel.

"Of course," cried Robinson from the car, supporting the justice of this demand, "you kept me waiting such a long time there. You must give him something more."

"Yes, that's so," said the taxi-driver.

"Yes, if I only had anything to give," said Karl, searching in his trouser pockets although he knew that it was useless.

"I have only you to look to," said the taxi-driver, planting himself squarely before Karl. "I can't ask anything from a sick man."

From the door a young lad with a nose half eaten away drew nearer and stood listening a few paces away. A policeman who was just making his round of the street lowered his head, took a good look at the figure in shirt-sleeves and came to a stop.

Robinson, who had noticed the policeman, made the blunder of shouting to him from the other window of the car: "It's nothing, it's nothing!" as if a policeman could be chased away like a fly. The children, who had been watching the policeman, saw him stop, had their attention drawn to Karl and the taxi-man, and came trotting up. In a doorway across the street an old woman stood stolidly at gaze.

"Rossmann!" shouted a voice from above them. It was Delamarche standing on the balcony of the top floor. It was difficult to see him against the pale blue sky, but he was obviously wearing a dressing-gown and observing the street through a pair of opera glasses. Beside him there was a big red sunshade, under which a woman seemed to be sitting. "Hello!" he shouted at the very top of his voice, to make himself understood, "is Robinson there too?"

"Yes," replied Karl, powerfully supported by a second, far louder "Yes" from Robinson in the car.

"Hello!" Delamarche shouted back, "I'm coming at once!" Robinson leaned out of the car. "That's a man," he said, and this praise of Delamarche was directed at Karl, at the driver, at the policeman and anyone else who cared to hear it. Up on the balcony, which they still kept watching absently, although Delamarche had already left it, from under the sunshade there rose a large figure which proved to be indeed a woman in a loose red gown; she lifted the opera glasses from the ledge of the balcony and gazed through them down at the people below, who began to turn their eyes away from her, though lingeringly. Karl looked at the house-door where Delamarche was to appear, and then right through it into the courtyard, which was being traversed by an almost unbroken line of workmen, each of whom bore on his shoulder a small but obviously very heavy box. The taxi-driver had stepped across to his car and to employ the time was polishing the lamps with a rag. Robinson felt all his limbs, seeming astonished because in spite of the most intent examination he could discover none but trivial aches, and then bent down and cautiously began to undo one of the thick bandages round his leg. The policeman held his black baton at a slant before him and quietly waited with that deep patience which policemen must have, whether they are on ordinary duty or on the watch. The lad with the eaten nose sat down on a doorstep and stretched his legs before him. The children gradually crept nearer to Karl, for although he paid no attention to them, he seemed the most important of all to them because of his blue shirt-sleeves.

By the length of time that elapsed before Delamarche's arrival one could measure the great height of the house. And Delamarche came in great haste, having stopped merely to tie the cord round his dressing-gown. "So here you are!" he cried, with both delight and severity in his tone. At each great stride he took his bright-coloured pyjamas could be seen for an instant. Karl could not quite make out how Delamarche could go about in such negligent attire here, in the town, in this huge tenement, on the open street, as if he were in his private villa. There was a big change in Delamarche, as well as in Robinson. His dark, clean-shaven, scrupulously clean face with its rough modelling of muscle looked proud and inspired respect. The hard glitter of his eyes, which he still kept half-shut, was startling; his violet-coloured dressing-gown was certainly old, spotted and too big for him, but from that squalid garment there emerged at the neck the folded swathes of an enormous scarf of heavy dark silk.

"Well?" he asked, addressing everybody. The policeman stepped a little nearer and leaned against the body of the car. Karl gave a brief explanation.

"Robinson's a bit wobbly, but he can easily climb the stairs if he tries; the driver here wants something extra besides the fare I have already paid him. And now I'm going, good day."

"You're not going," said Delamarche.

"I've told him that too," Robinson announced from the taxi.

"I'm going all the same," said Karl, taking a few steps. But Delamarche was already beside him, forcibly holding him back.

"I say you're staying here!" he cried.

"Let me go," said Karl, and he made ready to gain his freedom if necessary, little hope as he had of downing a man like Delamarche. Yet the policeman was standing by, and the taxi-driver, and the street was not so quiet but that occasional groups of workmen passed through it; would they tolerate it if Delamarche were to mishandle him? He would not like to be left alone with him in a room, but why not here? Delamarche was now quietly paying off the taxi-driver, who pocketed the unmerited and substantial addition to his fare with many bows and out of gratitude went up to Robinson and began to consult with him how he was best to be got out of the car. Karl saw that he was unobserved; perhaps Delamarche would mind it less if he just slipped away; it was best to avoid a quarrel if it could be avoided; and so he simply stepped on to the road as the quickest way of getting clear. The children rushed over to Delamarche to let him know that Karl was escaping, but Delamarche had no need to intervene, for the policeman stretched out his baton and said "Stop!"

"What's your name?" he asked, tucking his baton under his arm and slowly bringing out a notebook. Karl now looked at him carefully for the first time; he was a powerfully built man, but his hair was already almost white.

"Karl Rossmann," he said.

"Rossmann," the policeman echoed him, no doubt simply because he was a quiet and conscientious man, but Karl, who was now having his first encounter with the American Police, saw in this repetition of his words a certain mistrust. And indeed his position was probably precarious, for even Robinson, though he was so occupied with his own troubles, was making dumb imploring gestures from the car to Delamarche, begging him to help Karl. But Delamarche refused him with a hasty shake of the head and looked on without doing anything, his hands in the huge pockets of the dressing-gown. To a woman who had just come out of the house the lad on the doorstep explained the whole situation from the very beginning. The children stood in a half-circle behind Karl and silently looked up at the policeman.

"Show your identification papers," said the policeman. That could only be a formal question; for without a jacket one was not likely to have many identification papers in one's pockets.

213

So Karl remained silent, deciding to answer the next question fully and so if possible to gloss over his lack of identification papers.

But the next question was "So you have no papers?" And Karl had to answer: "Not with me."

"But that's bad," said the policeman, looking thoughtfully around him and tapping with two fingers on the cover of his notebook. "Have you an occupation?" he asked at last.

"I was a lift-boy," said Karl.

"You were a lift-boy, so you aren't one any longer; and in that case what are you living on now?"

"I'm going to look out for another job."

"I see; have you just been dismissed?"

"Yes, an hour ago."

"Suddenly?"

"Yes," said Karl, raising his hand as in apology. He could not tell the whole story here, and even if that had been possible, it seemed quite hopeless to think of averting a threatened injury by the recital of injuries already suffered. And if he had not been able to get his rights when faced by the kindness of the Manageress and the insight of the Head Waiter, he certainly could not expect to get them from the company gathered here in the street.

"And you were dismissed without your jacket?" asked the policeman.

"Why, yes," said Karl; so in America too it was the habit of authorities to ask questions about what they could see for themselves. (How exasperated his father had been over the pointless enquiries of the officials when he was getting Karl's passport!) Karl felt like running and hiding himself somewhere, if only to escape answering any more questions. And now the policeman put the very question which he feared most of all and which he had been so uneasily expecting that very likely he had behaved with less prudence than he might have done.

"In what hotel were you employed?"

Karl sank his head and did not reply; that was the last question he was prepared to answer. It simply must not happen for him to be escorted by a policeman to the Hotel Occidental again, to start investigations there into which his friends and enemies would all be drawn, to have the Manageress's wavering faith in him completely undermined, should the boy whom she thought was in the Pension Brenner turn up in the custody of a policeman, in his shirt-sleeves, without the card she had given him; while the Head Waiter would probably nod comprehendingly and the Head Porter mention the Hand of God which had at last caught the evil-doer.

"He was employed in the Hotel Occidental," said Delamarche, stepping over to the policeman.

"No," shouted Karl, stamping his foot, "that isn't true!" Delamarche surveyed him with his lips pursed in mockery, as if there were many things he could divulge. Among the children Karl's unexpected agitation produced great excitement, and they lined up beside Delamarche to get a better look at Karl. Robinson had stuck his head completely out of the car; he was so intent that he did not move except for an occasional flicker of the eyelids. The boy on the doorstep clapped his hands with delight; the woman beside him gave him a nudge with her elbow to keep him quiet. The porters in the courtyard had just stopped for breakfast and appeared in a bunch with great cans of black coffee, which they kept stirring with long rolls of bread. Several sat down on the edge of the pavement, and they all gulped down their coffee very loudly.

"You know this lad?" the policeman asked Delamarche.

"Better than I have a mind to," said Delamarche. "I have done him much kindness in my time, and he gave me little thanks for it, as you can probably imagine, even after the short encounter you've had with him."

"Yes," said the policeman, "he seems to be a hardened young rascal."

"He is all that," said Delamarche, "but even that isn't the worst thing about him."

"Is that so?" said the policeman.

"Oh," said Delamarche, who was now warming to his theme and swinging his dressing-gown to and fro with his hands in the pockets, "he's a fine bird, this fellow. I and my friend there in the car once picked him up when he was down and out, he had no idea at that time of American conditions, he had just come from Europe, where they had no use for him either; well, we took him with us, let him live with us, explained things to him and tried to get him a job, thinking in spite of everything that we'd make a decent human being out of him, and in the end he did the disappearing trick one night, simply vanished, and in circumstances I'd rather not mention now. Is that true or not?" asked Delamarche in conclusion, plucking at Karl's shirt-sleeve.

"Back there, you children!" shouted the policeman, for the children had pressed forward so far that Delamarche had almost stumbled over one of them. Meanwhile the porters, discovering that this cross-examination was more interesting than they had suspected, began to pay some heed to it and gathered in a close ring behind Karl, so that he could not retreat even by a step and had to suffer, too, at his very ear the incessant chatter of these same porters, who babbled rather than spoke in a quite incomprehensible jargon which was perhaps broken English interspersed with Slavonic words.

"Thanks for the information," said the policeman, saluting Delamarche. "In any case I'll take him with me and hand him back to the Hotel Occidental."

But Delamarche said: "May I ask you as a favour to leave the boy with me for the time being; I have some business to settle with him. I promise you that I'll personally take him back to the hotel afterwards."

"I can't do that," said the policeman.

Delamarche said: "Here is my card," and handed him the card.

The policeman looked at it respectfully, but said with a polite smile: "No, it can't be done."

Much as Karl had been on his guard against Delamarche hitherto, he saw in him now his only possible salvation. The way he was haggling with the policeman was certainly suspicious, but in any case Delamarche would be more easily induced than the policeman not to deliver him to the hotel. And even if he were brought back to the hotel by Delamarche, it would not be nearly so bad as to be escorted there by a policeman. For the moment, of course, he must not let it be seen that he really wanted to stay with Delamarche, or all was lost. And with an uneasy feeling he watched the policeman's hand, which might rise at any moment to seize him.

"I must at least find out why he was suddenly dismissed," said the policeman at last, while Delamarche looked away with an offended air and twisted the card between his finger-tips.

"But he isn't dismissed at all!" cried Robinson to everyone's surprise, leaning out of the taxi as far as he could reach, with one hand on the driver's shoulder. "Far from it; he has a very good job there. He's the head boy in the dormitory and can take anyone in there that he likes. Only he's terribly busy, and if you want to ask him for anything you have to wait for a long time. He's always in conference with the Head Waiter and the Manageress; his post is a confidential one. He's certainly not dismissed. I don't know why he said he was. How can he be dismissed? I got badly hurt in the hotel, and he had instructions to take me home, and since he wasn't wearing his jacket at the time he just came without it. I couldn't wait until he fetched his jacket."

"Well now," said Delamarche, spreading out his arms, in a tone which reproached the policeman for his lack of discernment; and these two words of his seemed to bring an incontestable clarity into the vagueness of Robinson's statement.

"But is this true?" asked the policeman, already weakening. "And if it is true, why does the boy give out that he is dismissed?"

"You'd better tell him," said Delamarche.

Karl looked at the policeman whose task it was to keep order here among strangers thinking only of their own advantage, and he had some intuition of the man's difficulties. That made him unwilling to tell a lie, so he kept his hands tightly clasped behind his back.

In the house-door an overseer appeared and clapped his hands as a signal that the porters should go back to work again. They shook the grounds out of their coffee cans and, falling silent, drifted reluctantly through the doorway.

"We'll never come to a conclusion this way," said the policeman, and he made to seize Karl by the arm. Karl involuntarily recoiled a little, became conscious of the free space at his back which the porters' departure had left open, turned about and with a few great bounds for a start set off at full speed. The children let out a single yell and with outstretched arms ran a few steps along with him.

"Stop him!" the policeman shouted down the long, almost empty street, and shouting this cry at regular intervals set out after Karl at an easy run which showed both great strength and practice. It was lucky for Karl that the chase took place in a working-class quarter. The workers had no liking for the authorities. Karl stuck to the middle of the road because there were fewer obstacles there, and he saw occasional workers calmly halting on the pavement to watch him while the policeman shouted "Stop him!" and kept pointing his baton at him as he ran a parallel course, keeping shrewdly to the smooth pavement. Karl had very little hope and almost lost that altogether when the policeman, as they were nearing some cross-streets where there were sure to be police patrols, began to blow really deafening blasts on his whistle. Karl's only advantage was his light attire; he flew, or rather plunged, down the street, which sloped more and more steeply; but confused by his lack of sleep he often made useless bounds, too high in the air and a vain waste of precious time. Besides, the policeman had his objective before his eyes and had no need to think, whereas Karl had to think first and attend to his running only in the intervals between weighing possibilities and making decisions. His plan, a somewhat desperate one, was to avoid the cross-streets for the time being, since he did not know what they concealed, perhaps for instance he might run straight into a police station; he wanted as long as possible to keep to this main thoroughfare which he could survey from end to end, since it did not terminate until far below, in a bridge vanishing suddenly into a haze of mist and sunshine in mid-air. Acting on this decision, he was just putting on a faster spurt so as to pass the first cross-street in a flash, when he saw not very far in front of him a policeman lurking watchfully by the dark wall of a house in shadow, ready to spring out on him at the right moment. There was nothing for it but to turn into the cross-street, and when from that very street someone gently called him by name—he thought it was a delusion at first, for there had been a ringing in his ears all the time—he hesitated no longer and made an abrupt turn, to take the police as much as possible by surprise, swinging round at a right-angle on one foot into the cross-street.

He had taken only two strides—he had already forgotten that someone had called his name, for the second policeman was now blowing his whistle too, obviously fresh and unwinded, and distant pedestrians ahead of him in the cross-street seemed to be quickening their steps—when an arm darting out from a little doorway seized him and he was drawn into a dark entry, while a voice said: "Don't move!" It was Delamarche, quite out of breath, his face flushed, his hair sticking damply to his head. He was clad only in his shirt and drawers, his dressing-gown tucked under his arm. The door, which was not a main door but only an inconspicuous side door, he shut and locked at once.

"Wait a minute," he said, leaning against the wall and breathing heavily with his head thrown back. Karl, almost lying in his arms and hardly knowing what he was doing pressed his face against his breast.

"There they go," said Delamarche, listening intently and pointing with his finger at the door. The two policemen were really running past, their feet ringing in the empty street like the striking of steel against stone.

"You've been fairly put through it," said Delamarche to Karl, who was still panting for breath and could not bring out a word. Delamarche laid him cautiously on the floor, knelt down beside him, passed a hand several times over his brow and regarded him.

"I'm all right now," said Karl, painfully getting up.

"Then let's go," said Delamarche, who had put on his dressing-gown again, and he pushed Karl, whose head still drooped with weariness, before him, giving him an occasional shake to liven him up.

"You say you're tired?" he said. "You had the whole street to career about in like a horse, but I had to double through these accursed passages and courtyards. It's a good thing that I'm a bit of a runner too." In his pride he gave Karl a mighty thump on the back. "A race with the police like this now and then is good practice."

"I was dog-tired before I began running," said Karl.

"There's no excuse for bad running," said Delamarche. "If it hadn't been for me they would have nabbed you long since."

"I think so too," said Karl. "I'm much obliged to you."

"No doubt of that," said Delamarche.

They went through a long narrow ground-floor lobby, which was paved with dark, smooth flagstones. Here and there to right and left a staircase opened out, or a passage giving on a more spacious hall-way. Scarcely any grown people were to be seen, but children were playing on the empty stairs. Beside a stair-railing a little girl was standing weeping so hard that her whole face glistened with tears. As soon as she caught sight of Delamarche she rushed up the stairs, gasping for air, her mouth wide open, and was not reassured until she was quite high up, after looking over her shoulder time and again to make certain that no one was chasing her or likely to chase her.

"I ran her down a minute ago," said Delamarche laughing, and he flourished his fist at her, whereupon she rushed up still farther, screaming.

The courtyards they threaded were also almost completely forsaken. An occasional porter pushed a two-wheeled handbarrow before him, a woman was filling a bucket with water at a pump, a postman was quietly making his round, an old man with a white moustache sat before a glass door smoking a pipe with his legs crossed, crates were being unloaded before a despatch agency while the idle horses imperturbably turned their heads from side to side and a man in overalls supervised the proceedings with a paper in his hand; behind the open window of an office a clerk, sitting at his desk, raised his head and looked thoughtfully out just as Karl and Delamarche went past.

"This is as quiet a place as you could wish for," said Delamarche. "In the evening it's pretty noisy for an hour or two, but all day long it's ideal." Karl nodded; it seemed a good deal too quiet for him. "I couldn't live anywhere else," said Delamarche, "for Brunelda simply can't stand any noise. Do you know Brunelda? Well, you'll soon see her. Take my advice anyhow, and keep as quiet as you can."

When they reached the stairway which led up to Delamarche's flat, the taxi had already gone and the boy with the half-eaten nose announced, without showing any surprise at Karl's reappearance, that he had lugged Robinson upstairs. Delamarche only nodded to him, as if he were a servant who had merely done his duty, and then drew Karl, who hesitated a moment and gazed out at the sunny street, up the stairs with him. "We'll soon be there," said Delamarche several times during the ascent, but his prophecy was tardy in fulfilling itself, for there was always another stair ahead of them, with a barely perceptible change in direction. Once Karl actually had to stop, not from weariness but from helplessness in face of such a length of stairs. "The flat's very high up," said Delamarche, as they went on, "but that has its advantages too. We're not tempted to go out much, we lounge about in our dressing-gowns all day, it's very comfortable. Of course, no visitors ever come up so far, either."

"And what visitors could they have?" thought Karl.

At last on a landing they caught sight of Robinson outside a closed door, and now they had arrived; the stairs were not at an end yet, but went on farther in the semi-darkness without any indication that an end was even in sight.

"I thought so!" said Robinson in a muted voice as if he were still suffering pain, "Delamarche has brought him! Rossmann, where would you be without Delamarche!" Robinson was standing in his underclothes, scantily wrapped in the small blanket he had been given at the Hotel Occidental; there was no visible reason why he did not go into the flat instead of standing here as a laughing-stock for any chance passer-by.

"Is she asleep?" asked Delamarche.

"I don't think so," said Robinson, "but I thought it better to wait till you came."

"We must see first whether she's sleeping," said Delamarche, bending down to the keyhole. After he had peered through it a long time, turning his head this way and that, he got up and said: "I can't see her clearly; the curtain's drawn. She's sitting on the couch, but she may be asleep."

"Why, is she ill?" asked Karl, for Delamarche was standing there as if at a loss for advice.

But he retorted in a sharp enough voice: "Ill?"

"He doesn't know her," said Robinson, in extenuation.

A few doors farther on two women stepped out into the passage; they wiped their hands on their aprons, eyeing Delamarche and Robinson, and seemed to be talking about them. A young girl with gleaming fair hair bounded out of a door and squeezed between the two women, hanging on to their arms.

"These are disgusting women," said Delamarche, lowering

his voice, it was evident, only out of consideration for the slumbering Brunelda, "sooner or later I'll report them to the police and then I'll be rid of them for years. Don't look their way," he snapped at Karl. But Karl had not seen any harm in looking at the women, since in any case he had to stand in the passage waiting for Brunelda to waken. And he shook his head angrily, as if he refused to take any admonitions from Delamarche, and he had just begun walking towards the women, to make his meaning clearer, when Robinson caught him by the sleeve with the words: "Rossmann, take care!", while Delamarche, already exasperated, was roused to such fury by a loud burst of laughter from the girl that whirling his arms and legs he made a great spring at the women, who vanished into their doors as if they had been blown away. "That's how I have often to clear the passages," remarked Delamarche, strolling back again; then he remembered that Karl had been refractory and said: "But I expect very different behaviour from you, or else you're likely to come up against me."

Then from the room a gentle voice queried in a tired tone: "Is that Delamarche?"

"Yes," answered Delamarche, looking tenderly at the door, "may we come in?"

"Oh yes," was the answer, and after casting one more glance at the two standing behind him, Delamarche slowly opened the door.

They stepped into complete darkness. The curtain before the balcony door—there was no window—was completely drawn and let very little light through; but the fact that the room was crammed with furniture and clothes hanging everywhere contributed greatly to make it darker. The air was musty and one could literally smell the dust which had gathered here in corners apparently beyond the reach of any hand. The first things that Karl noticed on entering were three trunks, set just behind one another.

On the couch was lying the woman who had been looking down earlier from the balcony. The red gown had got rumpled a little beneath her and hung in a great peak to the floor; her legs could be seen almost as far as the knee; she was wearing thick white woollen stockings; she had no shoes.

"How hot it is, Delamarche," she said, turning her face from the wall and languidly extending her hand in the direction of Delamarche, who seized it and kissed it. Karl could see only her double chin, which rolled in sympathy with the turning of her head.

"Would you like me to open the curtain?" asked Delamarche.

"Oh, not that," she said as if in despair, shutting her eyes, "that would only make it worse."

Karl had gone up to the foot of the couch so as to see the woman better; he was surprised at her lamentations, for the heat was nothing out of the common.

"Wait, I'll make you a little more comfortable," said Delamarche anxiously, and he undid a few buttons at her neck and pulled her dress open at the throat so that part of her breast was laid bare and the soft, yellowish lace border of her chemise appeared.

"Who is that," said the woman suddenly, pointing a finger at Karl, "why does he stare at me so hard?"

"You're being a great help, aren't you?" said Delamarche, pushing Karl aside, while he reassured the woman with the words: "It's only the boy I've brought with me to attend on you."

"But I don't want anyone!" she cried. "Why do you bring strange people into the house?"

"But you've always been asking for someone to attend to you," said Delamarche, kneeling down on the floor, for there was no room whatever on the couch beside Brunelda, in spite of its great breadth.

"Ah, Delamarche," she said, "you don't understand me, you don't understand me at all."

"Then, all right, I don't understand you," said Delamarche, taking her face between his hands. "But it doesn't really matter; he can go at once, if you like."

"Since he is here, he can stay," she said now, and tired as he was, Karl felt so grateful for these words, though they probably were not kindly meant, that still vaguely thinking of these endless stairs which he might have had to descend again, he stepped over Robinson, now peacefully asleep on his blanket, and said, in spite of Delamarche's angry gesticulations:

"I thank you anyway, for letting me stay here a little longer. I've had no sleep for twenty-four hours and I've done a lot of things and been rather upset. I'm terribly tired. I hardly know where I am. But after I have slept an hour or two you can pack me off straight away and I'll go gladly."

"You can stay here as long as you like," said the woman, adding ironically: "We have more than room enough here, as you see."

"Then, you'd better go," said Delamarche, "we haven't any use for you."

"No, let him stay," said the woman, this time in earnest.

And Delamarche said to Karl as if in obedience to her words: "Well then, go and lie down somewhere."

"He can lie down on the curtains, but he must take off his shoes, to keep from tearing them."

Delamarche showed Karl the place she meant. Between the

door and the three trunks a great pile of the most multifarious window curtains had been flung. Had they all been methodically folded, with the heavy ones below and the light ones on top, and had the curtain rods and wooden rings scattered through the pile been taken out, they might have made a tolerable couch, but as it was they made merely a tottering, unstable heap on which, however, Karl lay down at once, for he was too tired to make any particular preparations for sleeping and had also to guard against standing on too much ceremony with his host and hostess.

He had almost fallen into a genuine sleep when he heard a loud cry and started up to see Brunelda sitting erect on the couch, opening her arms wide and flinging them round Delamarche, who was kneeling before her. Karl, shocked at the sight, lay back again and curled up among the curtains to continue his sleep. That he would not be able to endure this place for two days seemed clear enough to him; yet it was all the more necessary to have a thorough sleep to begin with, so that he might have his wits about him and be able to decide quickly on the right course of action.

But Brunelda had been aware of Karl's eyes, big with fatigue, which had startled her once already, and she cried: "Delamarche, I can't bear this heat, I'm burning, I must take off my clothes, I must have a bath; send the two of them out of the room, wherever you like, into the passage, on to the balcony, so long as they are out of my sight! Here I am in my own home, and yet I can't get any peace. If I were only alone with you, Delamarche! Oh God, they're still here! Look at that shameless Robinson sprawling about in his underclothes in the presence of a lady. And look at that boy, that stranger, who has just been staring savagely at me, how he is pretending to lie down again to fool me. Turn them out, Delamarche, they're a burden on me, they're a weight on my breast; if I die now it will be their fault."

"Out you get at once, out of here!" said Delamarche, advancing on Robinson and stirring him up with one foot, which he put on his chest.

Then he shouted to Karl: "Rossmann, get up! Out on the balcony, both of you! And it'll be your funeral if you come in here before you're called! Now look slippy, Robinson"—at this he kicked Robinson more violently—"and you, Rossmann, look out or I'll come and attend to you too," and he clapped his hands loudly twice.

"How long you're taking!" cried Brunelda from the sofa; she had spread her legs wide where she sat so as to get more room for her disproportionately fat body; only with the greatest effort, gasping and frequently pausing to recover her breath, could she bend far enough forward to catch hold of her stockings at the top and pull them down a little; she could not possibly take off her own clothes; Delamarche would have to do that, and she was now impatiently waiting for him.

Quite dazed with weariness, Karl crept down from the heap of curtains and trailed slowly to the balcony door; a piece of curtain material had wrapped itself round his foot and he dragged it indifferently with him. In his distraction he actually said as he passed Brunelda: "I wish you good night," and then wandered past Delamarche, who was drawing aside the curtain of the balcony door, and went out on to the balcony. Immediately behind him came Robinson, who seemed to be equally sleep-sodden, for he was muttering to himself: "Always being ill-treated! If Brunelda doesn't come too I'm not going on to the balcony." But in spite of this pronouncement he went out meekly enough on the balcony, where, as Karl had already subsided into the easy chair, he immediately bedded himself on the stone floor.

When Karl awoke it was evening, the stars were already out and behind the tall houses on the other side of the street the moon was rising. Not until he had surveyed the unknown neighbourhood for a little and taken a few breaths of the cool, reviving air did Karl realise where he was. How imprudent he had been; he had neglected all the counsels of the Manageress, all Therese's warnings, all his own fears; here he was sitting calmly on Delamarche's balcony, where he had slept for half a day as if Delamarche, his mortal enemy, were not just on the other side of the curtain. Robinson, that lazy good-for-nothing, was sprawling on the floor and tugging him by the foot; he seemed indeed to have wakened him in this manner, for he was saying: "How you can sleep, Rossmann! That's what it is to be young and carefree. How long do you want to go on sleeping? I'd have let you go on sleeping, but in the first place I'm bored with lying on the floor, and in the second place I'm terribly hungry. Come on, get up for a minute, I've got something hidden under your chair, something to eat, and I want to get it out. I'll give you some too." And Karl, getting up, looked on while Robinson, without getting up, rolled over on his belly and reached under the chair to pull out a sort of silver salver such as is used for holding visiting-cards. On the salver lay one-half of a quite black sausage, a few thin cigarettes, an open sardine tin still nearly full and dripping with oil, and a number of sweets, most of them squashed into a mass. Then appeared a big hunk of bread and a kind of perfume bottle, which seemed to contain something else than perfume, however, for Robinson displayed it with particular satisfaction, licking his lips and looking up at Karl.

"You see, Rossmann," said Robinson, while he devoured sardine after sardine and now and then wiped the oil off his hands with a woollen scarf which Brunelda had apparently forgotten on the balcony, "you see, Rossmann, that's what you need to do if you don't want to starve. I tell you, I'm just kicked out of the way. And if you're always treated like a dog, you begin to think that you're actually one. A good thing you're here, Rossmann; I have at least someone to talk to. Nobody in the building speaks to me. They hate us. And all because of Brunelda. She's a marvellous woman, of course. I say,"—and he gave Karl a sign to bend down, so that he might whisper to him—"I once saw her naked. Oh"—and in the memory of that pleasure he began to pinch and slap Karl's leg until Karl shouted:

"Robinson, you're mad!" and forcibly pushed his hands away.

"You're still only a child, Rossmann," said Robinson, and from under his shirt he pulled out a dagger that he wore on a cord round his neck, removed the sheath and began to slice up the hard sausage. "You've still a lot to learn. But you've come to the right place to learn things. Do sit down. Won't you have something to eat too? Well, maybe you'll get an appetite watching me. You don't want a drink, either? So you don't want anything at all. And you're not much inclined to talk, either. But I don't care who's on the balcony with me, so long as there's somebody. For I'm often out on the balcony. It's great fun for Brunelda. She only has to get an idea in her head that she's too cold, that she's too hot, that she wants to sleep, that she wants to comb her hair, that she wants to loosen her corset, that she wants to put it on, and then she has me sent on the balcony. Sometimes she actually does what she says, but mostly she just lies on the couch the same as before and never moves. I used sometimes to draw the curtain a little and peep through, but once Delamarche—I know quite well that he didn't want to do it and only did it because Brunelda told him to—but once Delamarche on one of these occasions struck me across the face several times with the whip—can you see the marks?—and since then I haven't dared to peep again. And so I just lie here on the balcony and have nothing to do but eat. The night before last, as I lay up here alone all evening, I still had on the fine clothes which I had the bad luck to lose in your hotel—the swine, tearing a man's expensive clothes off his back—well, as I lay alone and looked down through the railings, everything seemed so miserable that I began to blubber. But it just happened, without my noticing it, that Brunelda had come out here in her red gown—that suits her far the best of them all—and she looked at me for a little while and said: 'Robinson, what are you crying for?' Then she lifted up her skirt and wiped my eyes with the hem. Who knows what more she might have done if Delamarche hadn't called her and she hadn't had to go back into the room again at once. I thought, of course, that it was my turn next, and I asked through the curtain if I couldn't come in. And what do you think Brunelda said? 'No!' said she, and 'what are you thinking of!' said she."

"But why do you stay here if they treat you like that?" asked Karl.

"Excuse me, Rossmann, but that's a stupid question," replied Robinson. "You'll stay here too, even if they treat you still worse. Besides they don't treat me so very badly."

"No," said Karl, "I'm certainly going away, and this very evening if possible. I'm not going to stay with you."

"And how, for instance, will you manage to get away tonight?" asked Robinson, who was digging out the soft inside

232

of the loaf and carefully dipping it into the oil in the sardine box. "How are you going to leave when you mustn't even go into the room?"

"And why shouldn't I go into the room?"

"Because, until we're rung for, we can't go in," said Robinson, opening his mouth to its full extent and devouring the oily bread, while in the hollow of one hand he caught the oil that dripped from it, making a kind of reservoir in which he dipped the rest of the bread from time to time. "Things are much stricter now. At first there was only a thin curtain; you couldn't actually see through it, but in the evenings you could watch their shadows on it. But Brunelda didn't like that, and so I had to turn one of her evening cloaks into a curtain and hang it up instead of the old one. Now you can see nothing at all. Then at one time I could always ask whether I might go in, and they used to say yes or no accordingly; but I suppose I took too much advantage of that and asked once too often. Brunelda couldn't bear it—and although she's so fat she's very delicate, she often has headaches and almost always gout in her legs— and so it was decided that I mustn't ask any more, but that I could go in whenever the table bell was rung. That rings so loudly that it can waken even me out of my sleep—I once had a cat here to cheer me up, but she was so scared at the bell that she ran away and never came back again; it hasn't rung today yet, you see, for when it does ring, I'm not only allowed to go in, I have to go in—and when such a long time goes by without ringing, it can take a good while before the bell rings again."

"Yes," said Karl, "but what applies to you needn't apply to me at all. Besides, that kind of thing only applies to those who put up with it."

"But," cried Robinson, "why shouldn't it apply to you as well? Of course it applies to you, too. You'd better stay quietly

233

here with me until the bell rings. Then of course you can at least try to get away."

"What is it really that keeps you here? Simply that Delamarche is your friend, or rather was your friend. Do you call this a life? Wouldn't it be better for you in Butterford, where you wanted to go first? Or even in California, where you have friends?"

"Well," said Robinson, "nobody could have told that this was going to happen." And before continuing, he said: "To your good health, my dear Rossmann," and took a long pull at the perfume bottle. "We were hard up against it that time when you let us down so meanly. We could get no work at all the first day or two; besides, Delamarche didn't want work, he could easily have got it, but he always sent me to look for it instead, and I never have any luck. He just loafed around, but by the evening all he brought back with him was a lady's handbag. It was fine enough, made of pearls; he gave it to Brunelda later, but there was almost nothing in it. Then he said we'd better try begging at the doors, you can always pick up something or other that way; so we went begging and I sang in front of the houses to make it look better. And it was just like Delamarche's luck, for we had only been a minute or two at the second door, a very grand flat on the ground floor, and sung a couple of songs to the cook and the butler, when the lady the flat belonged to, Brunelda herself, came up the front steps. Maybe she was too tightly laced; anyhow she couldn't get up to the top of these steps. But how lovely she looked, Rossmann! She was wearing a white dress with a red sunshade. You felt you could eat her. You felt you could drink her up. God, God, she was lovely. What a woman! Tell me yourself, how can such a woman be possible? Of course the cook and the butler rushed down to her at once and almost carried her up. We stood on either side of the door and raised our hats, as people do here. She stopped for a little, for she hadn't quite got her breath back, and I don't know how it actually happened, I was so hungry I didn't know quite what I was doing, and close at hand she was even handsomer, so broad and yet so firm everywhere because of the special stays she had on, I can let you see them in the trunk; well, I couldn't help touching her back, but quite lightly, you know, just a touch. Of course it's a shocking thing for a beggar to touch a rich lady. I only just touched her, but after all I did touch her. Who knows where it might have ended if Delamarche hadn't given me a clip on the ear, and such a clip that both my hands flew to my own face."

"What things to do!" said Karl, quite absorbed in the story, and he sat down on the floor. "So that was Brunelda?"

"Yes," said Robinson, "that was Brunelda."

"Didn't you say once that she was a singer?" asked Karl.

"Certainly she is a singer, and a great singer," replied Robinson, who was rolling a sticky mass of sweetmeats on his tongue and now and then pushing back with his finger some piece that had got crowded out of his mouth. "Of course we didn't know that at the time; we only saw that she was a rich and very fine lady. She behaved as if nothing had happened, and perhaps she hadn't felt anything, for I had touched her really only with the tips of my fingers. But she kept looking at Delamarche, who stared back straight into her eyes—he usually hits it off like that. Then she said to him: 'Come inside for a little,' and pointed with her sunshade into the house, and Delamarche had to go in front of her. Then the two of them went in and the servants shut the door after them. As for me, I was left forgotten outside, and since I thought it wouldn't be for very long, I sat down on the steps to wait for Delamarche. But instead of Delamarche the butler came out bringing me a whole bowl of soup. 'A compliment from Delamarche!' I told myself. The man stood beside me for a time while I ate and told me some things about Brunelda, and then I saw how important this visit might be for us. For Brunelda had divorced her husband, was very wealthy and completely independent! Her ex-husband, a cocoa manufacturer, was still in love with her, to be sure, but she refused to have anything whatever to do with him. He often called at the flat, always dressed in great style as if he were going to a wedding—that's true, word for word, I know the man myself—but in spite of the huge tips he got, the butler never dared to ask Brunelda whether she would receive her husband, for he had asked her before once or twice, and she had always picked up anything she had handy and thrown it at his head. Once she even flung her big hot-water bottle at him and knocked out one of his front teeth. Yes, Rossmann, you may well stare!"

"How do you come to know the husband?" asked Karl.

"He often comes up here," said Robinson.

"Here?" In his astonishment Karl struck the floor lightly with his hand.

"You may well be surprised," Robinson went on, "I was surprised myself when the butler stood there telling me all this. Just think, whenever Brunelda was out, the husband always asked the butler to take him to her room, and he always took away some trifle or other as a keepsake and left something rare and expensive for Brunelda in return and strictly forbade the butler to say who had left it. But once—the servant swears it and I believe it—when he left an absolutely priceless piece of porcelain, Brunelda must have recognised it somehow, for she flung it on the floor at once, stamped upon it, spat on it and did other things to it as well, so that the servant could hardly carry it away for disgust."

"But what had her husband done to her?" asked Karl.

"I really don't know," said Robinson. "But I think it wasn't anything very serious, at least he himself doesn't know. I have often talked to him about it. I have an appointment with him every day at the corner of the street over there; if I can come, I have always to tell him the latest news; if I can't come, he waits for half an hour and then goes away again. It was a nice extra for me at first, for he paid like a gentleman for the news, but after Delamarche came to know of it I had to hand over the money to him, and so I don't go down there so often now."

"But what's the man after?" asked Karl. "What on earth is he after? He surely knows that she doesn't want him."

"Yes," sighed Robinson, lighting a cigarette and fanning the smoke high in the air with great sweeps of his arm. Then he seemed to change his attitude and said: "What does that matter to me? All I know is that he would give a lot of money to be able to lie here on the balcony like us."

Karl got up, leant against the railing and looked down into the street. The moon was already visible, but its light did not yet penetrate into the depths of the street. Though it had been so empty during the day, the street was now crowded with people, particularly before the house doors; they were all drifting along slowly and heavily, the shirt-sleeves of the men and the light dresses of the women standing out faintly against the darkness; they were all bareheaded. The various balconies round about were now fully occupied; whole families were sitting there by the light of electric lamps, either round small tables, if the balcony were big enough, or in a single row of armchairs or merely sticking their heads out of their living-rooms. The men sat at ease with their legs stretched out, their feet between the bars of the railing, reading newspapers which extended almost to the floor, or playing cards, apparently without speaking but to the accompaniment of loud bangs on the table; the women's laps were full of sewing work, and they had nothing but a brief glance now and then for their surroundings or the street below. A fair, delicate woman on the next balcony kept on yawning, turning her eyes up and raising to her mouth a piece of underwear which she was mending; even on the smallest balconies the children managed to chase each other round and make themselves a nuisance to their parents. Inside many of the rooms gramophones could be heard grinding out songs or orchestral music; nobody paid any particular attention to this music, except that now and then the father of a family would give a sign and someone would hurry into the room to put on a new record. At some of the windows could be seen loving couples standing quite motionless; one of these couples was standing at a window opposite; the young man had his arm round the girl and was squeezing her waist.

"Do you know any of your neighbours here?" Karl asked Robinson, who had now also got to his feet, and feeling cold had huddled himself into Brunelda's wrap as well as his blanket.

"Hardly one of them, that's the worst of my situation," said Robinson, and he pulled Karl closer so as to whisper in his ear, "or else I wouldn't have much to complain about at the moment. Brunelda has sold everything she had for the sake of Delamarche, and has moved with all she possesses into this suburban flat in order to devote herself entirely to him with nobody to disturb her; besides, that was what Delamarche wanted too."

"And she has dismissed her servants?" asked Karl.

"That's so," said Robinson. "Where could you find accommodation for servants here? Servants like that expect the best of everything. In Brunelda's old flat Delamarche once simply kicked one of these pampered creatures out of the room, he just went on kicking him until the man was outside. The other servants of course took the man's side and staged a row before the door; then Delamarche went out (I wasn't a servant then, but a friend of the family, yet I was outside among the servants all the same) and asked: 'What do you want?' The oldest servant, a man called Isidor, told him: 'You have nothing to do with us; we are engaged by the mistress.' I suppose you notice that they had a great respect for Brunelda. But Brunelda paid no attention to them and ran up to Delamarche—she wasn't so heavy then as she is now—and embraced and kissed him before them all and called him 'darling Delamarche.' And then she said: 'Now send these fools away.' Fools—that's what she called the servants; you can imagine the expression on their faces. Then Brunelda took Delamarche's hand and drew it down to the purse she wore at her belt; Delamarche put in his hand and began to pay off the servants; Brunelda did nothing but stand there with the open purse at her waist. Delamarche had to put his hand in over and over again, for he paid out the money without counting it and without checking their claims. At last he said: 'Since you won't have anything to do with me, I'll only say in Brunelda's name: Get out, this instant,' So they were dismissed; there were some legal proceedings afterwards, Delamarche had actually to go once to court, but I don't know much more about it. Except that as soon as the servants had gone Delamarche said to Brunelda: 'So now you have no servants?' And she said: 'But there's still Robinson.' So Delamarche clapped me on the shoulder and said: 'Very well, then, you'll be our servant.' And then Brunelda patted me on the cheek. If you ever get a chance, Rossmann, you should get her to pat you on the cheek some time. You'll be surprised how lovely it feels."

"So you've turned into Delamarche's servant, have you?" said Karl, summing up.

Robinson heard the pity in his voice and answered: "I may be a servant, but very few people know about it. You see, you didn't know it yourself, although you've been here quite a while. Why, you saw how I was dressed last night in the hotel. I had on the finest of fine clothes. Are servants dressed like that? The only thing is that I can't leave here very often, I must always be at hand, there's always something to do in the flat. One man isn't really enough for all the work. You may have noticed that we have a lot of things standing about in the room; what we couldn't sell at the removal we took with us here. Of course it could have been given away, but Brunelda gives nothing away. You can imagine what it meant to carry these things up the stairs."

"Robinson, did you carry all these things up here?" cried Karl.

"Why, who else was there to do it?" said Robinson. "I had a man to help me, but he was a lazy rascal; I had to do most of the work alone. Brunelda stood down below beside the van, Delamarche decided up here where the things were to be put, and I had to keep rushing up and down. That went on for two days, a long time, wasn't it? But you've no idea whatever how many things are in that room; all the trunks are full and behind the trunks the whole place is crammed to the very roof. If they had hired a few men for the transport, everything would soon have been finished, but Brunelda wouldn't trust it to anyone but me. That was flattering, of course, but I ruined my health

240

for life during those two days, and what else did I have except my health? Whenever I try to do the least thing, I have pains here and here and here. Do you think these boys in the hotel, these young jumping-jacks—for that's all they are—would ever have got the better of me if I had been in good health? But broken down as I may be, I'll never say a word to Delamarche or Brunelda; I'll work on as long as I can and when I can't do it any longer I'll just lie down and die and then they'll find out, too late, that I was really ill and yet went on working and worked myself to death in their service. Oh Rossmann——" he ended, drying his eyes on Karl's shirt-sleeve. After a while he said: "Aren't you cold, standing there in your shirt?"

"Go on, Robinson," said Karl, "you're always blubbering. I don't believe you're so ill as all that. You look healthy enough, but lying about on the balcony all the time you fancy all sorts of things. You may have an occasional pain in the chest; so have I, so has everybody. If everybody blubbered like you about trifles, there would be nothing but blubbering on all these balconies."

"I know better," said Robinson, wiping his eyes with the corner of his blanket. "The student staying next door with the landlady who cooks for us said to me a little time ago when I brought back the dishes: 'Look here, Robinson, you're ill, aren't you?' I'm not supposed to talk to these people, and so I simply set down the dishes and started to go away. Then he came right up to me and said: 'Listen man, don't push things too far, you're a sick man.' 'All right then, what am I to do about it?' I asked him. 'That's your business,' he said and turned away. The others sitting at the table just laughed, they're all our enemies round here, and so I thought I'd better quit."

"So you believe anyone who makes a fool of you, and you won't believe anyone who means well by you."

"But I must surely know how I feel," exclaimed Robinson indignantly, beginning to cry again almost at once.

"You don't know what's really wrong with you; you should only find some decent work for yourself, instead of being Delamarche's servant. So far as I can tell from your account of it and from what I have seen myself, this isn't service here, it's slavery. Nobody could endure it; I believe you there. But because you're Delamarche's friend you think you can't leave him. That's nonsense; if he doesn't see what a wretched life you're leading, you can't have the slightest obligation to him."

"So you really think, Rossmann, that I would recover my health if I gave up working here?"

"Certainly," said Karl.

"Certainly?" Robinson asked again.

"Quite certainly," said Karl smiling.

"Then I can begin recovering straight away," said Robinson, looking at Karl.

"How's that?" asked Karl.

"Why, because you are to take over my work here," replied Robinson.

"Who on earth told you that?" asked Karl.

"Oh, it's an old plan. It's been discussed for days. It began with Brunelda scolding me for not keeping the flat clean enough. Of course I promised to put everything right at once. But, well, that was very difficult. For instance, in my state of health, I can't creep into all the corners to sweep away the dust; it's hardly possible to move in the middle of the room, far less get behind the furniture and the piles of stuff. And if the place is to be thoroughly cleaned, the furniture would have to be shifted about, and how could I do that by myself? Besides, it has all to be done very quietly so as not to disturb Brunelda, and she scarcely ever leaves the room. So I promised to give everything a clean-up, but I didn't actually clean it up. When Brunelda noticed that, she told Delamarche that this couldn't go on and that he would have to take on an assistant. 'I don't want you, Delamarche,' she said, 'to reproach me at any time for not running the house properly. I can't put any strain upon myself, you know that quite well, and Robinson isn't enough; in the beginning he was fresh and looked after everything, but now he's always tired and sits most of the time in a corner. But a room with so many things in it as ours needs to be kept in order.' So Delamarche considered how it was to be managed, for of course it wouldn't do to take anyone and everyone into such a household as ours, even on trial, since we're spied on from all sides. But as I was a good friend of yours and had heard from Rennell how you had to slave in the hotel, I suggested your name. Delamarche agreed at once, although you were so rude to him before, and of course I was very glad to be of some use to you. For this job might have been made for you; you're young, strong and quick, while I'm no good to anyone. But I must tell you that you're not taken on yet; if Brunelda doesn't like you, that's an end of it. So do your best to be pleasant to her; I'll see to the rest."

"And what are you going to do if I take on the job?" queried Karl. He felt quite free; he had got over the first alarm which Robinson's announcement had caused him. So Delamarche meant no worse by him than to turn him into a servant—if he had had more sinister intentions, the babbling Robinson would certainly have blabbed them—but if that was how things stood, Karl saw his way to get clear of the place that very night. No one could be compelled to take a job. And though at first he had been worried in case his dismissal from the hotel would hinder him from getting a suitable and if possible fairly respectable post quickly enough to keep him from starving, any post at all now seemed good enough compared with this proposal, which repelled him; he would rather be unemployed and destitute than accept it. But he did not even try to make that clear to Robinson, particularly as Robinson's mind was now completely obsessed by the hope of shifting his burdens on to Karl's shoulders.

"To begin with," said Robinson, accompanying the words with a reassuring wave of the hand,—his elbows were planted on the railings,—"I'll explain everything and show you all the things we have. You've had a good education and I'm sure your handwriting's excellent, so you could make an inventory straightaway of all our stuff. Brunelda has been wanting that done for a long time. If the weather's good tomorrow morning we'll ask Brunelda to sit out on the balcony, and we can work quietly in the room without disturbing her. For that must be your first consideration, Rossmann. Brunelda mustn't be disturbed. Her hearing's very keen; it's probably because she's a singer that her ears are so sensitive. For instance, say that you're rolling out a keg of brandy which usually stands behind the trunks, it makes a noise because it's heavy and all sorts of things are lying about on the floor, so that you can't roll it straight out. Brunelda, let us say, is lying quietly on the couch catching flies, which are a great torment to her. You think she's paying no attention to you, and you go on rolling the keg. She's still lying there quite peacefully. But all at once, just when you're least expecting it and when you're making least noise, she suddenly sits up, bangs with both hands on the couch so that you can't see her for dust—since we came here I have never beaten the dust out of the couch; I really couldn't, she's always lying on it—and begins to yell ferociously, like a man, and goes on yelling for hours. The neighbours have forbidden her to sing, but no one can forbid her to yell; she has to yell; though that doesn't happen often now, for Delamarche and I have grown careful. It was very bad for her, too. Once she fainted,—Delamarche was away at the time—and I had to fetch the student from next door, who sprinkled some fluid over her out of a big bottle; it did her good, too, but the fluid had an awful smell; even now you can smell it if you put your nose to the couch. That student is certainly an enemy of ours, like everybody here; you must be on your guard too and have nothing to do with any of them."

"But I say, Robinson," remarked Karl, "this is a heavy programme. A fine job this that you've recommended me for."

"Don't you worry," said Robinson, shutting his eyes and shaking his head, as if shaking off all Karl's possible worries. "This job has advantages that you wouldn't find in any other. You're always in close attendance on a lady like Brunelda; you sometimes sleep in the same room as she does, and, as you can imagine, there's lots of enjoyment to be got out of that. You'll be well paid, there's plenty of money about; I got no wages, being a friend of Delamarche, though every time I went out Brunelda always gave me something, but you of course will be paid like any other servant. That's what you are, after all. But the most important thing is that I'll be able to make your job much easier for you. Of course I won't do anything just at first, to give myself a chance of getting better, but as soon as I'm even a little better you can count on me. In any case, I'll do all the waiting on Brunelda, doing her hair, for example, and helping her to dress, so far as Delamarche doesn't attend to that. You'll only have to concern yourself with clean-ing the room, getting in what we need, and doing the heavy housework."

"No, Robinson," said Karl, "all this doesn't tempt me."

"Don't be a fool, Rossmann," said Robinson, putting his face quite close to Karl's, "don't throw away this splendid chance. Where will you get another job so quickly? Who knows you? What people do you know? The two of us, both full-grown men with plenty of practical skill and experience, wandered about for weeks without finding work. It isn't easy; in fact it's damned difficult."

Karl nodded, marvelling that Robinson could talk so reason-ably. Still, all this advice was beside the point so far as he was concerned; he couldn't stay here; there must be some place for him in the great city; the whole night, he knew, all the hotels were filled to bursting and the guests needed service, and he had had some training in that. He would slip quickly and unobtrusively into some job or other. Just across the street there was a small restaurant on the ground floor, from which came a rush of music. The main entrance was covered only with a big yellow curtain, which billowed out into the street now and then, as a draught of air caught it. Otherwise things were much quieter up and down the street. Most of the balconies were dark; only far in the distance a single light was twinkling here and there; but almost as soon as one fixed one's eye upon it the people beside it got up and thronged back into the house, while the last man left outside put his hand to the lamp and switched it off after a brief glance at the street.

"It's nightfall already," said Karl to himself, "if I stay here any longer I'll become one of them." He turned round to pull aside the curtain of the balcony door. "What are you doing?" said Robinson, planting himself between Karl and the curtain.

"I'm leaving," said Karl. "Let me go! Let me go!"

"But surely you're not going to disturb her," cried Robinson, "what are you thinking of!" And he threw his arms round Karl's neck, clinging to him with all his weight, and twisting his legs round Karl's legs, so that in a trice he had him down on the floor. But among the lift-boys Karl had learned a little fighting, and so he drove his fist against Robinson's chin, not putting out his whole strength, to avoid hurting him. Quickly and without any scruple Robinson punched him in the belly with his knee before beginning to nurse his chin in both hands, and let out such a howl that a man on the next balcony clapped his hands furiously and shouted: "Silence!" Karl lay still for a little so as to recover from the pain of Robinson's foul blow. He turned only his head to watch the curtain hanging still and heavy before the room, which was obviously in darkness. It looked as if no one were in the room now; perhaps Delamarche had gone out with Brunelda and the way was perfectly free. For Robinson, who was behaving exactly like a watchdog, had been finally shaken off.

Then from the far end of the street there came in fitful blasts the sound of drums and trumpets. The single shouts of individuals in a crowd soon blended into a general roar. Karl turned his head again and saw that all the balconies were once more coming to life. Slowly he got up; he could not stand quite straight and had to lean heavily against the railing. Down on the pavement young lads were striding along, waving their caps at the full stretch of their arms and looking back over their shoulders. The middle of the road was still vacant. Some were flourishing tall poles with lanterns on the end of them enveloped in a yellowish smoke. The drummers and the trumpeters, arrayed in broad ranks, were just emerging into the light in such numbers that Karl was amazed, when he heard voices behind him, turned round and saw Delamarche lifting the heavy curtain and Brunelda stepping out of the darkness of the room, in the red gown, with a lace scarf round her shoulders and a dark hood over her hair, which was presumably still undressed and only hastily gathered up, for loose ends straggled here and there. In her hand she held a little fan, which she had opened but did not use, keeping it pressed closed to her.

Karl moved sideways along the railing, to make space for the two of them. No one, surely, would force him to stay here, and even if Delamarche tried it Brunelda would let him go at once if he were to ask her. After all, she couldn't stand him; his eyes terrified her. Yet as he took a step towards the door she noticed it and asked: "Where are you going, boy?" Delamarche's severe eye held Karl an instant and Brunelda drew him to her. "Don't you want to see the procession down there?" she said, pushing him before her to the railing. "Do you know what it's about?" Karl heard her asking behind him, and he flinched in an involuntary but unsuccessful attempt to escape from the pressure of her body. He gazed down sadly at the street, as if the cause of his sadness lay there.

For a while Delamarche stood with crossed arms behind Brunelda; then he ran into the room and brought her the opera glasses. Down below the main body of the procession had now come into sight behind the band. On the shoulders of a gigantic man sat a gentleman of whom nothing could be seen at this height save the faint gleam of a bald crown, over which he was holding a top-hat upraised in perpetual greeting. Round about him great wooden placards were being carried which, seen from the balcony, looked blankly white; they were obviously intended to make a sloping rampart round the prominent central figure, against which they were literally leaning.

But since the bearers were moving on all the time, the wall of placards kept falling into disrepair and seeking to repair itself again. Beyond the ring of placards, so far as one could judge in the darkness, the whole breadth of the street, although only a trifling part of its length, was filled with the gentleman's supporters, who clapped their hands in rhythm and kept proclaiming in a chanting cadence what seemed to be the gentleman's name, a quite short but incomprehensible name. Single supporters adroitly distributed among the crowd were carrying motor-car lamps of enormous power, which they slowly shone up and down the houses on both sides of the street. At the height where Karl was the light was not unbearable, but on the lower balconies he could see people hastily putting their hands over their eyes whenever it flashed in their faces.

At Brunelda's request Delamarche enquired of the people on the next balcony what the meaning of the demonstration was. Karl was somewhat curious to note whether and how they would answer him. And actually Delamarche was forced to repeat his question three times before he received an answer. He was already bending threateningly over the railing and Brunelda had begun to tap with one foot in exasperation at her neighbours, for Karl could feel her knee moving. Finally some sort of answer was given, but simultaneously everyone on the next balcony, which was packed with people, burst out into loud laughter. At that Delamarche yelled a retort so loudly that, if the whole street had not been filled with noise for the moment, all the people round about must have pricked up their ears in astonishment. In any case it had the effect of making the laughter cease with unnatural abruptness.

"A judge is being elected in our district tomorrow, and the man they are chairing down there is one of the candidates," said Delamarche quite calmly, returning to Brunelda. "Oh!" he went on, caressing Brunelda's shoulder, "we've lost all idea of what's happening in the world."

"Delamarche," said Brunelda, reverting to the behaviour of her neighbours, "how thankful I would be to move out of here, if it wasn't such an effort. But unfortunately I can't face it." And sighing deeply she kept plucking restlessly and distractedly at Karl's shirt; as unobtrusively as he could he kept pushing away her plump little hand again and again, which was an easy matter, for Brunelda was not thinking of him; she was occupied with quite other thoughts.

But Karl soon forgot her and suffered the weight of her arms on his shoulders, for the proceedings in the street took up all his attention. At the command of small groups of gesticulating men, who marched just in front of the candidate and whose consultations must have had a particular importance, for one could see attentive faces turned to them from all sides, a halt was abruptly called before the little restaurant. A member of this authoritative group made a signal with his upraised hand which seemed to apply to the crowd and to the candidate as well. The crowd fell silent and the candidate, who tried several times to stand upright and several times fell back again on the shoulders of his bearer, made a short speech, waving his tophat to and fro at lightning speed. He could be seen quite clearly, for during his speech all the motor-car lamps were directed upon him, so that he found himself in the centre of a bright star of light.

Now, too, one could realise the interest which the whole street took in the occurrence. On the balconies where supporters of the candidate were packed, the people joined in chanting his name, stretching their hands far over the railings and clapping with machine-like regularity. On the opposition balconies, which were actually in the majority, a howl of retaliation arose which, however, did not achieve a unified effect, as it came from rival supporters of various candidates. However, all the enemies of the present candidate united in a general cat-calling, and even many of the gramophones were set going again. Between the separate balconies political disputes were being fought out with a violence intensified by the late hour. Most of the people were already in their night clothes, with overcoats flung over them; the women were enveloped in great dark wraps; the children, with nobody to attend to them, climbed dangerously about the railings of the balcony and came swarming more and more out of the dark rooms in which they had been sleeping. Here and there unrecognisable objects were being flung by particularly heated partisans in the direction of their enemies; sometimes they reached their mark, but most of them fell down into the street, where they provoked yells of rage. When the noise became too much for the leading man in the procession, the drummers and trumpeters received orders to intervene, and their blaring, long-drawn-out flourish, executed with all the force of which they were capable, drowned every human voice up to the very housetops. And then quite suddenly—almost before one realised it—they would stop, whereupon the crowd in the street, obviously trained for this purpose, at once launched their party song into the momentary general silence—one could see all their mouths wide open in the light of the motor-car lamps—until their opponents, coming to their senses again, yelled ten times as loudly as before from all the balconies and windows, and the party below, after their brief victory, were reduced to complete silence, at least for anyone standing at this height.

"How do you like it, boy?" asked Brunelda, who kept turning and twisting close behind Karl, so as to see as much as possible through her glasses. Karl merely answered with a nod of the head. He noticed out of the corner of his eye that Robinson was busily talking away to Delamarche, obviously about Karl's intentions, but that Delamarche seemed to attach no importance to what he said, for with his right arm round Brunelda he kept pushing Robinson aside with his left. "Wouldn't you like to look through the glasses?" asked Brunelda, tapping Karl on the chest to show that she meant him. "I can see well enough," said Karl.

"Do try," she said, "you'll see much better."

"I have good eyes," replied Karl, "I can see everything." He did not feel it as a kindness but as a nuisance when she put the glasses before his eyes, with the mere words "Here, you!" uttered melodiously enough but threateningly. And now the glasses were before Karl's eyes and he could see nothing at all.

"I can't see anything," he said, trying to get away from the glasses, but she held them firmly, and his head, which was pressed against her breast, he could move neither backwards nor sideways.

"But you can see now," she said, turning the screw.

"No, I still can't see anything," said Karl, and he thought that in spite of himself he had relieved Robinson of his duties after all, for Brunelda's insupportable whims were now being wreaked on him.

"When on earth are you going to see?" she said and turned the screw again; Karl's whole face was now exposed to her heavy breath. "Now?" she asked.

"No, no, no!" cried Karl, although he could actually distinguish everything now, though very vaguely. But at that moment Brunelda thought of something to say to Delamarche; she held the glasses loosely before Karl's face, and without her noticing it he could peep under the glasses at the street. After

252

that she no longer insisted on having her way and used the glasses for her own pleasure.

From the restaurant below a waiter had emerged and dashing in and out of the door took orders from the leaders. One could see him standing on his toes so as to overlook the interior of the establishment and summon as many of the staff as possible. During these preparations for what was obviously a round of free drinks, the candidate never stopped speaking. The man who was carrying him, the giant specially reserved for him, kept turning round a little after every few sentences, so that the address might reach all sections of the crowd. The candidate maintained a crouching posture most of the time, and tried with backward sweeps of his free hand and of the top-hat in the other to give special emphasis to his words. But every now and then, at almost regular intervals, the flow of his eloquence proved too much for him; he rose to his full height with outstretched arms, he was no longer addressing a group but the whole multitude; he spoke to all the people in the houses up to the very top floors, and yet it was perfectly clear that no one could hear him even in the lowest storeys; indeed, even if they could, nobody would have wanted to hear him, for every window and every balcony was occupied by at least one spouting orator. Meanwhile several waiters were carrying out of the restaurant a table covered with brimming, winking glasses, about the size of a billiard-table. The leaders organised the distribution of the drinks, which was achieved in the form of a march past the restaurant. But although the glasses on the table were always filled again, there were not enough for the mob of people, and two relays of bar-men had to keep slipping through the crowd on both sides of the table to supply further needs. The candidate had, of course, stopped speaking and was employing the pause in refreshing his energies. His bearer carried him slowly backwards and forwards, somewhat apart from the crowd and the harsh light, and only a few of his closest supporters accompanied him and threw remarks up to him.

"Look at the boy," said Brunelda, "he's so busy staring that he's quite forgotten where he is." And she took Karl by surprise, turning his face towards her with both hands, so that she was gazing into his eyes. But it lasted only a minute, for Karl shook her hands off at once and, annoyed that they would not leave him in peace and also eager to go down to the street and see everything close at hand, tried with all his might to free himself from Brunelda's grip and said:

"Please, let me go away."

"You'll stay with us," said Delamarche, without turning his eyes from the street, merely stretching out his hand to prevent Karl from going.

"Leave him alone," said Brunelda, pushing away Delamarche's hand, "he'll stay all right." And she squeezed Karl still more firmly against the railing, so that he would have had to struggle with her to get away from her. And even if he were to free himself, what could he gain by that! Delamarche was standing on his left, Robinson had now moved across to his right; he was literally a prisoner.

"Count yourself lucky that you're not thrown out," said Robinson, tapping Karl with the hand he had hooked through Brunelda's arm.

"Thrown out?" said Delamarche. "You don't throw out a runaway thief; you hand him over to the police. And that might happen to him the very first thing tomorrow morning if he doesn't keep quiet."

From that moment Karl had no further pleasure in the spectacle below. Simply because he could not help it, being crushed against Brunelda and unable to straighten himself, he leaned forward a little over the railing. Full of his own trouble, he gazed absently at the people below, who marched up to the table before the restaurant in squads of about twenty men, seized the glasses, turned round and waved them in the direction of the recuperating candidate, shouted a party slogan, emptied the glasses and set them down on the table again with what must have been a great clatter that was, however, inaudible at this height, in order to make room for the next noisy and impatient squad. On the instructions of the party leaders the brass band which had been playing in the restaurant came out into the street; their great wind instruments glittered against the dark crowd, but the music was almost lost in the general din. The street was now, at least on the side where the restaurant stood, packed far and wide with human beings. From up the hill, the direction from which Karl's taxi had arrived that morning, they came streaming down; from as far as the low-lying bridge they came rushing up; and even the people in the adjoining houses could not resist the temptation to take personal part in this affair; on the balconies and at the windows there was hardly anyone left but women and children, while the men came pouring out of the house-doors down below. By now the music and the free drinks had achieved their aim; the assembly was great enough at last; one of the leaders, flanked on either side by head-lamps, signalled the band to stop playing and gave a loud whistle, and at once the man carrying the candidate hastily turned back and could be seen approaching through a path opened for him by supporters.

The candidate had barely reached the restaurant door when he began a new speech in the blaze of the head-lamps which were now concentrated upon him in a narrow ring. But conditions were much less comfortable than before. His gigantic bearer had now no initiative at all in movement, for the crowd was too dense. His chief supporters, who had previously done their best in all kinds of ways to enhance the effect of his words, now had the greatest difficulty in keeping near him, and only about twenty of them managed to retain their footing beside the bearer. Even he, strong giant as he was, could not take a step of his own free will, and it was out of the question to think of influencing the crowd by turning to face this section or that, by making dramatic advances or retreats. The mob was flowing backwards and forwards without plan, each man propelled by his neighbour, not one braced on his own feet; the opposition party seemed to have gained a lot of new recruits; the bearer, after stemming the tide for a while outside the restaurant door, was now letting himself be swept up and down the street, apparently without resistance; the candidate still kept on uttering words, but it was no longer clear whether he was outlining his programme or shouting for help; and unless Karl were mistaken a rival candidate had made his appearance, or rather several rivals, for here and there, when a light suddenly flared up, some figure could be seen, high on the shoulders of the crowd, orating with white face and clenched fists to an accompaniment of massed cheering.

"What on earth is happening down there?" asked Karl, turning in breathless bewilderment to his warders.

"How it excites the boy," said Brunelda to Delamarche, taking hold of Karl's chin so as to turn his face towards her. But that was something Karl did not desire, and made quite reckless by the events down in the street he gave himself such a jerk that Brunelda not only let him go but recoiled and left him quite to himself. "You have seen enough now," she said, obviously angered by Karl's behaviour, "go into the room, make the bed and get everything ready for the night." She

pointed towards the room. That was the very direction Karl
had wanted to take for hours past, and he made no objection at
all. Then from the street came a loud crash of breaking glass.
Karl could not restrain himself and took a flying leap to the
railing for a last hasty look down. The opposition had brought
off a grand coup, perhaps a decisive one; the car head-lamps of
the candidate's party, which had thrown a powerful light on at
least the central figures and afforded a measure of publicity
which controlled the proceedings up to a point, had all been
simultaneously smashed and the candidate and his bearer were
now received into the embrace of the general uncertain street
lighting, which in its sudden diffusion had the effect of complete darkness. No one could have guessed even approxi-
mately the candidate's whereabouts, and the illusoriness of the
darkness was still more enhanced by a loud swelling chorus in
unison which suddenly broke out from the direction of the
bridge and was coming nearer.

"Haven't I told you what to do?" said Brunelda. "Hurry up.
I'm tired," she added, stretching her arms above her so that her
bosom arched out even more than before. Delamarche, whose
arm was still round her, drew her into a corner of the balcony.
Robinson followed them to push out of the way the remains of
his supper, which were still lying there.

Such a favourable opportunity was not to be let slip; this was
no time for Karl to look down at the street; he would see
enough of what was happening there once he was down below,
much better than from up here. In two bounds he was through
the room with its dim red lighting, but the door was locked
and the key taken away. It must be found at once; yet who
could expect to find a key in this disorder and above all in the
little space of precious time which Karl had at his disposal.
Actually he should be on the stairs by now, running and run-

ning. Instead of which he was hunting for a key! He looked in all the drawers that would open, rummaged about on the table, where various dishes, table napkins and pieces of half-begun embroidery were lying about, was allured next by an easy chair on which lay an inextricable heap of old clothes where the key might possibly be hidden but could never be found, and flung himself finally on the couch, which was indeed evil-smelling, so as to feel in all its nooks and corners for the key. Then he stopped looking and came to a halt in the middle of the room. Brunelda was certain to have the key fastened to her belt, he told himself; so many things hung there; all searching was in vain.

And blindly Karl seized two knives and thrust them between the wings of the door, one above and one below, so as to get the greatest purchase on it from two separate points. But scarcely did he brace himself against the knives when the blades of course broke off. He wished for nothing better; the stumps, with which he could now get closer in, would hold the more firmly. And now he wrenched at them with all his strength, his arms far outstretched, his legs wide apart, panting and yet carefully watching the door at the same time. It could not resist for much longer; he realised that with joy from the audible loosening of the lock; but the more slowly he went the better; the lock mustn't burst open, or else they would hear it on the balcony; it must loosen itself quite gradually; and he worked with great caution to bring this about, putting his face closer and closer to the lock.

"Just look at this," he heard the voice of Delamarche. All three of them were standing in the room; the curtain was already drawn behind them; Karl could not have heard them entering; and at the sight of them he let go the knives. But he was given no time to utter a word of explanation or excuse, for in a fit of rage far greater than the occasion merited Delamarche leapt at him, the loose cord of his dressing-gown describing a long figure in the air. At the very last moment Karl evaded his attack; he could have pulled the knives from the door and defended himself with them, but he did not do so; instead, ducking down and then springing up, he seized the broad collar of Delamarche's dressing-gown, jerked it upwards, then pulled it still farther over—the dressing-gown was far too big for Delamarche—and now by good luck had a hold on the head of Delamarche, who, taken completely by surprise, pawed wildly with his hands at first and only after a moment or two began to beat Karl on the back with his fists, but with less than his full strength, while Karl, to protect his face, flung himself against Delamarche's chest. Karl endured the blows, though they made him twist with pain and kept increasing in violence, for it was easy to bear them when he thought he saw victory before him. With his hands round Delamarche's head, the thumbs just over the eyes, he pushed him towards the part of the room where the furniture stood thickest and at the same time with the toe of his shoe tried to twist the cord of the dressing-gown round Delamarche's legs to trip him up.

But since he had to bend all his attention on Delamarche, whose resistance he could feel growing more and more and whose sinewy body was bracing itself with greater enmity against him, he actually forgot that he was not alone in the room with Delamarche. Only too soon the reminder came, for suddenly his feet flew from under him, being wrenched apart by Robinson, who was lying shrieking behind him on the floor. Panting, Karl let go his hold of Delamarche, who recoiled a little. Brunelda, her legs straddling, her knees bent, a bulky figure in the middle of the room, was following the fight with glittering eyes. As if she herself were taking part in it she was breathing deeply, screwing up her eyes and slowly advancing her fists. Delamarche flung back the collar of his dressing-gown and now had the use of his eyes; of course, it was no longer a fight but simply a punishment. He seized Karl by the shirt-front, lifted him nearly off the floor and without even looking at him in his contempt flung him so violently against a chest standing a few steps away that at first Karl thought the searing pains in his back and head caused by the collision were the direct result of Delamarche's handling. "You scoundrel!" he could hear Delamarche shouting in the darkness that rose before his wavering eyes. And as he sank down fainting beside the chest the words "You just wait!" still rang dimly in his ears.

When he came to his senses everything was dark around him; it seemed to be late in the night; from the balcony a faint glimmer of moonlight came into the room beneath the curtain. He could hear the regular breathing of the three sleepers; by far the loudest noise came from Brunelda, who snorted in her sleep as she sometimes did in talking; yet it was not easy to make out where the different sleepers were lying, for the whole room was filled with the sound of their breathing. Not until he had examined his surroundings for a little while did Karl think of himself, and then he was struck with alarm, for though he was quite cramped and stiff with pain he had not imagined that he could have been severely wounded to the effusion of blood. Yet now he felt a weight on his head, and his whole face, his neck, and his breast under the shirt were wet as if with blood. He must get into the light to find out exactly what condition he was in; perhaps they had crippled him, in which case Delamarche would be glad enough to let him go; but what could he hope to do if that were so; there would be no prospects for him at all. The lad with the nose half-eaten away occurred to him, and for a moment he buried his face in his hands.

Then involuntarily he turned towards the outside-door and groped his way towards it on all fours. Presently he felt a shoe and then a leg under his finger-tips. That must be Robinson; who else would sleep in his shoes? They must have ordered him to lie across the door so as to keep Karl from escaping. But didn't they know, then, the condition that Karl was in? For the moment he was not thinking of escape; he merely wanted to reach the light. So, as he couldn't get out by the door, he must make for the balcony.

He found the dining-table in a quite different place from the evening before; the couch, which he approached very cautiously, was to his surprise vacant; but in the middle of the room he came upon a high though closely compressed pile of clothes, blankets, curtains, cushions and carpets. At first he thought it was only a small pile, like the one he had found at the end of the couch the previous evening, and that it had merely happened to fall on the floor; but to his astonishment he discovered on creeping farther that a whole van-load of such things was lying there, which, presumably for use in the night, must have been taken out of the trunks where they were kept during the day. He crept right round the pile and soon realised that the whole formed a sort of bed, on top of which, as he discovered by feeling cautiously, Delamarche and Brunelda were sleeping.

So now he knew where they all were and made haste to reach the balcony. It was quite a different world on the other side of the curtain, and he quickly rose to his feet. In the fresh night air he walked up and down the balcony a few times in the full radiance of the moon. He looked down at the street; it was quite still; music was still issuing from the restaurant, but more subdued now; a man was sweeping the pavement before the door; in the street where only a few hours ago the tumult had been so great that the shouting of an electoral candidate could not be distinguished among a thousand other voices, the scratching of the broom on the flagstones could be distinctly heard.

The scraping of table-legs on the next balcony made Karl aware that someone was sitting there reading. It was a young man with a little pointed beard, which he kept continually twisting as he read, his lips moving rapidly at the same time. He was facing Karl, sitting at a little table covered with books; he had taken the electric lamp from the parapet and shored it between two big volumes, so that he sat in a flood of garish light.

"Good evening," said Karl, for he thought he noticed the young man glancing at him.

But that must have been an error, for the young man, apparently quite unaware of him, put his hand to his eyes to shield them from the light and make out who had suddenly spoken to him, and then, still unable to see anything, held up the electric lamp so as to throw some light on the next balcony.

"Good evening," he said then in return, with a brief, penetrating look, adding: "And what do you want?"

"Am I disturbing you?" asked Karl.

"Of course, of course," said the man, returning the lamp again to its former place.

These words certainly discouraged any attempt at intercourse, but all the same Karl did not quit the corner of the balcony nearest to the man. Silently he watched him reading his book, turning the pages, now and then looking up something in another book, which he always snatched up at lightning speed, and frequently making notes in a jotter, which he did with his face surprisingly close to the paper.

Could this man be a student? It certainly looked as if he were. Not very unlike this—a long time ago now—Karl had sat at home at his parents' table writing out his school tasks, while his father read the newspaper or did book-keeping and correspondence for a society to which he belonged, and his mother was busy sewing, drawing the thread high out of the stuff in her hand. To avoid disturbing his father, Karl used to lay only the exercise book and his writing materials on the table, while he arranged his reference books on chairs to right and left of him. How quiet it had been there! How seldom strangers had visited their home! Even as a small child Karl had always been glad to see his mother turning the key in the outside door of an evening. She had no idea that he had come to such a pass as to try breaking open strange doors with knives.

And what had been the point of all his studying? He had forgotten everything; if he had been given the chance of continuing his studies here, he would have found it a very hard task. Once, he remembered, he had been ill for a whole month at home; what an effort it had cost him afterwards to get used to his interrupted studies again. And now, except for the handbook of English commercial correspondence, he had not read a book for ever so long.

"I say, young man," Karl found himself suddenly addressed, "couldn't you stand somewhere else? You disturb me frightfully, staring at me like that. After two o'clock in the morning one can surely expect to be allowed to work in peace on a balcony. Do you want anything from me?"

"Are you studying?" asked Karl.

"Yes, yes," said the man, taking advantage of his wasted moment to bring new order among his books.

"Then I won't disturb you," said Karl, "I'm going indoors again, in any case. Good night."

The man did not even answer; with abrupt resolution he had returned to his book again after dealing with the disturbance, his head leaning heavily on his right hand.

But just before he reached the curtain Karl remembered why he had actually come out; he did not even know how much he had been hurt. What could it be that was lying so heavy on his head? He put his hand up and stared in astonishment. There was no blood-stained wound such as he had feared in the darkness of the room, but only a turban-like bandage which was still rather wet. To judge from little frills of lace hanging from it here and there, it had been torn from an old chemise of Brunelda's, and Robinson must have wrapped it hurriedly round his head. But he had forgotten to wring it out, and so while Karl was unconscious the water had dripped down his face and under his shirt, and that was what had given him such a shock.

"Are you still there?" asked the man, peering across.

"I'm really going now," said Karl, "I only wanted to look at something; it's quite dark indoors."

"But who are you?" said the man, laying his pen on the open book before him and advancing to the railing. "What's your name? How do you come to be with these people? Have you been long here? What did you want to look at? Turn on the electric light there, won't you, so that I can see you."

Karl obeyed, but before answering he drew the curtain more closely to keep those inside from noticing anything. "Excuse me," he said in a whisper, "for not raising my voice more. If they were to hear me there would be another row."

"Another?" asked the man.

"Yes," said Karl, "I had a terrible row with them this very

evening. I must still have a pretty bad bump on my head."
And he felt the back of his head.

"What was the trouble?" asked the man, and as Karl did
not at once reply, he added: "You can safely tell me anything
you have against these people. For I hate all three of them, and
the Madam in particular. Besides, I'd be surprised to find that
they hadn't put you against me already. My name is Joseph
Mendel and I am a student."

"Well," said Karl, "they've told me about you already, but
nothing bad. You doctored Brunelda once, didn't you?"

"That's right," said the student, laughing. "Does the couch
still stink of it?"

"Oh yes," said Karl.

"I'm glad of that, anyway," said the student, passing his
fingers through his hair. "And why do they give you bumps
on the head?"

"We had a quarrel," said Karl, wondering how he was to
explain it to the student. Then he checked himself and asked:
"But am I not disturbing you?"

"In the first place," said the student, "you have already disturbed me, and I am unluckily so nervous that I need a long
time to get into my stride again. Ever since you began to walk
about your balcony I haven't been able to get on with my
studies. And then in the second place I always have a breather
about three o'clock. So you needn't have any scruples about
telling me. Besides, I'm interested."

"It's quite simple," said Karl, "Delamarche wants me to be
his servant. But I don't want to. I should have liked to leave
this very night. He wouldn't let me go, and he locked the
door; I tried to break it open and then there was a row. I'm
unlucky to be still here."

"Why, have you got another job?" asked the student.

"No," said Karl, "but that doesn't worry me in the least if I could only get away from here."

"What," said the student, "it doesn't worry you in the least, doesn't it?" And both of them were silent for a moment. "Why don't you want to stay with these people?" the student asked at last.

"Delamarche is a bad man," said Karl, "I've encountered him before. I tramped for a whole day with him once and I was glad to be out of his company. And am I to be his servant now?"

"If all servants were as fastidious in their choice of masters as you are!" said the student, and he seemed to be smiling. "Look here, during the day I'm a salesman, a miserable counter-jumper, not much more than an errand-boy, in Montly's big store. This Montly is certainly a scoundrel, but that leaves me quite cold; what makes me furious is simply that the pay is wretched. Let that be an example to you."

"What?" said Karl. "You are a salesman all day and you study all night?"

"Yes," said the student, "there's nothing else to be done. I've tried everything possible, but this is the best way. For years I did nothing but study, day and night, and I almost didn't dare attend lectures in the clothes I had to wear. But that's all behind me now."

"But when do you sleep?" asked Karl, looking at the student in wonder.

"Oh, sleep!" said the student. "I'll get some sleep when I'm finished with my studies. I keep myself going on black coffee." And he turned round, drew a big bottle from under the table, poured black coffee from it into a little cup and tossed it down his throat as if it were medicine which he wanted to get quickly over to avoid the taste.

"A fine thing, black coffee," said the student. "It's a pity you're too far away for me to reach you some."

"I don't like black coffee," said Karl.

"I don't either," said the student, laughing. "But what could I do without it? If it weren't for black coffee Montly wouldn't keep me for a minute. I say Montly although of course he's not even aware of my existence. I simply don't know how I would get on in the shop if I didn't have a big bottle like this under the counter, for I've never dared to risk stopping the coffee-drinking; but you can believe me that if I did I would roll down behind the counter in a dead sleep. Unfortunately the others have tumbled to that, they call me 'Black Coffee,' a silly witticism which I'm sure has damaged my career already."

"And when will you be finished with your studies?" asked Karl.

"I'm getting on slowly," said the student, with drooping head. He left the railing and sat down again at the table; planting his elbows on the open book and passing his fingers through his hair, he said then: "It might take me another year or two."

"I wanted to study too," said Karl, as if that gave him a claim to be on a more confidential footing than the student, now fallen silent, had seen fit to grant.

"Indeed?" said the student, and it was not quite clear whether he was reading his book again or merely staring absently at it. "You can be glad that you've given up studying. I've studied for years now simply for the sake of mere consistency. I get very little satisfaction out of it and even less hope for the future. What prospects could I have? America is full of quack doctors."

"I wanted to be an engineer," put in Karl quickly, as the student seemed to be losing all interest.

"And now you're supposed to be a servant to these people," said the student, glancing up for a moment, "that annoys you, of course."

This conclusion sprang from a misunderstanding, but Karl felt that he might turn it to his advantage. So he asked: "Perhaps I could get a job in the store too?"

This question detached the student completely from his book, but the idea that he might be of some help to Karl in applying for such a post did not enter his mind at all. "You try it," he said, "or rather, don't you try it. Getting a job at Montly's is the biggest success I've ever scored. If I had to give up either my studies or my job, of course I'd give up my studies; I spend all my energy trying to keep off the horns of that dilemma."

"So it's as hard as that to get a job in Montly's," said Karl more to himself than to the student.

"Why, what do you think?" said the student. "It's easier to be appointed district judge here than a door-opener at Montly's."

Karl fell silent. This student, who was so much more experienced than he was and who hated Delamarche for some unknown reason and who certainly felt no ill-will towards himself, could not give him a single word of encouragement to leave Delamarche. And yet he didn't know anything about the danger threatening Karl from the police, which only Delamarche could shield him from at the moment.

"You saw the demonstration down there this evening, didn't you? Anyone who didn't know the ropes could easily imagine, couldn't he, that the candidate, Lobter is his name, would have some prospect of getting in or at least of being considered?"

"I know nothing about politics," said Karl.

"That's a mistake," said the student. "But you have eyes

and ears in your head, haven't you? The man obviously has friends and opponents; that surely can't have escaped you. Well, in my opinion the fellow hasn't the slightest prospect of being returned. I happen to know all about him; there's a man staying here who's an acquaintance of his. He's not without ability, and as far as his political views and his political past are concerned, he would actually be the most suitable judge for the district. But no one even imagines that he can get in; he'll come as big a cropper as anyone can; he'll have chucked away his dollars on the election campaign and that will be all."

Karl and the student gazed at each other for a little while in silence. The student nodded smilingly and pressed his hand against his weary eyes.

"Well, aren't you going to bed yet?" he asked. "I must start on my reading again. Look, how much I have still to do." And he fluttered over half the pages of the book, to give Karl an idea of the work that still awaited him.

"Well then, good night," said Karl, with a bow.

"Come over and see us sometime," said the student, who had sat down at the table again, "of course, only if you would like to. You'll always find lots of company here. And I can always have time for you from nine till ten in the evening."

"So you advise me to stay with Delamarche?" asked Karl.

"Absolutely," said the student, whose head was already bent over his book. It was as if not he but someone else had said the word; it echoed in Karl's ears as if it had been uttered by a voice more hollow than the student's. Slowly he went up to the curtain, glanced once more at the student, who now sat quite motionless in his ring of light, surrounded by the vast darkness, and slipped into the room. The united breathing of the three sleepers received him. He felt his way along the wall to the couch, and when he found it calmly stretched himself out on it as if it were his familiar bed. Since the student, who knew all about Delamarche and the queer circumstances, and who was moreover an educated man, had advised him to stay here, he had no qualms for the time being. He did not have such high aims as the student; perhaps even at home he would never have succeeded in carrying his studies to their conclusion; and if it were difficult to do that at home, no one could expect him to manage it here in a strange land. But his prospects of finding a post in which he could achieve something, and be appreciated for his achievement, would be greater if he accepted the servant's place with Delamarche for the time being and from that secure position watched for a favourable opportunity. In this very street there appeared to be many offices of middling or inferior status, which in case of need might not be too fastidious in picking their staff. He would be glad to take on a porter's job, if necessary, but after all it was not utterly impossible that he might be taken on simply for office work, and in the future might sit at his own desk as a regular clerk, gazing occasionally out of the open window with a light heart, like the clerk whom he had seen that morning on his expedition through the courtyards. As he shut his eyes he was comforted by the reflection that he was still young and that some day or other he was bound to get away from Delamarche; this household certainly did not look as if it were established for all eternity. Once he got such a post in an office, he would concentrate his mind on his office work; he would not disperse his energies like the student. If it should be necessary, he would devote his nights as well as his days to his office work, which at the start might be actually expected of him, considering his meagre knowledge of business matters. He would think only of the interests of the firm he had to serve, and undertake any work that offered, even work which the other clerks rejected as beneath them. Good intentions thronged into his head, as if his future employer were standing before the couch and could read them from his face.

On such thoughts Karl fell asleep, and only in his first light slumber was disturbed by a deep sigh from Brunelda, who was apparently troubled by bad dreams and twisted and turned on her bed.

VIII THE NATURE THEATRE OF OKLAHOMA

A͟T a street corner Karl saw a placard with the following announcement: The Oklahoma Theatre will engage members
for its company today at Clayton race-course from six o'clock
in the morning until midnight. The great Theatre of Oklahoma calls you! Today only and never again! If you miss your
chance now you miss it for ever! If you think of your future
you are one of us! Everyone is welcome! If you want to be an
artist, join our company! Our Theatre can find employment
for everyone, a place for everyone! If you decide on an engagement we congratulate you here and now! But hurry, so that
you get in before midnight! At twelve o'clock the doors will be
shut and never opened again! Down with all those who do not
believe in us! Up, and to Clayton!

A great many people were certainly standing before the
placard, but it did not seem to find much approval. There were
so many placards; nobody believed in them any longer. And
this placard was still more improbable than usual. Above all,
it failed in an essential particular, it did not mention payment.
If the payment were worth mentioning at all, the placard
would certainly have mentioned it; that most attractive of all
arguments would not have been forgotten. No one wanted
to be an artist, but every man wanted to be paid for his labours.

Yet for Karl there was one great attraction in the placard.

"Everyone is welcome," it said. Everyone, that meant Karl too. All that he had done till now was ignored; it was not going to be made a reproach to him. He was entitled to apply for a job of which he need not be ashamed, which, on the contrary, was a matter of public advertisement. And just as public was the promise that he too would find acceptance. He asked for nothing better; he wanted to find some way of at least beginning a decent life, and perhaps this was his chance. Even if all the extravagant statements in the placard were a lie, even if the great Theatre of Oklahoma were an insignificant travelling circus, it wanted to engage people, and that was enough. Karl did not read the whole placard over again, but once more singled out the sentence: "Everyone is welcome." At first he thought of going to Clayton on foot; yet that would mean three hours of hard walking, and in all possibility he might arrive just in time to hear that every available vacancy had been filled. The placard certainly suggested that there were no limits to the number of people who could be engaged, but all advertisements of that kind were worded like that. Karl saw that he must either give it up or else go by train. He counted over his money, which would last him for eight days yet if he did not take this railway journey; he slid the little coins backwards and forwards on the palm of his hand. A gentleman who had been watching him clapped him on the shoulder and said: "All good luck for your journey to Clayton." Karl nodded silently and reckoned up his money again. But he soon came to a decision, counted out the money he needed for the fare and rushed to the underground station. When he got out at Clayton he heard at once the noise of many trumpets. It was a confused blaring; the trumpets were not in harmony but were blown regardless of each other. Still, that did not worry Karl; he took it rather as a confirmation of the fact that the Theatre

273

of Oklahoma was a great undertaking. But when he emerged from the station and surveyed the lay-out before him, he realised that it was all on a much larger scale than he could have conceived possible, and he did not understand how any organisation could make such extensive preparations merely for the purpose of taking on employees. Before the entrance to the race-course a long low platform had been set up, on which hundreds of women dressed as angels in white robes with great wings on their shoulders were blowing on long trumpets that glittered like gold. They were not actually standing on the platform, but were mounted on separate pedestals, which could not however be seen, since they were completely hidden by the long flowing draperies of the robes. Now, as the pedestals were very high, some of them quite six feet high, these women looked gigantic, except that the smallness of their heads spoiled a little the impression of size, and their loose hair looked too short and almost absurd hanging between the great wings and framing their faces. To avoid monotony, the pedestals were of all sizes; there were women quite low down, not much over life-size, but beside them others soared to such a height that one felt the slightest gust of wind could capsize them. And all these women were blowing their trumpets.

There were not many listeners. Dwarfed by comparison with these great figures, some ten boys were walking about before the platform and looking up at the women. They called each other's attention to this one or that, but seemed to have no idea of entering and offering their services. Only one older man was to be seen; he stood a little to one side. He had brought his wife with him and a child in a perambulator. The wife was holding the perambulator with one hand and with the other supporting herself on her husband's shoulder. They were clearly admiring the spectacle, but one could see all the same

that they were disappointed. They too had apparently expected to find some sign of work, and this blowing of trumpets confused them. Karl was in the same position. He walked over to where the man was standing, listened for a little to the trumpets, and then said: "Isn't this the place where they are engaging people for the Theatre of Oklahoma?"

"I thought so too," said the man, "but we've been waiting here for an hour and heard nothing but these trumpets. There's not a placard to be seen, no announcers, nobody anywhere to tell you what to do."

Karl said: "Perhaps they're waiting until more people arrive. There are really very few here."

"Possibly," said the man, and they were silent again. Besides, it was difficult to hear anything through the din of the trumpets. But then the woman whispered to her husband; he nodded and she called at once to Karl: "Couldn't you go into the race-course and ask where the workers are being taken on?"

"Yes," said Karl, "but I would have to cross the platform, among all the angels."

"Is that so very difficult?" asked the woman.

She seemed to think it an easy path for Karl, but she was unwilling to let her husband go.

"All right," said Karl, "I'll go."

"That's very good of you," said the woman, and both she and her husband took Karl's hand and pressed it.

The boys all came rushing up to get a near view of Karl climbing the platform. It was as if the women redoubled their efforts on the trumpets as a greeting to the first applicant. Those whose pedestals Karl had to pass actually took their trumpets from their mouths and leaned over to follow him with their eyes. At the other side of the platform Karl discovered a man walking restlessly up and down, obviously only waiting for people so as to give them all the information they might desire. Karl was just about to accost him, when he heard someone calling his name above him.

"Karl!" cried an angel. Karl looked up and in delighted surprise began to laugh. It was Fanny.

"Fanny!" he exclaimed, waving his hand.

"Come up here!" cried Fanny. "You're surely not going to pass me like that!" And she parted her draperies so that the pedestal and a little ladder leading up to it became visible.

"Is one allowed to go up?" asked Karl.

"Who can forbid us to shake hands!" cried Fanny, and she looked round indignantly, in case anyone might be coming to intervene. But Karl was already running up the ladder.

"Not so fast!" cried Fanny. "The pedestal and both of us will come to grief!" But nothing happened, Karl reached the top in safety. "Just look," said Fanny after they had greeted each other, "just look what a job I've got."

"It's a fine job," said Karl, looking round him. All the women near by had noticed him and began to giggle. "You're almost the highest of them all," said Karl, and he stretched out his hand to measure the height of the others.

"I saw you at once," said Fanny, "as soon as you came out of the station, but I'm in the last row here, unfortunately, nobody can see me, and I couldn't shout either. I blew as loudly as I could, but you didn't recognise me."

"You all play very badly," said Karl, "let me have a turn."

"Why, certainly," said Fanny, handing him the trumpet, "but don't spoil the show, or else I'll get the sack."

Karl began to blow into the trumpet; he had imagined it was a roughly-fashioned trumpet intended merely to make a noise, but now he discovered that it was an instrument capable of almost any refinement of expression. If all the instruments

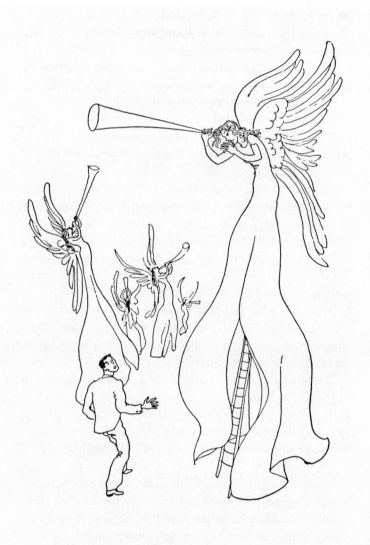

were of the same quality, they were being very ill-used. Paying no attention to the blaring of the others he played with all the power of his lungs an air which he had once heard in some tavern or other. He felt happy at having found an old friend, and at being allowed to play a trumpet as a special privilege, and at the thought that he might likely get a good post very soon. Many of the women stopped playing to listen; when he suddenly broke off scarcely half of the trumpets were in action; and it took a little while for the general din to work up to full power again.

"But you are an artist," said Fanny, when Karl handed her the trumpet again. "Ask to be taken on as a trumpeter."

"Are men taken on for it too?" asked Karl.

"Oh yes," said Fanny. "We play for two hours; then we're relieved by men who are dressed as devils. Half of them blow, the other half beat on drums. It's very fine, but the whole outfit is just as lavish. Don't you think our robes are beautiful? And the wings?" she looked down at herself.

"Do you think," asked Karl, "that I'll get a job here too?"

"Most certainly," said Fanny, "why, it's the greatest theatre in the world. What a piece of luck that we're to be together again. All the same, it depends on what job you get. For it would be quite possible for us not to see each other at all, even though we were both engaged here."

"Is the place really so big as that?" asked Karl.

"It's the biggest theatre in the world," Fanny said again, "I haven't seen it yet myself, I admit, but some of the other girls here, who have been in Oklahoma already, say that there are almost no limits to it."

"But there aren't many people here," said Karl, pointing down at the boys and the little family.

"That's true," said Fanny, "But consider that we pick up

people in all the towns, that our recruiting outfit here is always on the road, and that there are ever so many of these outfits."

"Why, has the theatre not opened yet?" asked Karl.

"Oh yes," said Fanny, "it's an old theatre, but it is always being enlarged."

"I'm surprised," said Karl, "that more people don't flock to join it."

"Yes," said Fanny, "it's extraordinary."

"Perhaps," said Karl, "this display of angels and devils frightens people off more than it attracts them."

"What made you think of that?" said Fanny. "But you may be right. Tell that to our leader; perhaps it might be helpful."

"Where is he?" asked Karl.

"On the race-course," said Fanny, "on the umpire's plat-form."

"That surprises me too," said Karl, "why a race-course for engaging people?"

"Oh," said Fanny, "we always make great preparations in case there should be a great crowd. There's lots of space on a race-course. And in all the stands where the bets are laid on ordinary days, offices are set up to sign on recruits. There must be two hundred different offices there."

"But," cried Karl, "has the Theatre of Oklahoma such a huge income that it can maintain recruiting establishments to that extent?"

"What does that matter to us?" said Fanny. "But you'd better go now, Karl, so that you don't miss anything; and I must begin to blow my trumpet again. Do your best to get a job in this outfit, and come and tell me at once. Remember that I'll be waiting very impatiently for the news."

She pressed his hand, warned him to be cautious in climbing down, set the trumpet to her lips again, but did not blow it until she saw Karl safely on the ground. Karl arranged the robe over the ladder again, as it had been before, Fanny nodded her thanks, and Karl, still considering from various angles what he had just heard, approached the man, who had already seen him up on Fanny's pedestal and had come close to it to wait for him.

"You want to join us?" asked the man. "I am the staff manager of this company and I bid you welcome." He had a slight permanent stoop as if out of politeness, fidgeted with his feet, though without moving from the spot, and played with his watch chain.

"Thank you," said Karl, "I read the placard your company put out and I have come here as I was requested."

"Quite right," said the man appreciatively. "Unluckily there aren't many who do the same." It occurred to Karl that he could now tell the man that perhaps the recruiting company failed because of the very splendour of its attractions. But he did not say so, for this man was not the leader of the company, and besides it would not be much of a recommendation for him if he began to make suggestions for the improvement of the outfit before even being taken on. So he merely said: "There is another man waiting out there who wants to report here too and simply sent me on ahead. May I fetch him now?"

"Of course," said the man, "the more the better."

"He has a wife with him too and a small child in a perambulator. Are they to come too?"

"Of course," said the man, and he seemed to smile at Karl's doubts. "We can use all of them."

"I'll be back in a minute," said Karl, and he ran back to the edge of the platform. He waved to the married couple and shouted that everybody could come. He helped the man to lift the perambulator on to the platform, and then they proceeded together. The boys, seeing this, consulted with each other, and then, their hands in their pockets, hesitating to the last instant, slowly climbed on to the platform and followed Karl and the family. Just then some fresh passengers emerged from the underground station and raised their arms in astonishment when they saw the platform and the angels. However, it seemed that the competition for jobs would now become more lively. Karl felt very glad that he was such an early arrival, perhaps the first of them all; the married couple were apprehensive and asked various questions as to whether great demands would be made on them. Karl told them he knew nothing definite yet, but he had received the impression that everyone without exception would be engaged. He thought they could feel easy in their minds. The staff manager advanced towards them, very satisfied that so many were coming; he rubbed his hands, greeted everyone with a little bow and arranged them all in a row. Karl was the first, then came the husband and wife, and after that the others. When they were all ranged up—the boys kept jostling each other at first and it took some time to get them in order—the staff manager said, while the trumpets fell silent: "I greet you in the name of the Theatre of Oklahoma. You have come early," (but it was already midday), "there is no great rush yet, so that the formalities necessary for engaging you will soon be settled. Of course you have all your identification papers."

The boys at once pulled papers out of their pockets and flourished them at the staff manager; the husband nudged his wife, who pulled out a whole bundle of papers from under the blankets of the perambulator. But Karl had none. Would that prevent him from being taken on? He knew well enough from experience that with a little resolution it should be easy to get round such regulations. Very likely he would succeed. The staff manager glanced along the row, assured himself that everyone had papers, and since Karl also stood with his hand raised, though it was empty, he assumed that in his case too everything was in order.

"Very good," said the staff manager, with a reassuring wave of the hand to the boys, who wanted to have their papers examined at once, "the papers will now be scrutinised in the employment bureaus. As you will have seen already from our placard, we can find employment for everyone. But we must know of course what occupations you have followed until now, so that we can put you in the right places to make use of your knowledge."

"But it's a theatre," thought Karl dubiously, and he listened very intently.

"We have accordingly," went on the staff manager, "set up employment bureaus in the bookmakers' booths, an office for each trade or profession. So each of you will now tell me his occupation; a family is generally registered at the husband's employment bureau. I shall then take you to the offices, where first your papers and then your qualifications will be checked by experts; it will only be a quite short examination; there's nothing to be afraid of. You will then be signed on at once and receive your further instructions. So let us begin. This first office is for engineers, as the inscription tells you. Is there perhaps an engineer here?"

Karl stepped forward. He thought that his lack of papers made it imperative for him to rush through the formalities with all possible speed; he had also a slight justification in putting himself forward, for he had once wanted to be an engineer. But when the boys saw Karl reporting himself they grew envious and put up their hands too, all of them. The staff manager rose to his full height and said to the boys: "Are you engineers?" Their hands slowly wavered and sank, but Karl stuck to his first decision. The staff manager certainly looked at him with incredulity, for Karl seemed too wretchedly clad and also too young to be an engineer; but he said nothing further, perhaps out of gratitude because Karl, at least in his opinion, had brought the applicants in. He simply pointed courteously towards the office, and Karl went across to it, while the staff manager turned to the others.

In the bureau for engineers two gentlemen were sitting at either side of a rectangular counter comparing two big lists which lay before them. One of them read while the other made a mark against names in his list. When Karl appeared and greeted them, they laid aside the lists at once and brought out two great books, which they flung open.

One of them, who was obviously only a clerk, said: "Please give me your identity papers."

"I am sorry to say I haven't got them with me," said Karl.

"He hasn't got them with him," said the clerk to the other gentleman, at once writing down the answer in his book.

"You are an engineer?" thereupon asked the other man, who seemed to be in charge of the bureau.

"I'm not an engineer yet," said Karl quickly, "but——"

"Enough," said the gentleman still more quickly, "in that case you don't belong to us. Be so good as to note the inscription." Karl clenched his teeth, and the gentleman must have observed that, for he said: "There's no need to worry. We can employ everyone." And he made a sign to one of the attendants who were lounging about idly between the barriers: "Lead this gentleman to the bureau for technicians."

The attendant interpreted the command literally and took Karl by the hand. They passed a number of booths on either side; in one Karl saw one of the boys, who had already been

signed on and was gratefully shaking hands with the gentleman in charge. In the bureau to which Karl was now taken
the procedure was similar to that in the first office, as he had
foreseen. Except that they now despatched him to the bureau
for intermediate pupils, when they heard that he had attended
an intermediate school. But when Karl confessed there that it
was a European school he had attended, the officials refused
to accept him and had him conducted to the bureau for European intermediate pupils. It was a booth on the outer verge of
the course, not only smaller but also humbler than all the
others. The attendant who conducted him there was furious at
the long pilgrimage and the repeated rebuffs, for which in his
opinion Karl alone bore the blame. He did not wait for the
questioning to begin, but went away at once. So this bureau
was probably Karl's last chance. When Karl caught sight of the
head of the bureau, he was almost startled at his close resemblance to a teacher who was presumably still teaching in
the school at home. The resemblance, however, as immediately
appeared, was confined to certain details; but the spectacles
resting on the man's broad nose, the fair beard as carefully
tended as a prize exhibit, the slightly rounded back and the
unexpectedly loud abrupt voice held Karl in amazement for
some time. Fortunately, he had not to attend very carefully, for
the procedure here was much simpler than in the other offices.
A note was certainly taken of the fact that his papers were lack-
ing, and the head of the bureau called it an incomprehensible
piece of negligence; but the clerk, who seemed to have the
upper hand, quickly glossed it over and after a few brief questions by his superior, while that gentleman was just preparing
to put some more important ones, he declared that Karl had
been engaged. The head of the bureau turned with open
mouth upon his clerk, but the clerk made a definitive gesture

with his hand, said: "Engaged," and at once entered the decision in his book. Obviously the clerk considered a European intermediate pupil to be something so ignominious that anyone who admitted to being one was not worth disbelieving. Karl for his part had no objection to this; he went up to the clerk intending to thank him. But there was another little delay, while they asked him what his name was. He did not reply at once; he felt shy of mentioning his own name and letting it be written down. As soon as he had a place here, no matter how small, and filled it satisfactorily, they could have his name, but not now; he had concealed it too long to give it away now. So as no other name occurred to him at the moment, he gave the nickname he had had in his last post: "Negro."

"Negro?" said the chief, turning his head and making a grimace, as if Karl had now touched the high water mark of incredibility. Even the clerk looked critically at Karl for a while, but then he said: "Negro" and wrote the name down.

"But you surely haven't written down Negro?" his chief shouted at him.

"Yes, Negro," said the clerk calmly, and waved his hand, as if his superior should now continue the proceedings. And the head of the bureau, controlling himself, stood up and said: "You are engaged, then, for the——" but he could not get any farther, he could not go against his own conscience, so he sat down and said: "He isn't called Negro."

The clerk raised his eyebrows, got up himself and said: "Then it is my duty to inform you that you have been engaged for the Theatre in Oklahoma and that you will now be introduced to our leader."

Another attendant was summoned, who conducted Karl to the umpire's platform.

At the foot of the steps Karl caught sight of the perambulator, and at that moment the father and mother descended, the mother with the baby on her arm.

"Have you been taken on?" asked the man; he was much more lively than before, and his wife smiled at Karl across her shoulder. When Karl answered that he had just been taken on and was going to be introduced, the man said: "Then I congratulate you. We have been taken on too. It seems to be a good thing, though you can't get used to everything all at once; but it's like that everywhere."

They said goodbye to each other again and Karl climbed up to the platform. He took his time, for the small space above seemed to be crammed with people, and he did not want to be importunate. He even paused for a while and gazed at the great race-course, which extended on every side to distant woods. He was filled with longing to see a horse-race; he had found no opportunity to do so since he had come to America. In Europe he had once been taken to a race-meeting as a small child, but all that he could remember was that he had been dragged by his mother through throngs of people who were unwilling to make room and let him pass. So that actually he had never seen a race yet. Behind him a mechanism of some kind began to whir; he turned round and saw on the board, where the names of the winners appeared, the following inscription being hoisted: "The merchant Kala with wife and child." So the names of those who were engaged was communicated to all the offices from here.

At that moment several gentlemen with pencils and notebooks in their hands ran down the stairs, busily talking to each other; Karl squeezed against the railing to let them pass, and then went up, as there was now room for him above. In one corner of the platform with its wooden railing—the whole looked like the flat roof of a small tower—a gentleman was

sitting with his arms stretched along the railing and a broad
white silk sash hanging diagonally across his chest with the inscription: "Leader of the tenth recruiting squad of the Theatre
of Oklahoma." On a table stood a telephone, doubtless in-
stalled for use during the races but now obviously employed in
giving the leader all necessary information regarding the various applicants before they were introduced, for he did not begin
by putting questions to Karl, but said to a gentleman sitting
beside him with crossed legs, his chin in his hands: "Negro, a
European intermediate pupil." And as if with that he had
nothing more to say to Karl, who was bowing low before him,
he glanced down the stairs to see whether anyone else was
coming. As no one came, he lent an ear to the conversation
which the other gentleman was having with Karl, but for the
most part kept looking at the race-course and tapping on the
railing with his fingers. These delicate and yet powerful, long
and nimble fingers attracted Karl's attention from time to time,
although he should really have been giving his whole mind to
the other gentleman.

"You've been out of work?" this gentleman began by
asking. The question, like almost all the other questions he
asked, was very simple and direct, nor did he check Karl's replies by cross-examining him at all; yet the way in which he
rounded his eyes while he uttered his questions, the way in
which he leaned forward to contemplate their effect, the way
in which he let his head sink to his chest while he listened to
the replies, in some cases repeating them aloud, invested his
enquiries with an air of special significance, which one might
not understand but which it made one uneasy to suspect.
Many times Karl felt impelled to take back the answer he had
given and substitute another which might find more approval,
but he always managed to refrain, for he knew what a bad

impression such shilly-shallying was bound to make, and how little he really understood for the most part the effect of his answers. Besides, his engagement seemed to be already decided upon, and the consciousness of that gave him support.

To the question whether he had been out of work he replied with a simple "Yes."

"Where were you engaged last?" the gentleman asked next.

Karl was just about to answer, when the gentleman raised his first finger and repeated again: "Last!"

As Karl had understood the question perfectly well, he involuntarily shook his head to reject the confusing additional remark and answered: "In an office."

That was the truth, but if the gentleman should demand more definite information regarding the kind of office, he would have to tell lies. However, the necessity did not arise, for the gentleman asked a question which it was quite easy to answer with perfect truth: "Were you satisfied there?"

"No!" exclaimed Karl, almost before the question was finished. Out of the corner of his eye he could see that the leader was smiling faintly. He regretted the impetuosity of his exclamation, but it was too tempting to launch that no, for during all his last term of service his greatest wish had been that some outside employer of labour might come in and ask him that very question. Still, his negative might put him at another disadvantage if the gentleman were to follow it up by asking why he had not been satisfied? But he asked instead: "For what kind of post do you feel you are best suited?" This question might contain a real trap, for why was it put at all since he had already been engaged as an actor? But although he saw the difficulty, he could not bring himself to say that he felt particularly suited for the acting profession. So he evaded the question and said, at the risk of appearing obstructive: "I read the placard in the town, and as it said there that you could employ anyone, I came here."

"We know that," said the gentleman, showing by his ensuing silence that he insisted on an answer to the question.

"I have been engaged as an actor," said Karl hesitantly, to let the gentleman see that he found himself in a dilemma.

"Quite so," said the gentleman, and fell silent again.

"No," said Karl, and all his hopes of being settled in a job began to totter, "I don't know whether I'm capable of being an actor. But I shall do my best and try to carry out all my instructions."

The gentleman turned to the leader, both of them nodded; Karl seemed to have given the right answer, so he took courage again and standing erect waited for the next question: It ran: "What did you want to study originally?"

To define the question more exactly—the gentleman seemed to lay great weight on exact definition,—he added: "In Europe, I mean," at the same time removing his hand from his chin and waving it slightly as if to indicate both how remote Europe was and how unimportant were any plans that might have been made there.

Karl said: "I wanted to be an engineer." This answer almost stuck in his throat; it was absurd of him, knowing as he did the kind of career he had had in America, to bring up the old day-dream of having wanted to be an engineer—would he ever have become an engineer even in Europe?—but he simply did not know what other answer to make and so gave this one.

Yet the gentleman took it seriously, as he took everything seriously. "Well, you can't turn into an engineer all at once," he said, "but perhaps it would suit you for the time being to be attached to some minor technical work."

"Certainly," said Karl. He was perfectly satisfied; true, if he accepted the offer, he would be transferred from the acting profession to the lower status of technical labourer, but he really believed that he would be able to do more justice to himself at technical work. Besides, he kept on telling himself, it was not so much a matter of the kind of work as of establishing oneself permanently somewhere.

"Are you strong enough for heavy work?" asked the gentleman.

"Oh yes," said Karl.

At that, the gentleman asked Karl to come nearer and felt his arm.

"He's a strong lad," he said, then pulling Karl by the arm towards the leader. The leader nodded smilingly, reached Karl his hand without changing his lazy posture, and said: "Then that's all settled. In Oklahoma we'll look into it again. See that you do honour to our recruiting squad!"

Karl made his bow, and also turned to say goodbye to the other gentleman, but he, as if his functions were now discharged, was walking up and down the platform gazing at the sky. As Karl went down the steps, the announcement board beside them was showing the inscription: "Negro, technical worker."

As everything here was taking an orderly course, Karl felt that after all he would not have minded seeing his real name on the board. The organisation was indeed scrupulously precise, for at the foot of the steps Karl found a waiting attendant who fastened a band round his arm. When Karl lifted his arm to see what was written on the band, there, right enough, were the words "technical worker."

But wherever he was to be taken now, he decided that he must first report to Fanny how well everything had gone. To his great sorrow he learned from the attendant that both the angels and the devils had already left for the next town on the recruiting squad's itinerary, to act as advance agents for the arrival of the troop next day.

"What a pity," said Karl; it was the first disappointment that he had had in this new undertaking, "I had a friend among the angels."

"You'll see her again in Oklahoma," said the attendant, "but now come along; you're the last."

He led Karl along the inner side of the platform on which the angels had been posted; there was nothing left but the empty pedestals. Yet Karl's assumption that if the trumpeting were stopped more people would be encouraged to apply was proved wrong, for there were now no grown-up people at all before the platform, only a few children fighting over a long, white feather which had apparently fallen out of an angel's wing. A boy was holding it up in the air, while the other children were trying to push down his head with one hand and reaching for the feather with the other.

Karl pointed out the children, but the attendant said without looking: "Come on, hurry up, it's taken a long time for you to get engaged. I suppose they weren't sure of you?"

"I don't know," said Karl in astonishment, but he did not believe it. Always, even in the most unambiguous circumstances, someone could be found to take pleasure in suggesting troubles to his fellow men. But at the friendly aspect of the Grand Stand which they were now approaching, Karl soon forgot the attendant's remark. For on this stand there was a long wide bench covered with a white cloth; all the applicants who had been taken on sat on the bench below it with their backs to the race-course and were being fed. They were all happy and excited; just as Karl, coming last, quietly took his seat several of them were rising with upraised glasses, and one of them toasted the leader of the tenth recruiting squad, whom he called the "father of all the unemployed." Someone then remarked that the leader could be seen from here, and actually the umpire's platform with the two gentlemen on it was visible at no very great distance. Now they were all raising their glasses in that direction, Karl too seized the glass standing in front of him, but loudly as they shouted and hard as they tried to draw attention to themselves, there was no sign on the umpire's platform that the ovation had been observed or at least that there was any wish to observe it. The leader lounged in his corner as before, and the other gentleman stood beside him, resting his chin on his hand. Somewhat disappointed, everybody sat down again; here and there one would turn round towards the umpire's platform again; but soon they were all well occupied with the abundant food; huge birds such as Karl had never seen before were carried round with many forks sticking into the crisply roasted meat; the glasses were kept filled with wine by the attendants—you hardly noticed it, you were busy with your plate and a stream of red wine simply fell into your glass—and those who did not want to take part in the general conversation could look at views of the Theatre of Oklahoma which lay in a pile at one end of the table and were supposed to pass from hand to hand. But few of the people troubled much about the views, and so it happened that only one of them reached Karl, who was the last in the row. Yet to judge from that picture, all the rest must have been well worth seeing. The picture showed the box reserved in the Theatre for the President of the United States. At first glance one might have thought that it was not a stage box but the stage itself, so far-flung was the sweep of its breastwork. This breastwork was made entirely of gold, to the smallest detail. Between its slender columns, as delicately carved as if cut out by a fine pair of scissors, medallions of former Presidents were arrayed side by side; one of these had a remarkably straight nose, curling lips and a downward-looking eye hooded beneath a full, rounded eye-lid. Rays of light fell into the box from all sides and from the roof; the foreground was literally bathed in light, white but soft, while the recess of the background, behind red damask curtains falling in changing folds from roof to floor and looped with cords, appeared like a duskily-glowing empty cavern. One could scarcely imagine human figures in that box, so royal did it look. Karl was not quite rapt away from his dinner, but he laid the photograph beside his plate and sat gazing at it. He would have been glad to look at even one of the other photographs, but he did not want to rise and pick one up himself, since an attendant had his hand resting on the pile and the sequence probably had to be kept unbroken; so he only craned his neck to survey the table, trying to make out if another photograph were being passed along. To his great amazement—it seemed at first incredible—he recognised among those most intent upon their plates a face which he knew well: Giacomo. At once he rose and hastened up to him. "Giacomo!" he cried.

Shy as ever when taken by surprise, Giacomo got up from his seat, turned round in the narrow space between the benches, wiped his mouth with his hand and then showed great delight at seeing Karl, suggesting that Karl should come and sit beside him, or he should change his own place instead; they had a lot to tell each other and should stick together all the time. Karl, not wanting to disturb the others, said perhaps they had better keep their own places for the time being, the meal would soon be finished and then of course they would stick together. But Karl still lingered a moment or two, only for the sake of looking at Giacomo. What memories of the past were recalled!

What had happened to the Manageress? What was Therese doing? Giacomo himself had hardly changed at all in appearance; the Manageress's prophecy that in six months' time he would develop into a large-boned American had not been fulfilled; he was as delicate looking as before, his cheeks hollow as ever, though at the moment they were bulging with an extra large mouthful of meat from which he was slowly extracting the bones, to lay them on his plate. As Karl could see from his arm-band, he was not engaged as an actor either, but as a lift-boy; the Theatre of Oklahoma really did seem to have a place for everyone! But Karl's absorption in Giacomo had kept him too long away from his own seat. Just as he was thinking of getting back, the Staff Manager arrived, climbed on to one of the upper benches, clapped his hands and made a short speech while most of the people rose to their feet, those who remained in their seats, unwilling to leave their dinners, being nudged by the others until they too were forced to rise.

"I hope," said the Staff Manager, Karl meanwhile having tip-toed back to his place, "that you have been satisfied with our reception of you and the dinner we have given you. The recruiting squad is generally supposed to keep a good kitchen. I'm sorry we must clear the table already, but the train for Oklahoma is going to leave in five minutes. It's a long journey, I know, but you'll find yourselves well looked after. Let me now introduce the gentleman in charge of your transport arrangements, whose instructions you will please follow."

A lean little man scrambled up on the bench beside the Staff Manager and, scarcely taking time to make a hasty bow, began waving his arms nervously to direct them how to assemble themselves in an orderly manner and proceed to the station. But he was at first ignored, for the man who had made a speech at the beginning of the dinner now struck the table with his hand and began to return thanks in a lengthy oration, although—Karl was growing quite uneasy about it—he had just been told that the train was leaving in five minutes. He was not even deterred by the patent inattention of the Staff Manager, who was giving various instructions to the transport official; he built up his oration in the grand manner, mentioning each dish that had been served and passing a judgement on each individually, winding up with the declaration: "Gentlemen, that is the way to our hearts!" Everyone laughed except the gentlemen he was addressing, but there was more truth than jest in his statement, all the same.

This oration brought its own penalty, since the road to the station had now to be taken at a run. Still, that was no great hardship, for—as Karl only now remarked—no one carried any luggage; the only thing that could be called luggage was the perambulator, which the father was pushing at the head of the troop and which jolted up and down wildly as if no hand were steadying it. What destitute, disreputable characters were here assembled, and yet how well they had been received and cared for! And the transport official must have been told to cherish them like the apple of his eye. Now he was taking a turn at pushing the perambulator, waving one hand to encourage the troop; now he was urging on stragglers in the rear; now he was careering along the ranks, keeping an eye on the slower runners in the middle and trying to show them with swinging arms how to run more easily.

When they reached the station the train was ready for departure. People in the station pointed out the newcomers to each other, and one heard exclamations such as: "All these belong to the Theatre of Oklahoma!" The Theatre seemed to be much better known than Karl had assumed; of course, he had never taken much interest in theatrical affairs. A whole carriage was specially reserved for their troop; the transport official worked harder than the guard at getting the people into it. Only when he had inspected each compartment and made a few re-arrangements did he get into his own seat. Karl had happened to get a window-seat, with Giacomo beside him. So there they sat, the two of them, close together, rejoicing in their hearts over the journey. Such a carefree journey in America they had never known. When the train began to move out of the station they waved from the window, to the amusement of the young men opposite, who nudged each other and laughed.

For two days and two nights they journeyed on. Only now did Karl understand how huge America was. Unweariedly he gazed out of the window, and Giacomo persisted in struggling for a place beside him until the other occupants of the compartment, who wanted to play cards, got tired of him and voluntarily surrendered the other window-seat. Karl thanked them— Giacomo's English was not easy for anyone to follow—and in the course of time, as is inevitable among fellow-travellers, they grew much more friendly, although their friendliness was sometimes a nuisance, as for example whenever they ducked down to rescue a card fallen on the floor, they could not resist giving hearty tweaks to Karl's legs or Giacomo's. Whenever that happened Giacomo always shrieked in renewed surprise and drew his legs up; Karl attempted once to give a kick in return, but suffered the rest of the time in silence. Everything that went on in the little compartment, which was thick with cigarette-smoke in spite of the open window, faded into comparative insignificance before the grandeur of the scene outside.

The first day they travelled through a high range of mountains. Masses of blue-black rock rose in sheer wedges to the railway line; even craning one's neck out of the window, one could not see their summits; narrow, gloomy, jagged valleys opened out and one tried to follow with a pointing finger the direction in which they lost themselves; broad mountain streams appeared, rolling in great waves down on to the foothills and drawing with them a thousand foaming wavelets, plunging underneath the bridges over which the train rushed; and they were so near that the breath of coldness rising from them chilled the skin of one's face.

AFTERWORD

FRANZ KAFKA's manuscript bears no title. In conversation he used to refer to this book as his "American novel," but later he called it simply *The Stoker*, after the title of the first chapter, which had appeared separately (1913). He worked at it with unending delight, mostly in the evenings and late into the night; the pages show amazingly few corrections and deletions. Kafka knew quite well, and discussed the fact, that this novel was more optimistic and "lighter" in mood than any of his other writings.

In this connection perhaps I may say that Franz Kafka was fond of reading travel books and memoirs, that Franklin's biography was one of his favourite books, from which he liked reading passages aloud, and that he had always a longing for free space and distant lands. He never actually travelled farther than France and Upper Italy, so that the innocence of his fantasy gives this book of adventure its peculiar colour.

Kafka broke off his work on this novel with unexpected suddenness. It remained unfinished. From what he told me I know that the incomplete chapter about the Nature Theatre of Oklahoma (a chapter the beginning of which particularly delighted Kafka, so that he used to read it aloud with great effect) was intended to be the concluding chapter of the work and should end on a note of reconciliation. In enigmatic language Kafka used to hint smilingly, that within this "almost limitless" theatre his young hero was going to find again a profession, a stand-by, his freedom, even his old home and his parents, as if by some celestial witchery.

The parts of the narrative immediately preceding this chapter are also incomplete. Two large fragments, describing Karl's service with Brunelda, are extant, but do not fill up the gaps. . . . Only the first six chapters were divided and given titles by Kafka. . . .

MAX BROD.